THE GRAYWOLF SHORT FICTION SERIES

1 9 8 9

•　　•　　•　　•　　•　　•　　•

The Invisible Enemy

EDITED BY MIRIAM DOW

& JENNIFER REGAN

• • • • • • • •

Graywolf Press / St. Paul / 1989

Introduction copyright © 1989 by Miriam Dow and Jennifer Regan.
Other material included in this anthology remains under copyright protection,
as specified on the acknowledgment pages.

Publication of this anthology is made possible by the generous donations Graywolf Press
receives from corporations, foundations and individuals, including the Minnesota State Arts
Board and the National Endowment for the Arts. Special contributions for *The Invisible Enemy*
were made by: the James R. Thorpe Foundation, the Archie D. and Bertha H. Walker
Foundation, and the Patrick and Aimee Butler Family Foundation. Graywolf is a member
organization of United Arts, Saint Paul.

Library of Congress Catalog Number 89-00000.
ISBN 1-55597-118-0

Library of Congress Cataloging-in-Publication Data

The Invisible enemy / edited by Miriam Dow and Jennifer Regan.
     p.   cm. — (The Graywolf short fiction series)
   ISBN 1-55597-118-0 (alk. paper) : $9.50
   1. Alcoholics—Fiction.   2. Alcoholism—Fiction.   3. Short
stories, American.   4. American fiction—20th century.   I. Dow,
Miriam.   II. Regan, Jennifer.   III. Series.
PS648.A42I58   1989
813'.0108'353—dc20   89-31690
                                CIP

Published by GRAYWOLF PRESS
Post Office Box 75006
Saint Paul, Minnesota 55175.
All rights reserved.

9 8 7 6 5 4 3 2

A C K N O W L E D G M E N T S

A L I C E   A D A M S . "Beautiful Girl." Copyright © 1979 by Alice Adams. Reprinted from *Beautiful Girl* by Alice Adams, by permission of Alfred A. Knopf, Inc. Originally appeared in *The New Yorker*.

A R N A   B O N T E M P S . "The Cure." Copyright © 1973 by Alberta Bontemps, Executrix. Reprinted from *The Old South: A Summer Tragedy and Other Stories of The Thirties* (Dodd Mead), by permission of Harold Ober Associates Incorporated.

H O R T E N S E   C A L I S H E R . "In Greenwich There Are Many Gravelled Walks." Copyright © 1945–75 by Hortense Calisher. Reprinted from *The Collected Stories of Hortense Calisher*, by permission of Arbor House, a division of William Morrow, Inc. Originally appeared in *The New Yorker*.

R A Y M O N D   C A R V E R . "Where I'm Calling From." Copyright © 1983 by Raymond Carver. Reprinted from *Cathedral* by Raymond Carver, by permission of Alfred A. Knopf, Inc. Originally appeared in *The New Yorker*.

J O H N   C H E E V E R . "The Sorrows of Gin." Copyright © 1953 by John Cheever. Reprinted from *The Stories of John Cheever* by John Cheever, by permission of Alfred A. Knopf, Inc. Originally appeared in *The New Yorker*.

L O U I S E   E R D R I C H . "Crown of Thorns." Copyright © 1984 by Louise Erdrich. Reprinted from *Love Medicine* (Henry Holt & Co.), by permission of the author.

W I L L I A M   G O Y E N . "Where's Esther?" Copyright © 1985 by Doris Roberts and Charles William Goyen. Reprinted from *Had I a Hundred Mouths*, by William Goyen, by permission of Clarkson N. Potter, Inc.

J U L I E   H A Y D E N . "Day-Old Baby Rats." Copyright © 1972 by Julie Hayden. Reprinted from *The Lists of the Past*, by permission of Viking Penguin, Inc. Originally appeared in *The New Yorker*.

L A N G S T O N   H U G H E S . "Minnie Again." Copyright © 1961 by Langston Hughes. Reprinted from *The Best of Simple*, by permission of Hill & Wang, a division of Farrar, Strauss & Giroux, Inc.

S U S A N   M I N O T . "The Navigator." Copyright © 1986 by Susan Minot. Reprinted from *Monkeys* by permission of E. P. Dutton, a division of Penguin Book USA.

TABLE OF CONTENTS

Delusions

Trying to Stop

For Raymond Carver

THE INVISIBLE ENEMY

•　　•　　•　　•　　•　　•　　•

I N T R O D U C T I O N

W hether its purpose is social or business, to celebrate or to mourn, Americans have come to expect the presence of alcohol whenever they come together. If anyone should drink too much, it is not seen as a problem but rather shrugged off as a mistake or an amusing pecadillo. Few people are comfortable making an issue of drinking because alcohol is such an accepted ingredient in our way of life.

With the proliferation of self-help groups, treatment centers and celebrities' accounts of addiction and recovery, tolerance of alcohol abuse may be changing. The popularity of many books which present facts and statistics about alcoholism and propose strategies for addressing the problems it creates is another signal of change.

Although the abundance of information now available can educate the intellect, it may not reach a deeper level of emotional understanding. Much of the literature of the "field" seems didactic and programatic. *The Invisible Enemy* presents stories which, through the artist's vision, probe alcohol's profound emotional effects. As in any successful work of art, the reader is drawn into the artist's world to experience directly and decipher the complexities of human experience. In many of these stories alcoholism is not the main focus. This is exactly the way it occurs in our daily lives, subtly and painfully woven through all our experiences. These stories invite the reader to participate in alcoholic situations and thereby heighten his awareness and understanding of alcoholism.

The alcoholic is the most obvious victim of alcoholism, but his friends and loved ones also play parts which aggravate the problem. In an alcoholic family a predictable system of behaviors is established, dominated by denial that anything is wrong. Family members who remain silent, resigned and resentful, rather than confront the alcoholic, perpetuate the alcoholic system as surely as if they themselves filled up the drinker's glass. The alcoholic, when not challenged about his drinking, feels such shame and guilt that his only relief is to take another drink.

The children we meet in these stories live in a world pervaded by fear and mistrust. They may suspect that they are responsible for the chaos around them and feel obliged to take care of their parents. Despite their efforts to bring order to their environments, they see themselves as ineffectual and unable to please their parents. Throughout their lives their self-image and relationships with others are colored by growing up in this alcoholic family system.

These stories in *The Invisible Enemy* teach us a great deal about the alcoholic, whose repeated strategies to justify and hide dependence on alcohol end in isolation and loss of control. Inevitably, this behavior spirals downward until the only thing that matters is the bottle.

To those who have not been directly involved with alcoholism, this collection of stories exposes the enormous task of giving up drinking. The alcoholic's attempts to get well by joining AA or seeking treatment are often greeted with skepticism. Furthermore, the powerful lure of drinking is always there.

Each story in *The Invisible Enemy* demonstrates that love and understanding are no match for alcohol's devastating grip. The book is divided into five sections that explore the intricate family dynamics which come into play in the presence of alcoholism, the debilitating impact suffered by children of alcoholics, the progressive stages of the disease, the web of denial and delusion which the alcoholic weaves in defense, and finally, the greatest challenge of all, stopping drinking.

The Family and Alcoholism

. . . .

•   •   •   •   •   •   •

The Navigator

In the summer they ate early, everyone drifting home like particles in a tide. By evening most of the people had disappeared from the wharf and the North Eden harbor was quiet, the thoroughfare running by as flat as a slab of granite. Tonight there was a fog coming in. It was the end of August and all seven of the Vincent children were up there in Maine.

Gus came in off the dock. The screen door ticked out its long yawn, and when he reached the kitchen at the end of the short hall it clapped shut.

The girls were making dinner. Delilah shook salt into the pots on the stove; Sophie peeled a cucumber.

Gus propped his foot against the icebox and bumped against the doorframe.

"Work hard?" Sophie said.

Gus nodded. He had been house painting all summer; his dark skin was specked with white.

Sophie ran a fork down the side of the cucumber while she held it up next to Gus's face. "For your skin," she said. He closed his eyes to feel the spray.

Delilah folded her arms. "It's just us tonight," she said. "Mum and Dad are going to the Irvings'."

"Dad is?" Gus said. "What is it, skit night?"

"Practically," Sophie said. She picked up a cigarette from the ashtray, took a drag, and gave it to Gus. "They're playing find-the-button."

Gus smiled. "Which one's that?"

"You know. They hide the things—a thimble on the lampshade or a golf tee in the peanuts—the button camouflaged in some flowers. When you spot it, you write it down."

"How'd Mum get him to go?" Gus rubbed the ash into his pants. The bottoms were rolled up in doughnuts.

"God knows," said Sophie.

"It was a choice between that and the Kittredges' clambake on Sunday," Delilah said.

They all laughed.

Delilah was crumbling hamburger. "Poor guy," she said to the frying pan.

"He can handle it," Sophie said.

Gus left them and went into the living room. Chicky, the youngest of the boys, was sitting on the creaking wicker sofa. Going by, Gus swatted the back of his head. On the record player, Bob Dylan was singing "Tangled Up in Blue" for the millionth time. Certain records stayed in North Eden all year long—they were the rejects, hopelessly warped. Still, they got put on again and again. Hearing those songs straight through somewhere else was always a surprise.

Gus took his book off the pile of *National Geographic* and *Harvard* magazines. He stretched out on the window seat, opened the book, and set it facedown on his stomach.

"Went to the quarry," Chicky said. He was whittling at a stick with his Swiss Army knife. "The bottomless one."

"Right," Gus said. He smiled out the window at the floats. The Jewel girls were down there climbing out of their stinkpot. A light mist drifted by in thin trails.

"It was," Chicky said. Shavings littered the floor by his bare feet.

"Chicky, it's impossible," his older brother said. "Quaries're man-made."

Chicky worked over a little knot. "You can think what you want," he said.

From the kitchen, Sophie called, "Where's Minna?" The boys didn't answer. The screen door slammed. "I'm right here," came the six-year-old voice from the hall. Sophie and little Miranda came into the living room at the same time from separate doors.

Sophie said, "Will someone go tell Ma?"

"Is it supper?" Gus asked.

"Five minutes."

"Good," Chicky said.

"Who's going to tell Ma?" Sophie said, holding a stack of napkins at her throat.

Minnie climbed onto Gus's lap and perched on her shins. Gus said, "Minnie will, won't she, Minniana?"

"Do I have to?"

"I would but we're getting supper," Sophie said. She stepped into the dining room but stayed within earshot.

"I always do," said Minnie, collapsing on her brother.

Caitlin walked in. "You always do what?" she asked. Her hair was set and she hit at it from underneath to dry.

"Well, somebody better go," Sophie said from the dining room. Her head appeared. "Gus, will you?"

Gus winced.

"What?" Caitlin said.

"Why don't you ask Sherman?" Chicky said. He pointed out the window. "He never goes."

Sherman, the middle brother, was standing outside at the dock railing. He was spitting over the edge and watching it land in the water. Someone must have tapped on the window above him—Mum and Dad were upstairs getting dressed—because Sherman turned and looked up. His eyes revealed nothing, like Indian eyes.

"Sure," Sophie said. "Good luck."

Minnie kept her head against Gus's chest. "*He's* not about to get Ma," she said.

"Why not?" Caitlin said. She huffed over to the window and lifted it. A damp mist came rolling over the sill. "Sherman," she said, her voice sounding cottony outside. "Go tell Ma it's supper."

Sherman turned his head. "Why don't you?" he said.

"Because I'm asking you to."

Sherman glanced past her. "Why doesn't Chicky go?" he said.

"I don't believe this." Sophie said.

Chicky's knife peeled a long curl. "She'll come over anyway," he said.

Caitlin turned around to him with her mouth set.

Delilah stood in the doorway with a potholder mitten on. "Has someone gone to get Ma?"

"Gee, Delilah," Gus said. "We thought you'd gone."

"This is ridiculous," Caitlin said. "Come on, Minnie. Go."

Minnie's little back went stiff. "I always do." She shifted off Gus.

"It's not going to kill you," Caitlin said.

Minnie trudged out of the room. They heard the screen door swing, then slam. From where he sat, Gus could see her padding over on the dock to Ma's house. He made a moping face and rocked from side to side, imitating her.

The girls laughed.

The dining room had cream-colored walls and two windows that faced the harbor. At high tide, the water rose right up to the shingles and the light made crisscrossing patterns on the low ceiling. It was a small room, just fitting the long table.

Ma, Dad's mother, lived by herself in the far house. Her cook, Livia, had gone back to Ireland, so the kitchen was no longer used. Before supper, Ma read in her living room and had glasses of sherry. By the time she got to the other house for dinner with her grandchildren, her face was flushed.

She sat down, wobbling, at her usual place.

Delilah had a plate at the side table. "Sherman, can you wait? I'm getting this for Ma."

Ma had on a smile. She smiled at the children, smiled at the candle flame, smiled at the blue bowl of grated cheese. "Isn't this nice," she said, smiling. Four small vases of nasturtiums from the garden were on the table.

Gus stood at the window, holding his plate over his chest. "Foggy," he said.

"Is it?" Sophie said. She was busy with wooden spoons in the salad. Everyone bustled around. Caitlin poured milk for Minnie.

Gus nodded and touched his forehead to the pane. "Everything's disappearing," he said.

They'd been eating for a while when Dad came in. He rubbed his hands together. "Evening, evening," he said, shifting from one foot to the other.

"You look pretty snappy," Sophie said. He was wearing a yellow blazer and a tie with green anchors on it. His face looked freshly slapped.

"Mum assures me I won't be allowed in Lally Irving's house without the proper attire," he said, bent slightly at the waist.

"You look great," Caitlin said.

Dad smiled dismissively.

Mum came in smelling of perfume, wearing a long skirt. "See you later, monkeys," she said. She plucked a carrot stick from the salad.

Ma beamed at Mum. "Rosie," she said.

Mum's real name was Rose Marie—it was Irish—but she'd changed it, thanks to Dad. He called her Rosie after the schoolteacher in *The African Queen* who dumps out all of Humphrey Bogart's gin in order to get them down the river. Mum never drank at all.

She looked at her family in the candlelight. "Okey-dokey," she said.

"Good luck finding the button," Gus said.

"Who needs luck?" Mum said, kicking out her foot. "You're looking at last year's champ. Come on, Uncs, off we go."

Dad bowed, putting his palms together, and followed after her. Everyone at the table chuckled. Ma was smiling. She held her fork over her plate but still had not touched her food.

Early the next morning Gus woke up the boys to explain what had happened.

"They got home from the Irvings'," Gus said, "and Mum couldn't get him down the steps."

There were five flights of granite that led down from the street. Gus and the girls had heard Mum call "Yoo hoo." Gus went up the steps to help Dad down. The girls stood in the floodlight of the underpass, watching in the fog. Gus and Mum brought him into the light. Collapsed between them, Dad had been smiling grandly. He caught sight of his daughters in a semicircle and beamed toward them. Receiving no response, he had made a *whoops* expression and covered his mouth, giggling.

Gus sat on Sherman's bed but faced Chicky. "We're going to talk to him this morning," he said.

"What for?" Sherman said. "Let the guy do what he wants."

The girls were downstairs with Mum, except for Minnie, who was at sailing class.

"He didn't want to go in the first place," Mum said, washing dishes at the sink. "I shouldn't have made him."

Caitlin waited by the toaster. "What happened?" she asked.

"He was okay till dinner," Mum said. She gazed through the window in front of her; the shingles of the house next door were a foot away. "Then half-way through the roast beef he decided he was finished and plopped his plate down on top of Mrs. Aberdeen's."

They all smiled in spite of themselves.

"What did Mrs. Aberdeen do?" Delilah said.

Mum shook her head.

Caitlin was serious. "Then what?"

"He collapsed on his place mat with his hands over his head." Mum turned to her daughters. "He said, 'This is so *boring*.'"

Caitlin was still. "You're kidding."

"Then—" Mum took a breath. "Everyone pretended it was time to go and they put their jackets back on and we all said good-bye and they helped Dad find his way to the car. After we drove off, I imagine they went back in and finished dinner."

Sophie said, "You mean they faked going home?"

Mum shrugged: that was nothing.

The boys were shuffling in. Mum said, "He won't listen to me. I'm like a buzz in his ear."

They waited at the table, the girls at the near end, the boys next to the windows.

Sophie heard Dad and set down her knife. Delilah straightened her spine. Dad came in with his plate and put it down. Caitlin bit delicately into her muffin, stealing glances in Dad's direction. Dad went back into the kitchen and returned with a carton of orange juice. He poured a glass and drank it standing up.

Mum was beside him, holding the back of her chair. Her scarf was rolled into a hairband above her wide forehead. She had on a lavender turtleneck.

"The kids want to talk to you, Uncs," she said and slipped into her seat.

Dad pulled out his chair noisily. He buttered his toast, not waiting for the butter to melt. "You ready for a little golf today, Sherman?" he said, not looking up.

Gus looked at Sherman, then at his father, then at Mum. Mum was pressing crumbs with her fingers and brushing them off, making a little pile. Chicky was interested in something under the table. He made a noise to call the cat. Sherman sat heavily, no breakfast plate in front of him, his hands in his lap.

Caitlin spoke first. "Do you remember last night?"

Dad's chin traced out a long nod.

"How's your arm?" Delilah asked.

"My hand," he said and held it up. "Stiff." He put it back down and with his good hand folded some toast around his bacon and took a bite.

Halfway down the steps, he had broken free of Gus and Mum and keeled over into the unguarded rubble. There had been a trickling of small stones after him. The girls watched helplessly as he got onto his hands and knees. His head had wobbled like one of those toy dogs people have on their dashboards. The girls looked away.

"Dad, do you remember talking to me?" Gus said.

"Yes," said his father, addressing the jar of beachplum jelly before him.

"What?" Delilah said.

Dad's frown was like a twitch. "Yes," he repeated.

"Do you remember what you said you'd do?" Gus asked.

Dad dipped his rolled-up toast into his mug of coffee. He nodded.

"Well?" Caitlin said. "What about it?"

Dad chewed, keeping his mouth closed. He looked around the table with an innocent expression.

Sophie said, "We have to talk about it."

"Fine," he said.

While Gus was bringing him upstairs, the girls had lingered in the hall with Mum. Above them, they heard Gus's urgent voice. They sat on the bottom step, transfixed. His voice was pleading, "We all do. . . because whenever we try. . . can't stand it when you. . . "

Outside some footsteps had banged by—two figures in yellow slickers passed the doorway—their steps ringing woodenly on the dock. But the girls hardly noticed, glancing over like sleepwalkers. The fog blew by through the underpass.

Above them they had heard Dad say, "Imagine that."

Caitlin covered her knuckles and slouched forward on the table. "So will you stop?" She looked at Mum. Mum was gazing out the window.

Dad looked at Caitlin as if she were speaking another language.

Sophie said, "You have to, Dad," and her voice wavered. Dad turned to her with the same face, blank but suspecting insult.

"Well?" Caitlin said.

Chicky pointed toward the water. "Look," he said.

Everyone turned. A huge green cattle boat had entered the window frame, undulating behind the tiny streaks in the glass. The white sails were as flat as building sides. It changed the light in the dining room.

"Looks like the *Horn of Plenty*," Mum said brightly.

Everyone watched it glide into the second window.

"No," Sherman said. It was a mystery how he knew these things. "That's *Captain's Folly*."

When Dad was young he had worked summers on a cattle boat that cruised through the islands. He'd been the navigator. He still had an astronomy book on the bottom shelf of his bedside table.

"Is it anchoring?" Sophie said.

Delilah shook her head. "It's just passing through."

The sailboat slipped out of the window frame. Gus tipped back his chair to keep it in sight. It continued through the thorofare. At the outer cove, its sails buckled and a tiny figure at the bow lowered a huge anchor into the water. Gus set his chair down and faced back in.

Dad hit the table with his hand like a gavel and started to get up.

"Wait," Caitlin said. "Dad." His frown was attentive. She ducked and went on, "We think you need help."

Dad glanced at Mum. She was fiddling with her pearl earring. Her other hand came up for an adjustment.

"You do, Dad," Sophie said.

Dad's gaze went over the table—the green vases of red nasturtiums, some Sugar Pops casting pebble shadows. . . . He reached into his pocket, hitching up his whole side as if mounting a horse. "Okay," he said uncertainly. He brought out a pack of cigarettes and stirred his finger in the opening. When he lit one, it burned halfway down in the first drag.

Sophie covered her forehead. "Okay what?" she said.

Dad looked at her with a cold eye. Delilah nudged her; she kept facing Dad. His posture was stiff and erect and his lips were pressed smartly together.

Caitlin lifted her chin toward him. "Okay what?" she said.

His eyes glared. She shrank back. As he put out his cigarette, his throat seemed to swell, as if his Adam's apple were expanding and the whole of his uncomfortable being were struggling there in his throat. He coughed. "I won't drink," he said.

Was that it? Caitlin began to smile. Sophie picked up a muffin crust and tapped it on her plate.

Gus said, "But, Dad, do you think—?"

"I said, 'I won't drink.'"

"I know, but . . . " Gus inspected his hands lying flat in front of him. Delilah said, "That's great, Dad."

Dad's chair scraped the floor and he stood up. Mum had a satisfied face. "Okay, monkeys," she said, "where shall we take the picnic?"

The sky was smooth, blue and clear. Ma watched from her balcony while they streamed out to the boat. A book lay in her lap. She had stopped going on picnics. Each one said good-bye to her, passing beneath her with their towels and books and baskets. Ma held a cigarette pinched elegantly between thumb and finger. The skirt of her print dress stirred against the chair.

Random River was at the end of one of the coves that scalloped off the thorofare. A tidal river, it was a muddy bed dotted with boulders at low tide. When the tide was high, a boat could motor up there. Even then, rocks appeared, just breaking the surface.

Dad stood at the wheel of the fiber-glass motorboat. His seven children were arranged in various perches; the motor gurgled at a slow speed. Mum sat beside him behind the windshield with her round sunglasses on. Usually there was much advice about the rocks, or Dad would appoint a lookout. "You're heading right for one!" "No no! To the left!" Today, there wasn't a peep. Dad navigated his way down the swirling turns, over the dimpled water.

It was glassy along the shore, the water dark green and shaded, bugs leaving pinpricks here and there. Bristling out of the rocks was the stiff grass—a porous leaf that slashed your calves when you were wading. There were tiny slugs clinging to the blades.

The Vincents glided toward their rock. They always went to the same rock. It had a plateau where the picnic basket got put and a scooped-out place where you could lie in the sun. In the photo albums there were lots of pictures taken here.

Gus stepped over the bow railing and crouched at the front.

"Careful," Mum said.

He leapt onto the rock and turned to fend off the bow.

"Eggshell landing," Caitlin said.

They all felt the crunch. "Whoops," Sophie said. But nothing was going to disturb the dreamy contentment that had taken over.

They unloaded, balancing cushions and coolers, lowering Minnie by her armpits. Delilah gripped Mum's arm while she stepped down. At the stern, Dad flung the anchor into the water. Gus led the painter into a jumble of rocks.

The sun steaked across the long ripples of the lagoon. Had Ma been there, she'd have already been in. Sophie tested the water. Everyone moved about politely. Caitlin squinted into the sun, then laid out her towel. She tugged the towel over to make room for Sophie. Mum pulled Minnie's sweatshirt over her head and her pigtails popped out.

"Listen to this," Delilah said. She had a magazine across her thighs. "'The two hundred couples exchanged vows beneath a grape bower on the Reverend's California estate.'"

"Sick," Mum said. She settled her head back on Minnie's life jacket.

"'Afterwards, the wedded devotees reaffirmed their faith in a baptismal ceremony in the garden fountains.'"

"Unbelievable," Caitlin said.

Sherman was rummaging around in the picnic basket. He stood up with a handful of Fritos and crunched them one at a time. Dad carried the cooler up higher into the shade. There was a toppled tree up there, with roots that spread in a fan. When they were younger, the kids used to stand in front of it and hoot and listen for the echo. It was like a half-shell, the way the sounds reverberated. Up close, the roots and moss made intricate designs, like an ancient chart. Chicky was digging at a groove in the rock with a stick, idly but persistently. Gus and Minnie squatted over some curly black lichen. "Indian cornflakes," Gus said. Minnie laughed. It was quiet and pleasant and there was no noise except the drone of a motorboat somewhere out on the water.

Then they all heard the sound.

They sometimes heard noises far off—a *crack* like that—someone with a shotgun who knew what he was doing, or a pickup backfiring on the South Eden bridge farther down the river. But none of the picnickers mistook this sound.

Some heads jerked toward Dad; some looked down. Above them, Dad was facing the root screen, his back to the family. Mum didn't move, lying on the life jacket, eyes hidden behind her sunglasses. Sophie hugged her shins and bit her knee. Gus's neck was twisted into a tortured position; he glared at Dad's back.

Dad turned around. He gazed with an innocent expression out over the snaking water. If aware of the eyes upon him, Dad did not betray it, observing the scenery with contentment; nothing more normal than for him to be standing in the shade at a family picnic holding a can of beer. He twisted the ring from its opening and, squinting at a far-off view, stooped to lap up the nipple foam at the top of the can.

The silence was no longer tranquil.

Sometimes on still, black nights they had had throwing contests off the dock. They threw stones into the thorofare and listened to hear them land. Sometimes the darkness would swallow up a stone and they'd wait, but no sound would come. It seemed then as if the stone had gone into some further darkness, entered some other dimension where things went on falling and falling.

Beautiful Girl

Ardis Bascombe, the tobacco heiress, who twenty years ago was a North Carolina beauty queen, is now sitting in the kitchen of her San Francisco house, getting drunk. Four-thirty, an October afternoon, and Ardis, with a glass full of Vodka and melted ice, a long cigarette going and another smoldering in an almost full ashtray, is actually doing several things at once; drinking and smoking, of course, killing herself, her older daughter, Linda, has said (Ardis is no longer speaking to Linda, who owns and runs a health food store), and watching the news on her small color Sony TV. She is waiting for her younger daughter, Carrie, who goes to Stanford but lives at home and usually shows up about now. And she is waiting also for a guest, a man she knew way back when, who called this morning, whose name she is having trouble with. Black? White? Green? It is a color name; she is sure of that.

Twenty years ago Ardis was a small and slender black-haired girl, with amazing wide, thickly lashed dark-azure eyes and smooth, pale, almost translucent skin—a classic Southern beauty, except for the sexily curled, contemptuous mouth. And brilliant too: straight A's at Chapel Hill. An infinitely promising, rarely lovely girl: everyone thought so. A large portrait of her then hangs framed on the kitchen wall: bare-shouldered, in something gauzy, light—she is dressed for a formal dance, the Winter Germans or the May Frolics. The portrait is flyspecked and streaked with grime from the kitchen fumes. Ardis despises cleaning up, and hates having maids around; periodically she calls a janitorial service, and sometimes she has various rooms repainted, covering the grime. Nevertheless, the picture shows the face of a beautiful young girl. Also hanging there, gilt-framed and similarly grimed, are several family portraits: elegant and upright ancestors, attesting to family substance—although in Ardis's messy kitchen they have a slightly comic look of inappropriateness.

Ardis's daughter Carrie, who in a couple of years will inherit several of those tobacco millions, is now driving up from the peninsula, toward home, in her jaunty brown felt hat and patched faded jeans, in her dirty battered Ford pickup truck. She is trying to concentrate on Thomas Jefferson (History I) or the view: blond subdivided hills and groves of rattling dusty eucalyptus trees that smell like cat pee. She is listening to the conversations on her CB radio, but a vision of her mother, at that table, with her emptying glass and heavy aura of smoke, fills Carrie's mind; she is pervaded by the prospect of her mother and filled with guilt, apprehension, sympathy. Her mother, who used to be so much fun, now looks as swollen and dead-eyed, as thick-skinned, as a frog.

Hoping for change, Carrie has continued to live at home, seldom admitting why. Her older sister, Linda, of the health food store, is more severe, or simply fatalistic. "If she wants to drink herself to death she will," says Linda. "Your being there won't help, or change a thing." Of course she's right, but Carrie sticks around.

Neither Linda nor Carrie is as lovely as their mother was. They are pretty girls—especially Linda, who is snub-nosed and curly-haired. Carrie has straight dark hair and a nose like that of her father: Clayton Bascombe, former Carolina Deke, former tennis star, former husband of Ardis. His was a nice straight nose—Clayton was an exceptionally handsome boy—but it is too long now for Carrie's small tender face.

Clayton, too, had a look of innocence; perhaps it was his innocent look that originally attracted Ardis's strong instinct for destruction. In any case, after four years of marriage, two daughters, Ardis decided that Clayton was "impossible," and threw him out—out of the house that her parents had given them, in Winston-Salem. Now Clayton is in real estate in Wilmington, N.C., having ended up where he began, before college and the adventures of marriage to Ardis.

Ardis has never remarried. For many years, in Winston-Salem, as a young divorcee, she was giddily popular, off to as many parties and weekends out of town as when she was a Carolina coed. Then, after the end of an especially violent love affair, she announced that she was tired of all that and bored with all her friends. With the two girls, Ardis moved to San Francisco, bought the big house on Vallejo Street, had it fashionably decorated, and began another round of parties with new people—a hectic pace that gradually slowed to fewer parties, invitations, friends. People became "boring" or "impossible," as the neglected house decayed. Ardis spent more and more time alone. More time drunk.

The girls, who from childhood had been used to their mother's lovers (suitors, beaux) and who by now had some of their own, were at first quite puzzled by their absence: Ardis, without men around? Then Linda said to Carrie, "Well, *Lord*, who'd want her now? Look at that face. Besides, I think she'd rather drink."

In some ways Ardis has been a wonderful mother, though: Carrie sometimes says that to herself. Always there were terrific birthday parties, presents, clothes. And there was the time in Winston-Salem when the real-estate woman came to the door with a petition about Negroes—keeping them out, land values, something like that. Of course Ardis refused to sign, and then she went on: "And in answer to your next question, I sincerely hope that both my daughters marry them. I understand those guys are really great. *Not*, unfortunately, from personal experience." *Well.* What other mother, especially in Winston-Salem, would ever talk like that?

Ardis dislikes paying bills—especially small ones; for instance, from the garbage collectors, although she loves their name: Sunset Scavenger Company. Thus the parking area is lined with full garbage cans, spilling over among all the expensively imported and dying rhododendrons and magnolia trees, the already dead azaleas in their rusted cans. Seeing none of this, Carrie parks her truck. She gets out and slams the door.

Five o'clock. Ardis will have had enough drinks to make her want to talk a lot, although she will be just beginning to not make sense.

Carrie opens the front door and goes in, and she hears her mother's familiar raucous laugh coming from the kitchen. Good, she is not alone. Carrie walks in that direction, as Ardis's deep hoarse voice explains to someone, "That must be my daughter Carrie. You won't believe—"

Carrie goes into the kitchen and is introduced to a tall, thin, almost bald, large-nosed man. He is about her mother's age but in much better shape: rich, successful. (Having inherited some of her mother's social antennae, Carrie has taken all this in without really thinking.) In Ardis's dignified slur, his name sounds like Wopple Grin.

"Actually," Ardis tells Carrie later on, "Walpole Greene is very important in Washington, on the Hill." This has been said in the heavily nasal accent with which Ardis imitates extreme snobs; like many good mimics, she is aping an unacknowledged part of herself. Ardis is more truly snobbish than anyone, caring deeply about money, family and position. "Although he certainly wasn't much at Carolina," she goes on, in the same tone.

Tonight, Ardis looks a little better than usual, her daughter observes. She did a very good job with her makeup; somehow her eyes look O.K.—not as popped out as they sometimes do. And a gauzy scarf around her throat has made it look less swollen.

Walpole Greene, who is indeed important in Washington, although, as the head of a news bureau, not exactly in Ardis's sense "on the Hill," thinks how odd it is that Ardis should have such a funny-looking kid.

Carrie, reading some of that in his face, thinks, "What a creep." She excuses herself to go upstairs. She smiles privately as she leaves, repeating, silently, "Wopple Grin."

In Chapel Hill, all those years ago, in the days when Walpole Greene was certainly not much—he was too young, too skinny and tall; with his big nose he looked like a bird—he was always acutely and enragedly aware of Ardis. So small and bright, so admired, so universally lusted after, so often photographed in the *Daily Tarheel* and *Carolina Magazine*, with her half-inviting, half-disdainful smile; she was everywhere. One summer, during a session of summer school, Walpole felt that he saw Ardis every time he left his dorm: Ardis saying "Hey, Walpole" (Wopple? was she teasing him?) in the same voice in which she said "Hey" to everyone.

He saw her dancing in front of the Y, between classes, in the morning—smiling, mocking the dance. He glimpsed her through the windows of Harry's, drinking beer, in the late afternoon. She was dressed always in immaculate pale clothes: flowered cottons, cashmere cardigans. And at night he would see her anywhere at all: coming out of the show, at record concerts in Kenan Stadium ("Music Under the Stars"), emerging from the Aboretum, with some guy. Usually she was laughing, which made even then a surprisingly loud noise from such a small, thin girl. Her laugh and her walk were out of scale; she *strode*, like someone very tall and important.

Keeping track of her, Walpole, who had an orderly mind, began to observe a curious pattern in the escorts of Ardis: midmornings at the Y, evenings at the show, or at Harry's, she was apt to be with Gifford Gwathmey, a well-known S.A.E., a handsome blond Southern Boy. But if he saw her in some more dubious place, like the Arboretum, late at night, she would be with Henry Mallory, a Delta Psi from Philadelphia.

Ardis always looked as if she were at a party, having a very good time but at the same time observing carefully and feeling just slightly superior to it all. And since his sense of himself and of his presence at Carolina was precisely opposite to that, Walpole sometimes dreamed of doing violence to Ardis. He hated her almost as much as he hated the dean of men, who in a conference had suggested that Walpole should "get out more," should "try to mix in."

It was a melancholy time for Walpole, all around.

One August night, in a stronger than usual mood of self-pity, Walpole determined to do what he had all summer considered doing: he would stay up all night and then go out to Gimghoul Castle (the Gimghouls were an undergraduate secret society) and watch the dawn from the lookout bench there. He did just that, drinking coffee and reading from "The Federalist Papers," and then riding on his bike, past the Arboretum and Battle Park, to the Castle. The lookout bench was some distance from the main building, and as he approached it Walpole noted that a group of people, probably Gimghouls and their dates, were out there drinking *still*, on one of the terraces.

He settled on the hard stone circular bench, in the dewy predawn air, and focussed his attention on the eastern horizon. And then suddenly, soundlessly—and drunkenly: she was plastered—Ardis appeared. Weaving towards him, she sat down on the bench beside him, though not too near.

"You came out here to look at the sunrise?" she slurred, conversationally. "God, Wopple, that's wonderful." Wunnerful.

Tears of hatred sprang to Walpole's eyes—fortunately invisible. He choked; in a minute he would hit her, very hard.

Unaware that she was in danger, Ardis got stiffly to her feet; she bent awkwardly toward him and placed a cool bourbon-tasting kiss on Walpole's mouth. "I love you, Wopple," Ardis said. "I truly and purely do." The sun came up.

He didn't hate her anymore—of course he would not hit her. How could he hit a girl who had kissed him and spoken of love? And although after that night nothing between them changed overtly, he now watched her as a lover would. With love.

"Lord, you're lucky I didn't rape you there and then," says Ardis now, having heard this romantic story. She is exaggerating the slur of her speech, imitating someone even drunker than she is.

Walpole, who believes that in a way he has loved her all his life, laughs sadly, and he wonders if at any point in her life Ardis could have been—he backs off from "saved" and settles on "retrieved." Such a waste: such beauty gone, and brains and wit. Walpole himself has just married again, for the fourth time: a young woman who, he has already begun to recognize, is not very nice, or bright. He has little luck with love. It is not necessarily true that Ardis would have been better off with him.

She is clearly in no shape to go out to dinner, and Walpole wonders if he shouldn't cook something for the two of them to eat. Scrambled eggs? He looks around the impossibly disordered kitchen, at stacks of dishes, piled-up newspapers, a smelly cat box in one corner, although he has seen no cat.

He reaches and pours some more vodka into his own glass, then glances over at Ardis, whose eyes have begun to close.

By way of testing her, he asks, "Something I always wondered. That summer, I used to see you around with Gifford Gwathmey, and then later you'd be with Henry Mallory. Weren't you pinned to Gifford?"

Ardis abruptly comes awake, and emits her laugh. "Of course I was pinned to Giff," she chortles. "But he and all those S. A. E. s were almost as boring as Dekes, although he did come from one of the oldest and *richest* families in Charleston." (This last in her nasal snob-imitating voice.) "So I used to late-date on him all the time, mainly with Henry, who didn't have a dime. But the Delta Psis were *fun*—a lot of boys from New York and Philadelphia." She laughs again. "Between dates, I'd rush back to the House and brush my teeth—talk about your basic fastidious coed. Henry teased me about always tasting of Pepsodent." For a moment Ardis looks extremely happy, and almost young; then she falls slowly forward until her head rests on the table in front of her, and she begins to snore.

Carrie, who has recently discovered jazz, is upstairs listening to old Louis Armstrong records, smoking a joint. "Pale moon shining on the fields below . . . "

She is thinking, as she often does, of how much she would like to get out of this house for a while. She would like to drop out of school for a term or two, maybe next spring, and just get into her truck with a few clothes and some money, and maybe a dog, and drive around the country. There is a huge circular route that she has often imagined: up to Seattle, maybe Canada, Vancouver, down into Wyoming, across the northern plains to Chicago—she knows someone there—New England, New York, and down the coast to her father, in Wilmington, N.C.;

Charleston, New Orleans, Texas, Mexico, the Southwest, L.A.; then home, by way of Big Sur. Months of driving, with the dog and the CB radio for company.

In the meantime, halfway through her second joint, she sighs deeply and realizes that she is extremely hungry, ravenous. She carefully stubs out the joint and goes downstairs.

Walpole Greene, whose presence she has forgotten, is standing in the pantry, looking lost. Ardis has passed out. Having also forgotten that she thought he was a creep, Carrie experiences a rush of sympathy for the poor guy. "Don't worry," she tells him. "She'll be O.K."

"She sure as hell doesn't look O.K.," says Walpole Greene. "She's not O.K. No one who drinks that much—"

"Oh, well, in the long run you're right," says Carrie, as airily as though she had never worried about her mother's health. "But I mean for now she's O.K."

"Well. I'd meant to take her out to dinner."

"Why bother? She doesn't eat. But aren't you hungry? I'm starved."

"Well, sort of." Walpole looks dubiously around the kitchen. He watches Carrie as she goes over to the mammoth refrigerator and extracts a small covered saucepan from its incredibly crowded, murky interior.

"She likes to make soup," says Carrie. "Lately she's been on some Southern kick. Nostalgia, I guess. This is white beans and pork. Just made yesterday, so it ought to be all right."

The soup, which Carrie has heated and ladled into bowls, is good but too spicy for Walpole's ulcer; the next day he will feel really terrible. Now he and Carrie whisper to each other, like conspirators, above the sound of Ardis's heavy breathing.

"Does she do this often?" asks Walpole.

"Pretty often. Well—like, every day."

"That's not good."

"No."

Having drunk quite a bit more than he usually does, Walpole feels that his perceptions are enlarged. Looking at Carrie, he has a sudden and certain vision of her future: in ten or so years, in her late twenties, early thirties, she will be more beautiful than even Ardis ever was. She will be an exceptional beauty, a beautiful woman, whereas Ardis was just a beautiful girl. Should he tell Carrie that? He decides not to; she wouldn't believe him, although he is absolutely sure of his perception. Besides, even a little drunk he is too shy.

Instead, in an inspired burst, he says, "Listen, she's got to go somewhere. You know, dry out. There's a place in Connecticut. Senators' wives—"

Carrie's bright young eyes shine, beautifully. "That would be neat," she says.

"You'd be O.K. by yourself for a while?"

"I really would. I'm thinking about getting a dog—our cat just disappeared. And there's this trip. But how would you get her there?"

"Leave that to me," says Walpole, with somewhat dizzy confidence.

Carrie clears the table—without, Walpole notices, washing any dishes.

Carrie goes back upstairs, her heart high and light.

She considers calling her sister, Linda, saying that Walpole Greene is taking their mother to Connecticut. But Linda would say something negative, unpleasant.

Instead, she puts on another record, and hears the rich pure liquid sound of Louis's horn, and then his voice. Beale Street Blues, Muskrat Ramble. A Son of the South. She listens, blows more joints.

Downstairs, seated at the table, Walpole is talking softly and persuasively, he hopes, to Ardis's ear (her small pink ears are still pretty, he has noticed), although she is "asleep."

"This lovely place in Connecticut," he is saying. "A wonderful place. You'll like it. You'll rest, and eat good food, and you'll feel better than you've felt for years. You'll see. I want you to be my beautiful girl again—"

Suddenly aroused, Ardis raises her head and stares at Walpole. "I am a beautiful girl," she rasps out, furiously.

PETER TAYLOR
· · · · · · · ·

The Captain's Son

There is an exchange between the two cities of Nashville and Memphis which has been going on forever—for two centuries almost. (That's forever in Tennessee.) It's like this: A young man of good family out at Memphis, for whom something has gone wrong, will often take up residence in Nashville. And of course it works the other way round. A young man in Nashville under similarly unhappy circumstances may pack up and move out to Memphis. This continuing exchange can explain a lot about the identical family names you find among prominent people in the two places, and about the mixup and reversal of names. Henderson Smith in one place, for instance, becomes Smith Henderson in the other. Or an habitual middle name in Nashville, say, may appear as a first or last name in Memphis. But whether I have made this entirely clear or not, it is an old story with us in Tennessee and was familiar before my sister Lila and her husband, Tolliver Bryant Campbell, were born even.

In nearly all versions of the old story the immigrant from Memphis arrives in Nashville (or the other way round) and falls in love at first sight with a distant connection whom he meets by chance at a party. They get married. They have children (giving them those mixtures of names). And the children grow up without ever having a very clear idea about what the original connection was or why their father chose to live in one city instead of the other.

The comical thing, though, in the case of Tolliver Campbell and my sister Lila, was that their chief connection was a quarrel—a quarrel which our two families had once had and which Tolliver, being from Memphis, still took quite seriously. For that's the way people are out at Memphis. They tend to take themselves and everything relating to themselves and their families too seriously. If Tolliver's family and ours had had a different sort of connection, he would have been no less intense about it. He was what we in Nashville used to think of as the perfect Memphis type. Yet he was not really born in Memphis. He was raised and educated out there but he was born on a cotton plantation fifty miles below Memphis—in Mississippi, which, as anybody in Nashville will tell you, is actually worse.

To my sister Lila that old family quarrel seemed merely a joke. Even Tolliver Campbell's name was not a serious-sounding name. And his own father (not his grandfather) had fought at San Juan Hill! That alone could send Lila into a fit of laughter. Our own grandfather was wartime governor of Tennessee—Spanish War (broad smiles), not Civil—and he had got Tolliver's father his captaincy! Later they quarreled, the Governor and the Captain of San Juan Hill (laughter). At our house we tended to laugh at anything that was far in the past or far in the future. We were more or less taught to. And our mother and father would say they were glad neither of us children was a young person who took himself too seriously or set too great store by who his forebears had been. We know who we were without talking about it or thinking about it even. Simply to be what we were in Nashville, circa 1935, seemed good enough.

Well, the long-ago Captain came back from Cuba a hero. But he didn't show his face in Nashville. And he didn't come to the Wartime Governor's support when the Governor made his subsequent race for the Senate. Such an ingrate! And what a silly old business! Even Mother would throw back her head and go into gales of laughter, though it had been her papa who was governor and who *didn't* get elected to the Senate. It was all so long ago that any reference to it could set us guffawing. It was like someone's mentioning "Remember the Maine" or "Break the News to Mother."

And so when Lila came home from a dinner party and told us she had met Tolliver Campbell, who had just moved in to Nashville (it was not clear why; and Lila would have been the last person to ask), we burst into laughter—Mother and Father and I. The two of them had been seated by each other at the dinner party just by chance. Or possibly some knowing old Nashvillian had arranged the place cards that way in jest. Anyhow, what a handsome pair they made, Tolliver Bryant Campbell in his white sharkskin suit, with his dark hair and eyes, his military bearing, and his politely grave manner, there beside my pretty, vivacious, honey-haired sister Lila. Lila was twenty-one then and was reckoned a kind of second-year girl, though, since it was during the Depression, she hadn't actually come out at all. And she looked like a girl of seventeen. Tolliver himself wasn't yet thirty and so couldn't properly be termed an old bachelor. Their ages were just right for a match. They made a striking pair. When they were introduced each of them knew at once who the other was or who—within reason, considering their names—the other must be.

Lila made their meeting sound very funny, especially Tolliver's formality, especially his notion that he ought to call on Father before trying to make a real date with Lila, that he ought ("in view of past events") to explain to Father his family's version of the old quarrel, which *was* that by the time the Senate race came up Captain Campbell had married the daughter of the biggest landowner in Mississippi, a man who disapproved of his son-in-law's taking part in politics. It was a question of loyalties, don't you see? In the end, what else could the Captain do but abide by his father-in-law's wishes? Lila repeated this argument to us, but even after she and Tolliver got married my parents would never permit Tolliver to defend his father to them. At the time of the wedding, they received old Captain Campbell and Mrs. Campbell as though nothing had ever happened. The ancient quarrel was water over the dam, Mother and Father insisted, and was best forgotten. Besides, it was all too absurd. Mother was fond of saying, "It's just too absurd to be ridiculous."

On the night of the party where Tolliver and Lila met, we sat up rather later than usual at our house, the four of us in the upstairs sitting room, listening to Lila's account of her evening. In her stocking feet, but still wearing her evening dress and clutching her high-heeled slippers in one hand and her silver evening bag in the other, she went on and on about Tolliver. Then finally she announced to us—rather belatedly, we three thought—that Tolliver Campbell was, in fact, coming to pay a call on Father. What she said came as a considerable surprise—that is, after all her merriment about their meeting. Father directed a knowing grin at Mother and me and he accused Lila of having given "young Campbell" encouragement. Mother said, "Tell us the truth, Lila. You must have found the young man somewhat attractive."

Lila rolled her eyes about the room for a moment. It was as though she were summoning Tolliver's face to her mind's eye. "Oh, he's good enough looking, I guess," she said. "Like all the Campbells are. And he's rich as Crocsus, everyone says." Resting her head on the chair back, she added, "But I think he's a little too Mississippi for our tastes. . . . Don't you?"

It was barely six months later, though, that my sister Lila and Tolliver Bryant Campbell got married at the West End Methodist Church. They had a honeymoon in the Caribbean and then, at the insistence of my parents, they came to live with us at our house on Elliston Place. That they should move into the house with us was something nobody would have predicted when they first got engaged—least of all Tolliver, so it seemed. He certainly appeared to have had other plans. He had already bought a house out in the Belle Meade section, and when the decision was made about where they would live he sold the house at a shocking loss—sold it without asking my father's advice, without even trying to get a good price for the place.

They were supposed to stay with us only temporarily but they remained for more than three years. Lila would often say, with a laugh, that she and Tolliver seemed to have been struck by a paralysis of some kind. But it was Father, actually, who never quite let them go. He would always come up with a reason for them to linger another month—or another year. In the beginning I think he was afraid Tolliver might turn out to be a high liver and big spender and so, during times when nearly everybody else was hard up, be a source of embarrassment to us all.

Yet once Lila and Tolliver had settled into the house with us, what worried Father, and worried us all, was the simple fact that Tolliver Campbell had no occupation—no calling or profession of any kind. He was content to stay home every day and attend to his financial affairs— his rents and royalties, as he referred to them—sitting either at the desk in the library or at a card table in the sun parlor. He employed a secretary to come to the house twice a week, to take dictation and to attend to the most tedious details of his banking and to the bookkeeping which he had to do in connection with his landholdings. As Father pointed out, all of this was hardest on Mother. She "just wasn't prepared" to have a man around the house all the time. That might be how you did things on a Mississippi plantation, but not in Nashville. In Nashville, any man was expected to have a career of some kind. Or at least to go to an office somewhere every weekday that dawned.

I was four years younger than my sister and was just finishing high school when she married. I attended Hume-Fogg High School, the public school, because during those Depression years our family was doing whatever it decently could to cut corners. Naturally, at that time I knew precious little about any life at all outside Hume-Fogg or outside the neighborhood around Elliston Place. To have someone as different as Tolliver Campbell suddenly moving into our house, a young man so rich that he hadn't given thought to taking up some line of work—to have him living there under our roof seemed to me an extraordinary thing. He was so different from us in so many ways that we knew from the start we would have to do a lot just to make him feel comfortable with us. My mother said, in advance, that it would be only good manners to put ourselves out for him a great deal and make many allowances for him because of all that he was accustomed to having done for him at his parents' house in Memphis. She was right, of course. But as it turned out we also had to do a good many things and take a certain care just to preserve our *own* comfort, with Tolliver around. He had a way of taking you up on things you didn't quite mean for him to—such as polite offers to fetch something for him that he could very well fetch for himself. If you came into a room drinking a Coca-Cola and said politely, "Could I get you a Coke, Tolliver?" he was apt to reply, "Yes, if you would be so kind." And so you would find yourself going back to the kitchen and opening a bottle for him. Even in quite serious matters, you had to watch out for yourself.

The first time this became apparent to me was one night when Father was talking at the dinner table, over coffee. He was remarking on the high cost of everything and how the Depression had made it necessary for *everyone* to watch expenses. Tolliver was present. Though this was well before the wedding, it was after the engagement was announced and he was already coming to the house regularly. Father's remarks about economy included questions about the house Tolliver had bought and about the costs involved in its renovation. Tolliver held nothing back. For instance, he told Father exactly what the house painter's estimate "amounted to." And Father, after first carefully setting his coffee cup in its saucer, exploded in a fit of ironic laughter. "What it amounts to," he said, "is highway robbery!" And he said, still laughing, that rather than pay such bills Tolliver and Lila ought just to come and live in the house with us. How that did make us all laugh! But Tolliver's unexpected reply made us laugh even louder. "I'd just like to take you up on that, sir," he said. We thought surely he was clowning—or I did. I hadn't learned yet that Tolliver didn't ever clown.

I can see in retrospect, of course, that there was more involved that night than just Tolliver Campbell's characteristic directness. Father's own characteristic way of proceeding was involved. The fact is, he had been giving Tolliver rope. One of Father's favorite sayings was "Give a fool enough rope and he'll hang himself." He didn't consider Tolliver a fool exactly, but still he had been operating on that principle with him. He had agreed to the kind of wedding Tolliver insisted upon having. I believe he would have agreed even to their marrying at Christ Church Episcopal if Tolliver had insisted upon it, instead of at West End, which was our church. And Father had not openly protested the extravagant kind of honeymoon Tolliver and Lila were going on. When Tolliver wasn't present, of course, he had made his joke about wishing they wouldn't go so near to Cuba and maybe stir Tolliver's family memories. But he had said nothing like that to Tolliver. In retrospect it is perfectly clear to me that my father was fully prepared for that "unexpected" reply he got about their coming to live with us. As soon as we had all stopped our laughing, he said, "Well, I don't know what could suit us better, Tolliver."

As I sat there stunned by this exchange, I found it somehow reassuring to observe the smile of genuine pleasure on Father's face. Presently he glanced at Mother and me as if for support. I smiled and nodded, because I knew that's what was expected of me. Mother said, "Don't you think that before making such a momentous commitment perhaps Tolliver ought to confer privately with his bride-to-be?" But even while she was pretending to protest Mother wore a look made of all sweet accord.

Without a moment's hesitation Tolliver answered, "I've already done that, ma'am."

And as for Lila, she seemed even more delighted than Father by the prospect. "It's a grand idea," she said, "if Tolliver thinks he can stand having so many of us around him for a while." It was evident how thoroughly she and Tolliver had already gone into the subject.

Mother said, "We'll certainly try to make you comfortable here, Tolliver."

It seemed a victory for Tolliver at the time. It appeared he was still having his way, as he had been allowed to have it about the wedding plans (a large church wedding with all of Nashville and half of Memphis invited, with eight bridesmaids and groomsmen, and a reception at the Centennial Club afterward; Father said that when the Campbell clan came down the aisle he was himself going to step forward and sing "The Campbells are coming, I owe, I owe!") and as he had been allowed to have it about where they would go on their honeymoon. (Mother thought it would seem less ostentatious, in view of how hard the times were for most people, if they merely went for a week's stay at Flat Rock. But Tolliver insisted upon his romantic notion that it wouldn't seem like a real honeymoon if they didn't cross over a border somewhere.) But it only *seemed* that Tolliver was once again having his own way. Looking back, I cannot imagine he and Lila would have been permitted to set up in a house of their own, especially not in a house of the grand sort that Tolliver had bought in Belle Meade. If they had been allowed to, one can't know what might have happened or how happily it all might have turned out. They might be living right here in Nashville and might have a house full of children with a scramble of names from our two families.

But I think even Tolliver may have shared Father's uneasy feeling that the Campbell affluence might become a source of embarrassment to us. Tolliver Campbell seemed to want to have some sort of restraint put upon himself. I don't know how else to explain his behavior. I have never since seen a young man who so plainly felt the urgency to marry not just a certain girl but that girl's whole family. And I suppose it was merely a fatal coincidence that my parents felt a similar compulsion to take Tolliver Campbell completely under their wing—even if it meant having him there in the house.

The worst of it was, he was always there. He found our house infinitely comfortable. And clearly our way of living in it was just as much to his liking. There were the afternoons when he played tennis and the afternoons when he played bridge and the evening hours when he and Lila were usually out with their friends. but, except for those times, one was apt to come upon him at any hour almost anywhere in the house. I had never before fully realized what great opportunities for comfort our house afforded or how many cozy corners we had. It got so I could wander into a room and sit down without observing for some time that he was present. It was as if Tolliver Campbell had become more at home in our house than we were ourselves. When suddenly I did see him, he simply gazed over his newspaper or his book or his pipe or raised his eyes from his game of solitaire and smiled at me warmly. And then he went on with whatever he was doing. His smile seemed to say, "Isn't this great, our life in this house?" Sometimes Lila would be there beside him and they would be playing double sol or reading from the same newspaper or just talking so quietly that you could not really hear them across the room. But Lila would still smile at you in her old way as if she were suppressing a giggle about the situation. This was surprising to me, because I somehow felt that it meant she wasn't taking her marriage seriously. But often as not I wouldn't really notice whether Lila was with

3 2 / T H E   I N V I S I B L E   E N E M Y

him. I would just register his presence and his smile and think how extraordinary it was for a grown man to be at home so much and to behave so like somebody my age, like a teen-ager lounging around the house in the summertime.

Yet you couldn't help liking *his* liking his life with us so much. It inevitably made you speculate on how he must have hated his life in Memphis. If he had had more frankness in his nature, if he had been a more talkative person than he was, he would surely—or so I used to imagine—have said how much he preferred my parents to his own parents out at Memphis and preferred our kind of household to theirs.

The truth is, we knew quite well by this time that Tolliver's parents were the "something" in Memphis that had gone wrong in his life. Once he and Lila were safely married, once they had been pronounced man and wife, and when we were all finally leaving the Centennial Club reception and were about to take the bride and groom to their train, Tolliver called Father aside to thank him for everything and to tell him also—at what he considered the first appropriate moment—his reason for having left Memphis and come to Nashville to live. I don't know how long before that night Father had already known all about it, but I am sure he *had* known. Perhaps he knew the night when, over coffee, he committed Tolliver to coming to live with us. Perhaps Tolliver knew he knew even then. Perhaps everyone except me knew, and that only because I was thought too young to know. But even I knew from the first moment that the senior Campbells arrived in Nashville for the wedding. They stepped down from their Pullman car, early on the morning of the wedding, both of them reeking so of alcohol that I saw the colored porter who had received their tip turn away with a pained expression.

At the wedding itself they both clearly were so drunk that each had to be supported as they walked down the aisle on the arm of an usher. It was at the reception that I got my best look at them. I was at an age when I knew almost nothing about such matters, of course, but I did have the distinct impression that they were the best-dressed people present; that, despite a certain disarray in their clothes, they were of the highest style. And I was aware of how well nature had endowed them both, of what good-looking people they were, or had once been. And though they were among the oldest people present, it was hard for me to think of them as such. What was most difficult of all was to remember that he was none other than Captain Lester Campbell of the Spanish-American War and San Juan Hill.

There was only a fruit punch served at the reception, but the senior Campbells staggered about, unable to make any sensible conversation, now and then disappearing into the rest rooms and reappearing noticeably refreshed but wearing a stunned expression on their faces, as though they were not quite sure where they were or what company they were in. Finally they were taken away to their train to Memphis by a person obviously in the employ of Tolliver and described by him as a "hired chauffeur." It was then that Tolliver asked Father if he might have a few words with him in private. Looking Father directly in the eye, and with no apology in his manner, he told him that from his earliest recollection both his parents had been in and out of the famous Memphis sanitarium that treated alcoholics in those days, committed sometimes the one by the other, sometimes both of them by Tolliver himself after he came of age. He told Father that they were well known in Memphis (as Father no doubt already knew) for their public fights with each other and their brawling at the Country Club or at the Silver Slipper or on the Peabody Hotel Roof. Tolliver had finally bolted and come to Nashville, but only after years of degrading experiences at home and endless humiliation in public and only after he had realized at last that he could no longer be of help to them and could not make a satisfactory life of his own while continuing to live in the same city with them.

Father tried to reassure him. He said how sad it was that a person with Tolliver's fine qualities should have been born into such a situation and brought up in such a world. "Yes," said Tolliver, manifesting an impatient satisfaction, "yes." But the "yes" did not imply that he agreed with Father. It seemed to mean that this was just the line he had known Father would take. And that the real purpose of their exchange was for him to dispel any notion on Father's part that he was not happy and proud to be who and what he was. It was not till a number of years later that Father reported the incident to me. It was his impression then that Tolliver had taken this opportunity—that it had perhaps been the sole purpose of his ostensible revelation—to say that although he rejected his parents' alcoholism he did not reject the kind of Deep South Planter life that he and his kind were heir to, and did not accept the idea that a life of leisure, supported by the labor of others or maintained by an un-earned income, was necessarily an immoral sort of existence. "I regret that my parents have been destroyed by their weakness for bourbon whiskey," he said. "But that doesn't mean I discount my good luck in having been born their son or having grown up in their house. I look for-ward to living in your house for a time, sir," he concluded, "but, still, remember that I come there as my father's son." Then he added that he had waited till after the wedding ceremony to speak of his parents' un-happy state because otherwise he would have been speaking of it to someone outside his family. That was all he said. After that night he never made reference to the subject again. And we never again set eyes on Captain and Mrs. Campbell.

I must say something now about the drinking habits—or, more pre-cisely, the non-drinking habits—of my own parents during those years. From the day that the Eighteenth Amendment became law no liquor was served in our house. My father even gave up his toddy before dinner. The only liquor in the house was kept under lock and key in a cabinet in his bedroom. And then, fourteen years later, on the day when the Repeal became official, Father brought forth his bottle of bourbon and renewed his old habit of a single toddy before dinner and a neat jigger at bedtime. This observance of the law of the land was not so strait-laced or unusual on his part as it may sound. Other people like my parents, in Nashville, were as strict about observing the changeable laws of the land as they were about observing their own unchangeable codes of decent conduct. We had a cousin, a federal judge, who declined to serve alcoholic drinks throughout the period of national Prohibition. His younger friends assumed that he had never during his life served drinks and that it was out of personal conviction. They always fortified themselves well before going to dinner at the Judge's house. At his first party after the Repeal, the guests came as usual in a fortified state. When the Judge served cocktails that night, the young people all got shockingly drunk. Deciding Prohibition had been a good thing after all, the Judge never again served liquor.

My father, even in those days, even in a Southern place like Nashville, thought that, since it was the law of the land, Negro people ought to be allowed to vote. He would sometimes make special trips home from town to take our servants to register and to vote, just to make sure there was no interference with what was supposed to be. Only our old cook Betsy refused to go along with him. "Don't come bothering me about voting," said she. "That's something white folks know how to do, and what I say is, 'Let the white folks do any little old thing for themselves that they can do.'"

But my parents were not merely law-abiding. And they did not merely conform to social conventions. They believed that they acted always from the right instincts—right instincts which they shared with all the sensible and well-bred people they knew in Nashville. During the Depression they entertained very little, because they thought it would look bad to be dressing up and giving parties, as if to show that they had been sensible enough to stash something away when there were so many people of their own background who had not. To have done otherwise would have revealed a lack of the right instinct. And it was for the same reason, really, that Lila had been discouraged from making her début. Similar reasoning no doubt had something to do with their wish to bring Tolliver Campbell to live in our house Wasn't *everybody*'s son-in-law coming to live with them in those difficult days? And if your son-in-law was very rich and saw fit to come and live with you, weren't you and he the most sensible, most modest people of all?

As I have indicated, Tolliver never expressly praised our way of living. No more than he ever made direct references to the shortcomings of his parents or to what his parents had provided him or failed to provide him in the way of an upbringing. But sometimes when I came in from school he would look on as Mother and Lila and I seated ourselves around the dining-room table and reported to each other the events of our day. Usually old Betsy would come through the pantry and, standing with the swinging door half open, would ask me what I had done-eat for lunch. If

I had had the very kind of cake she had baked that day, she would say, "Oh, pshaw!" But she would always manage to produce some other sweet that I liked, and bring it and a glass of milk and set them before me on the bare table.

"You are a lucky young fellow," Tolliver would say then. That was the nearest he came to saying anything direct about his upbringing. But once, when I was in the hammock out in the yard and somebody called to ask if I wanted a slice of cake or a piece of pie, he told me about some friend or other of his in Memphis, somebody that he, when he was my age, used to go home with sometimes after school, and how his friend's family seemed always to be just sitting around, laughing and talking with each other, telling each other everything there was to tell about themselves, and making no pretense about anything whatsoever, and expressing no dissatisfaction with the life they had.

When I reported to my father how Tolliver implied a comparison between us and those people in Memphis, Father sat smiling to himself. Then he broke into derisive laughter. Of *course* Tolliver knew people like us in Memphis! And was kin to them, too. Anyone would know that. And didn't Tolliver think we had just such relatives as the Campbells? Of *course* we did have. Even I didn't need to be told that. We had many rich cousins in New York and St. Louis and Chicago. And we had any number of them right in Nashville, for that matter! But from Father's tone of voice I knew the kind of relative that he was talking about: We had what he called our Old South cousins. Some of them lived around Nashville, out on the various pikes and lanes toward Brentwood. They kept horses and rode to hounds and lived in antebellum houses or in houses built to look antebellum. But most of our cousins and connections of that sort lived a little farther off, in such snooty old towns as Franklin and Gallatin and Shelbyville. They would talk to you as though Gallatin or Franklin, for instance, were places as big as Nashville or Memphis. It was as though they were all of them blind and couldn't see what a city Nashville had become and didn't know what a difference that made in the way you looked at things. They thought too much of themselves and their pasts to observe that some places and some people in

Tennessee had changed and had kept up with the times. Moreover, Father always reminded us, too, that he had country kin who were poor as church mice and would never be anything but dirt farmers. He said he didn't like one sort any better than he did the other. He said he thought everybody ought to manage to be merely representative, and ought to be modest about who they were and what they had. "The Campbells have plenty of poor, up-country kin, too," he said. "But the Campbells are people who have always managed to marry *up*—in one sense or another. I hope that may never be said of us."

When Tolliver and Lila had been married about two years my parents suddenly began to entertain. At first Lila made humorous references to this entertaining, though without being really critical of it. She said, "Don't you see you're upsetting Tolliver's routine?" She meant there was always a flurry of housecleaning on the day people were coming to dinner and that Tolliver had to keep shifting from room to room to get out of old Betsy's way. But, more important, she had meant that Tolliver had to dress for dinner, had to put on his tuxedo and participate in the party. Because it was soon apparent, even to me, that it was for Tolliver that the parties were given. The dinner guests were for the most part (as Mother would have said, and no doubt did say to Father in private) sensible, representative people like themselves—representative, one supposes of the old social values in Nashville, people who maintained standards that only they could understand and that even their children never pretended to understand entirely, people who did nothing to excess, especially who did not fail or succeed in life to excess. But sprinkled among these, from the first, would be a cousin or two, from Gallatin or Shelbyville, say, who had great tone. And then, always, there would be an example of what Father would previously have spoken of laughingly as Nashville's business tycoons, a shoe manufacturer or an insurance executive, who was happy—or whose wife was happy—to meet those horsy, high-living, Middle Tennessee, non-Nashville relatives of ours. Those dinner parties were actually rather swell affairs, with Mother producing from her store of possessions silver and plate and crystal and table linen that Lila and I hardly knew existed. Even at the time of the wedding there had been no such display. At each party, one of the out-of-town Old South kin would be the guest of honor—guests of honor, I should say, because they always came in couples, of course—and naturally it was they who would invariably be seated at Mother's and Father's right. And however else the seating might be arranged, Tolliver would invariably be seated directly across from the business tycoon. And inevitably Tolliver would, a few days afterward, receive an invitation to lunch with the man. It became as clear as Mother's best crystal that Father was determined now to find Tolliver a career, an occupation which would finally get him out of the house during daylight hours.

The offers of jobs that came to Tolliver—even offers of partnerships, offers to let him buy into something good—were discussed openly in the family. During this period Father emerged from a state of gloom that had been of many months' duration, a state of which I, and possibly the rest of the family, had not taken sufficient notice. To resort to those entertainments that he and Mother gave, for him to actually initiate such a program, undoubtedly constituted an act of desperation. But he and Mother had obviously realized that there *had* to be a change. Tolliver's comfort in our house had become my father's utter discomfort. Although I frequently failed to observe Tolliver's presence in a room, Father could step inside the front door and sense in precisely what spot in the house his son-in-law was "lolling." "Lolling" was of course not the correct word, though it was the word Father used. Tolliver never lolled in his life. He always sat fairly erect in a chair, and his attention was always occupied by a game or by some matter of his income or by his thorough perusal of the daily newspaper and the various weekly magazines that came to us. Father never failed to ask him what he was reading—especially if, as sometimes, he had a book instead of the newspaper or a magazine in his hand—and then Father's only comment would be a snort of laughter. Tolliver always rose when Father addressed him. He gave Father the title of the book or the subject of the article, but he never said more than that. Father's snort of laughter was Tolliver's signal to sit down again and return to his reading. And after pretending to suppress further signs of amusement Father would go off into another room and close the door.

The discussions of Tolliver's job offers were not discussions of how worthwhile they might be for him but of the nature of each particular line of business or segment of industry. Tolliver would reveal that he had considerable information on the subject at hand and could reel off impressive statistics. He was willing to discuss with us types of business organization, methods of production, distribution, et cetera. But he always ended it there, making it clear that he understood what it was that was being offered him, but also that it was something that he could not by any stretch of the imagination interest himself in.

At last it was the Governor of Tennessee himself that my parents had to dinner. The Governor's wife was my mother's second cousin—not that that had anything to do with their being invited or with their acceptance of the invitation, either. Before the Depression, we had always made a practice of having each new governor and his lady to dinner. My father was not directly influential in politics, but it goes without saying, I suppose, that we were the kind of people whose invitation to dinner a governor recently arrived in Nashville was not likely to refuse. The long and short of it was, Tolliver was asked up to the Capitol the very next week and was offered a place on the Governor's staff. When the subject of his offer came up at home, over coffee that night—it was Mother's rule that subjects which might possibly be controversial should not be introduced until the meal was substantially over—Tolliver tried to dismiss it with a shake of his head and with the application of a new match to his pipe. There was no discussion of the job itself or of how the state government functioned. That, of course, would have been superfluous in our company. Father gazed up at the ceiling for a long time. The room was silent except for Tolliver's raspy drawing on his pipe. Finally Father dropped his eyes to his hands, which he had clasped before him. Then he looked up at Tolliver, a self-deprecating smile on his face, and said, "As your father-in-law I ask you to accept the Governor's appointment."

The silence in the room seemed to deepen. Tolliver didn't even take another draw on his pipe. Mother's suggestion that we all "go into the other room" to finish our coffee was very welcome. And two days later Tolliver reported to the Governor's office on the main floor of the Capitol building.

By this time I was in my second year out at the University—at Vanderbilt, that is—but I still lived at home because of the money it saved us. And though I spent a lot of time at my fraternity house I always came home for dinner at night and frequently I came in during the early afternoon. I remember two or three times having the feeling that something was missing in the house. It was Tolliver, of course. He wasn't over there in the leather chair in the library, with his book or his newspaper, and wasn't on the wicker settee in the sun parlor, with a game of old sol going on the cushion beside him. This happened only two or three times, though. Because it was just a matter of weeks after he went to work for the Governor that I came home one afternoon and found him again in the upstairs sitting room. It was just as it had been before. I didn't notice he was in the room at first. I wandered into the room, eating a bowl of dry cereal with sugar and cream and a sliced banana on it. My thoughts must have been on something over at the University. When I saw him I was so startled that I almost dropped the china cereal bowl. I was startled beyond all reason, much more than I had been even the first time I ever came into a room without realizing he was present. It seems to me now at least that I sensed at once that his being over there would never be *quite* the same as his being there before had been. I asked him if had "a holiday or something." He said no, he was home to stay. He just wasn't cut out, he said, for the kind of work required of somebody on a governor's staff. He said not an hour of the day passed without your having to tell a big lie or do something else that went against the grain. "You know what I mean, don't you, Brother?" he said. ("Brother" was what Lila and my parents always called me. This was the first time Tolliver had taken it up, and I was never to hear him use it again.) I said I did understand, of course—though I didn't at all know what he meant. After a second he said. "I thought *you* might." Clearly he saw now that I didn't. And I felt terribly guilty. I felt that, if I had let him, he would have talked to me about things long before this. And that he would never try again. I felt vaguely responsible somehow for whatever was going to happen now, though I could not have said why. I got out of the room as fast as I could. When I went back downstairs I found Mother and Lila in the front part of the house, in the living room. They had been talking and they went on talking. I ambled into the big front room and sat down, still taking a spoonful of cereal now and then. They saw me, naturally, yet they seemed really unaware that I had sat down there in the room with them.

They had already been over Tolliver's resignation a number of times. They had covered that ground and now they were preparing themselves for Father's coming home from town. They would tell him all about it at once, they agreed. There was no use postponing it. "The inevitable result must be—" said Mother, standing before Lila, who was seated on the couch. "The end result will be—though it will not be to my liking, Lila—that you and Tolliver must find a house of your own now. You must console yourself with that. No matter what bitter words Father may utter and how difficult the moment may be, you must bear in mind that it all means that you will finally have a place of your own. I am sure that is something you must have wished for many times, dear."

Lila, in her characteristic way, dropped her head on the back of the couch and let her eyes roll about the room. "Well, no," she said at last. "It can't be that, Mother. That *can't* be the outcome."

"I am afraid, in the end, it will have to be that," Mother insisted.

"No it *can't* be that, Mother," Lila repeated, with new firmness in her tone. "Not yet."

I could tell from Mother's expression, and Lila obviously could tell too, that Mother thought that something had happened to Tolliver Campbell's fortune, that his money was gone.

Lila gave way to giggles. Then, pulling herself up, she said "It's worse than you think, Mother darling. We can't, we *must not* go to a house of our own. I couldn't quite face that now. It's too late. Or maybe it's only too soon. You see, Tolliver and I are not really married."

"Lila, do be serious for once in your life."

"I have never been more serious, Mother. You might as well know now that what we call our marriage is a marriage that has never been consummated."

Mother was plainly unable to speak for half a minute or so. Lila sat looking at her. Finally Lila said, "You mustn't ask me what it is he and I have been waiting on—or what *he* has been waiting on—for I can't tell you." Then the two of them looked at each other for a longer time without speaking.

At last Mother sat down on the fire bench and said, "Lila, my dear unhappy child, why haven't you spoken before? But it is not too late. Don't you see this may be a godsend? It may be that it's the privacy of his own house he has been waiting on?"

"Except that he didn't ever really want a house," Lila said. "That house he bought was just to make him seem serious about things. And he didn't really want a wife. He's a little boy still. He never *was* what he seemed. He wasn't the mysterious young man I imagined him to be, whose immoral life had made his leaving Memphis a necessity. He's only a little boy. What he wanted of us here was a mama and a papa and a little sister and maybe a little brother." Suddenly she looked over at me and snickered.

Now Mother was saying, "That may be how it *was*, Lila, and how it *has* been. but it is up to you from this moment forward, daughter. You must change matters. You know what I mean, don't you?"

"Yes," said Lila, "even Brother over there knows what you mean, Mother." My mother looked at me and blushed. She had completely forgotten my presence. Perhaps it would be true to say that for the moment she had forgotten my existence even. I think it must have been among the worst moments in her life. I rose to leave, and Lila said— more to me than to Mother, it seemed—"It's not up to me. It never will be up to me. It's still up to Tolliver. It's his problem, and he must solve it in his own way, whatever that may turn out to be." I could hear Mother crying now as I went out through the dining room toward the pantry.

My mother never kept anything from my father. And so there was no doubt that before the next morning he knew all that she knew about the state of affairs. At dinner nothing was said of Tolliver's failure at the State House and nothing, of course, of his failure upstairs. After dinner Tolliver and Lila went out for a while, and I noticed that Tolliver had his briefcase with him. But they didn't dress up as they usually did when they were going out for the evening. And they were back in less than an hour, with Tolliver still lugging his briefcase. They went directly up to their room and they did not reappear until lunchtime the following day. It was something that had never happened before. But during the two following spring months it was never any other way than that. They would disappear upstairs immediately after dinner at night, and we wouldn't see them again until noon the next day. Our house was one of those big houses built in Nashville around the turn of the century, and the walls were fairly soundpoof. But sometimes in the night, during this period, I would hear Lila's and Tolliver's voices coming from their room. Sometimes they would seem to be laughing almost hysterically, and sometimes I was sure both voices were raised in anger. And no one was allowed in their room at any time during those months. Even old Betsy wasn't let in to change the linen. On a few occasions, at the beginning, they went out with some of their friends to dinner. And I would hear Lila locking the bedroom door as they left. Soon they altogether gave up seeing their friends in the evening. Lila seldom left the house. Often she returned to their room after lunch. Tolliver had now begun leaving the house to play either bridge or tennis every afternoon—even on the weekend. During all this, my parents struck me as being in a kind of daze. Most of the time they didn't even make conversation with each other.

Then one morning early in June, Tolliver appeared at the breakfast table, though without sitting down to join us. He announced that he had rented a small office a few blocks away from the house. He planned to go there every morning and attend to all of his business matters. Father looked up at him and smiled uncertainly. It seemed to me it was the first time he had smiled at all for two months past. I thought I read hope in the smile as it began to spread across his face. Then as the smile became more fully formed and expressive I saw that what it clearly expressed was regret. I understood Father's feeling at once: Why couldn't

Tolliver have made such a gesture six months earlier? It would have mattered then. It didn't matter now to any of us. It was too late—though I could sense that even Father didn't know exactly why it was too late. He and Mother were sitting across the table from me. Tolliver was standing at the place just beside me. It was apparent he was not going to have breakfast with us. He just stood there behind the chair, with his two hands on the chair back. I could barely keep from fixing my eyes on his gold wedding band, but I managed to look up at his face, and I heard Mother saying, "You will be better able to concentrate on your work in an office, won't you?" As she spoke, and as I watched Tolliver's face, I thought that in his brown eyes there was none of the respect and admiration for my parents that formerly one always read there. Afterward, it seemed to me I had read in his eyes that morning a certain vengeful gleam. But I can never be certain of that. At any rate, while I looked at him I became aware of something considerably more powerful than anything that his eyes expressed. He smelled the way some of the older boys in my fraternity did on the morning after a big drunk. And I had smelled it once before, on the platform at the Union Depot. It was the odor, at once sour and musky, of a person whose system has been saturated with bourbon whiskey. I could imagine almost that he was standing close to me on purpose, so that I would be sure to smell him. Once I had recognized the odor, the vaguely bloodshot eyes and the tired expression about the mouth were unmistakable signs. He was like a hung-over fraternity boy with an eight-o'clock class to make.

I said nothing until he had gone. But when he had lumbered out through the front hall with his briefcase and pulled the front door behind him, I said at once, "Boy! Has *he* been boozing!"

Almost before the words were out of my mouth Father said, "Nonsense! What idiocy has come over you? You don't know what you are talking about."

And Mother said, "I often wonder, Brother, what it is you *are* learning over at Vanderbilt University!"

With my two parents' eyes on me I began eating my breakfast again. Though I could recognize the outrage in their faces and knew that nothing I might add would convince them if they did not already believe me,

I did say, with my mouth full of food, "I'm just telling you. He's been boozing. And I don't mean he's just had a 'social' drink or two." I felt as though this were almost the first observation about a member of my family that I had ever made for myself, and I knew I had to insist upon it.

"Well," Father said, "*I'm* telling you to keep such mistaken observations to yourself."

Still I did not give in. He got up from the table and kissed Mother goodbye. But before he had got halfway across the front hall, there was a noise from upstairs, a loud thump, as though a piece of furniture had fallen over or someone had dropped a heavy object. Father turned and moved quickly toward the foot of the stairs. Mother sprang up from the table and overtook him. "Let me go to her, dear," she said.

At the top of the stairway she knocked on Lila's door. And she called her name. "May I come in, Lila?" she asked.

Lila's voice rang out: "No, you may not. You may not come in here. It's *my* room, and Tolliver's!"

"What's happened, darling?"

"You just may not come in. Do you hear me? You just may *not*."

Mother glanced down the steps at Father. He nodded. "Go in," he whispered. Mother tried the door to see if it was locked. It wasn't. She cracked the door, leaning forward. She seemed frozen in that position for several seconds. Presently she made a gesture, indicating that Father and I should stay downstairs. I think Father would have gone on up except that he knew I would follow, sheeplike, and he was afraid there was something up there that I shouldn't see.

He and I might as well have gone up, because when Mother came down, half an hour later, she concealed nothing, not even from me. She described what she had seen so graphically that I have ever afterward imagined that I actually did look into the room with her. As she opened the door she beheld Lila stark naked except for her hat and shoes and just picking herself up—herself and her handbag—from where she had fallen, in the center of the large room. She had plainly been preparing to come downstairs and then go out on the streets of Nashville just as she was. She seemed unaware that the only clothing she had put on was her narrow-brimmed straw hat and her spectator pumps. Mother said to us,

"In the old days, before Prohibition, I saw any number of drunk persons in all kinds of public places in Nashville. But Lila is the most thoroughly inebriated person I have ever set eyes on." Upstairs she had struggled with Lila to get her into her nightgown and then back into bed. She was able to do so, she told us, only after making a solemn promise to Lila. "And," she asserted, more to herself now than to us, "I intend to keep my promise to her."

While she seemed to be wandering off in her own reflections, Father declared, "The first thing is to get a doctor here." That recalled Mother from her reverie.

"No," she asserted, "there will be no doctor here. Our concern from here out is to protect Lila. And only that. She is married to an unholy fiend. Since he is her lawful husband, we may not be able to protect her from him, but we can protect her from the eyes of the world. Within a few months he has managed to reduce her to a complete dependence upon liquor. He has done it right here in our house. You should see the room. The mantel shelf and the tops of the bureaus are lined with empty bottles."

I could not make out from what she said whether she thought Tolliver, as he had turned to drinking himself, had done this thing unconsciously or had purposely corrupted Lila. The question would occupy my mind for a long time and of course no one—possibly not even Tolliver—could ever give an assured answer to it. And now Mother was saying to Father, "I want you to go to your liquor cabinet and bring me a bottle of bourbon whiskey. That's what she's come to like. If I give her one drink now, she says she will sleep till noon. That's become her practice."

During the hours before lunchtime I wondered if Tolliver would come back for lunch or even if he would ever come back at all. I doubted that the office he spoke of existed. It seemed possible that, with full knowledge of her present condition and probably what was her fixed habit, he had left her in the house without any liquor and without the means of obtaining any unless she came downstairs to beg some of her father or went out in the town somewhere to purchase it. In either case she was bound to expose her wretched condition to her parents. On the other hand, in his own present hung-over state it seemed possible—even quite likely—that Tolliver was incapable of such purposeful action. The worst possibility—and one which I could not even entertain—was that Tolliver was so base as to have consciously planned an act of vengeance months before and was now mindlessly carrying it out.

We were all somewhat reassured when Tolliver did return for lunch. Father had been persuaded by Mother to go on downtown as usual. It is hard to believe he was able to concentrate on his work there. I was supposed to be studying for my examinations, and so I stayed at home all morning, but only pretending to study, actually waiting to see if there was any word from Tolliver. He came in at noon with the predictable briefcase, and went directly up to his and Lila's room. At half past twelve he and Lila and Mother and I sat down to lunch in the dining room. Since Father never came home to lunch, he was not there. But Mother had gone to the telephone and called him to report Tolliver's return the moment it occurred. My first thought when Tolliver opened the front door was how I dreaded the four of us sitting down at the table together. But, though I doubted my own senses almost, it was no different from other lunches in past months. And I knew then that dinner that night would be no different from other dinners. It was not like old times before Tolliver resigned his place on the Governor's staff, but it was like all the times since his resignation. There was no laughing or giggling on our part and no warm smiles on the part of Tolliver. And at dinner that night Father did not, of course, tease or attempt any of his old jokes. But still there was merely a subdued or modulated tone to our talk and to our behavior in general. The fact is, that noon and that night I observed changes which had clearly taken place but which had escaped me before or which I had been unwilling to take cognizance of. Lila was no longer my pretty second-year-girl sister, careless of what she said in the bosom of the family and making her giggly comments on everything. I felt that even the way she asked for a second cup of coffee nowadays was different. She considered how it would sound. Would she seem to be *needing* too much coffee? But what was more noticeable even was that before answering any question at all—of the least consequence—she would glance at Tolliver. I noticed, too, that the same, more or less, was true of Tolliver. Whenever a remark was addressed to him, he would glance at Lila before responding. They had become exclusively dependent upon each other—in a way that was altogether unpleasant to the rest of us. We seemed no longer a real part of their existence. It is hard for me to believe that my parents had not noticed such changes or had not detected at some time or other—even though *I* had failed to—the smell of alcohol on their breath or the odor of alcohol in the vicinity of their bedroom. But I must confess that from that day forward it became harder for me to understand the behavior of my parents than that of my alcoholic sister and brother-in-law.

The incident of that morning wasn't again mentioned within my hearing. There was never any mention made, either, of the drinking that had gone on upstairs in the past months and that continued to go on up there. Sometimes in the night one would still hear voices—drunken voices, as I thought of them now—but that of course was never commented upon. The only oblique reference, even, made to what had happened came on the Sunday afternoon following the incident.

It was just after our big midday Sunday meal. I was still studying for my exams. I drifted into the library, intending to look up something in the encyclopedia. Suddenly I became aware that Tolliver and Lila were talking quietly in a corner of the room. Mother and Father observed my quick withdrawal from the library and were able to surmise what it meant. Father began talking to me at once about how happy he and Mother had been from the very start to have Lila and Tolliver live with us. Presently Mother commenced repeating her old bit about our wanting to make Tolliver comfortable. Only this time it was Tolliver's *and* Lila's comfort she referred to. She and Father both insisted that their feelings about this had not changed at all. Mother, who only those few months before had spoken plainly to Lila about the desirability of their finding another place to live, now said that Lila and Tolliver must not be tempted by anything any of us said or did to leave our house and go into a house of their own.

"We are thinking only of their own good," Father said. "It would be a costly, a very dangerous move for them."

From then on there could be no doubt that my parents had only one concern: Tolliver and Lila must not be subjected to the public gaze of Nashville. Lila was hardly ever allowed to leave the house without Mother at her side. It was even suggested that the upstairs sitting room be converted into an office for Tolliver. Above all, life in the house must go on just as it had before, so long as Tolliver and Lila could be kept at home. The only obvious change was that Tolliver, instead of accepting the offer of the sitting room, continued to rise early every morning— though not so early as on that first day—and set out for his office, always without breakfast, always with his briefcase in hand. Meanwhile, Lila continued to sleep every morning until almost noon.

My two parents did seem to regain some of their old spirit and composure. Or at least they feigned it. Sometimes at the dinner table Father would actually make a sort of imitation of his old jokes. And Lila would make a feeble effort to respond with something like a girlish giggle. It went on like that all summer. Since I had failed two of my examinations, I went to summer school and was away from the house even more than in the winter. I even spent a good many nights at the fraternity house. It was mostly empty, and so I didn't have to pay to stay there. I did my first real drinking that summer, and from time to time all of us who were putting up there brought girls to the house, which was on Twenty-third Avenue and only a few blocks from Elliston Place. I don't know that that has any relevance except that I embraced almost any opportunity that summer that might help me interpret for myself what was going on at home.

Then, toward the end of August, at Sunday dinner, Tolliver announced that he was going to make a trip to Memphis that week—to attend to some business there. He had barely taken his seat at the table when he made the announcement. Father had just begun to carve the hen and he continued with his carving. Still not looking at Tolliver, he said, "I wasn't listening carefully just now. But did I understand you to say, Tolliver, that you were *moving* to Memphis—you and Lila?" He looked up then with a smile on his face which would allow Tolliver to take what he said as a joke if he so wished. I may have imagined it but I thought I saw a blush rising in Tolliver's cheek. He didn't speak until he had accepted a plate and passed it on to Mother. When he did speak, he enunciated with great care, as if to make certain there was no misunderstanding: "Yes, sir. The fact is, Lila and I have decided to buy a house in Memphis, and I am going out there this week to look around." Lila's face told me nothing. There was no telling whether or not she and Tolliver had really discussed such a plan before. She was in perfect control. But when I glanced at my mother I saw at once that she and Father had already gone into this possibility very thoroughly.

I went back to the fraternity house that afternoon and spent the night there. I didn't have a girl or do any drinking. I sat on the upstairs porch with my feet on the banister railing half the night, thinking about what had happened and then trying for a while, now and then, not to think about it.

Within two weeks Lila and Tolliver had bought a house in Memphis. Within less than a month, before the fall session began at Vanderbilt, they took their leave of Elliston Place. Only on the morning of their departure did Lila manage to get up in time for breakfast. They had done all their packing during the previous day or two. (I don't know what ever became of all the bottles. They were not in the room when I went up to help with their luggage. Perhaps they went out as they came in, two at a time in Tolliver's briefcase.) Lila drank her coffee but ate almost no breakfast. There was again no mistaking the odor of liquor about her or Tolliver. As they sat down at the table, I suddenly remembered the ugly face the porter had made when the senior Campbells got off the train on the morning of the wedding. But Father and Mother didn't bat an eye, much less turn up a nose. You would have thought we had never had a bad moment in the house and that Lila and Tolliver were off on a lark to Memphis or were facing some bright new prospect out there. We said our goodbyes at the curb, and Father said that he would have the wedding presents, which were all stored in our attic, sent on to them within a week. Mother said she could hardly wait to come out and see their house.

But she and Father never made such a trip to visit them in Memphis. Sometimes Lila would come home for a one-night stay. No more than that, though. From then on, Lila and Tolliver lived always in Memphis. They had one child, a son. He was not named for Father or for our family at all but for his Campbell grandfather, who died just before the baby was born.

Both my mother and my father are dead now and have been dead for several years. After Lila and Tolliver left Nashville—that fall—I decided to try living in the fraternity house, despite all Father had to say about the expense of it. And though I have never married, I never lived at home again. After Vanderbilt, I took an apartment in one of the suburban developments off Hillsboro Road. There was no pressure at all put on me to move back to Elliston Place. Mother and Father continued to live there alone during the rest of their lives, dying within a few months of each other.

Nowadays, two or three times a year I get a letter from Lila. One letter will be full of her old fun or full of reminiscences about our childhood. But the next may make no sense at all. Or there will be one that is almost entirely illegible and that I don't work very hard at deciphering, because I can see at a glance it consists mostly of complaints about troubles they are having with their son. It is easy to imagine the kind of life she and Tolliver have had out there. (And what a life the boy must have had, growing up with them!) It sometimes seems a wonder to me that they have managed to stick together at all. Yet I know couples just like them right here in Nashville. Something happened to them that nobody but the very two of them could ever understand. And so they can't separate. They are too dependent on each other and on the good bourbon whiskey they drink together. Theirs is a sort of joint boozing that sustains them in a way that solitary boozing or casual boozing with a stranger or even with some old friend can't do. They go on drinking together year after year. If their livers stand up under it, they may actually survive to a very old age. In fact, one imagines sometimes, waking in the middle of the night and thinking about them, that Tolliver and Lila just might have the bad luck to live forever—the two of them, together in that expensive house they bought, perched among other houses just like it, out there on some godforsaken street in the flat and sun-baked and endlessly sprawling purlieus of Memphis.

Children

. . . .

The Sorrows of Gin

I t was Sunday afternoon, and from her bedroom Amy could hear the Beardens coming in, followed a little while later by the Farquarsons and the Parminters. She went on reading *Black Beauty* until she felt in her bones that they might be eating something good. Then she closed her book and went down the stairs. The living-room door was shut, but through it she could hear the noise of loud talk and laughter. They must have been gossiping or worse, because they all stopped talking when she entered the room.

"Hi, Amy" Mr. Farquarson said.

"Mr. Farquarson spoke to you, Amy," her father said.

"Hello, Mr. Farquarson," she said. By standing outside the group for a minute, until they had resumed their conversation, and then by slipping past Mrs. Farquarson, she was able to swoop down on the nut dish and take a handful.

"Amy!" Mr. Lawton said.

"I'm sorry, Daddy," she said, retreating out of the circle, toward the piano.

"Put those nuts back," he said.

"I've handled them, Daddy," she said.

"Well, pass the nuts, dear," her mother said sweetly. "Perhaps someone else would like nuts."

Amy filled her mouth with the nuts she had taken, returned to the coffee table, and passed the nut dish.

"Thank you, Amy," they said, taking a peanut or two.

"How do you like your new school, Amy?" Mrs. Bearden asked.

"I like it," Amy said. "I like private schools better than public schools. It isn't so much like a factory."

"What grade are you in?" Mr. Bearden asked.

"Fourth," she said.

Her father took Mr. Parminter's glass and his own, and got up to go into the dining room and refill them. She fell into the chair he had left vacant.

"Don't sit in your father's chair, Amy," her mother said, not realizing that Amy's legs were worn out from riding a bicycle, while her father had done nothing but sit down all day.

As she walked toward the French doors, she heard her mother beginning to talk about the new cook. It was a good example of the interesting things they found to talk about.

"You'd better put your bicycle in the garage," her father said, returning with the fresh drinks. "It looks like rain."

Amy went out onto the terrace and looked at the sky, but it was not very cloudy, it wouldn't rain, and his advice, like all the advice he gave her, was superfluous. They were always at her. "Put your bicycle away." "Open the door for Grandmother, Amy." "Feed the cat." "Do your homework." "Pass the nuts." "Help Mrs. Bearden with her parcels." "Amy, please try and take more pains with your appearance."

They all stood, and her father came to the door and called her. "We're going over to the Parminters' for supper," he said. "Cook's here, so you won't be alone. Be sure and go to bed at eight like a good girl. And come and kiss me good night."

After their cars had driven off, Amy wandered through the kitchen to the cook's bedroom beyond it and knocked on the door. "Come in," a voice said, and when Amy entered, she found the cook, whose name was Rosemary, in her bathrobe, reading the Bible. Rosemary smiled at Amy. Her smile was sweet and her old eyes were blue. "Your parents have gone out again?" she asked. Amy said that they had, and the old woman invited her to sit down. "They do seem to enjoy themselves, don't they? During the four days I've been here, they 've been out every night, or had people in." She put the Bible face down on her lap and smiled, but not at Amy. "Of course, the drinking that goes on here is all sociable, and what your parents do is none of my business, is it? I worry about drink more than most people, because of my poor sister. My poor sister drank too much. For ten years, I went to visit her on Sunday afternoons, and most of the time she was *non compos mentis*. Sometimes I'd find her huddled up on the floor with one or two sherry bottles empty beside her. Sometimes she'd seem sober enough to a stranger, but I could tell in a second by the way she spoke her words that she'd drunk enough not to be herself any more. Now my poor sister is gone, I don't have anyone to visit at all."

"What happened to your sister?" Amy asked.

"She was a lovely person, with a peaches-and-cream complexion and fair hair," Rosemary said. "Gin makes some people gay—it makes them laugh and cry—but with my sister it only made her sullen and withdrawn. When she was drinking, she would retreat into herself. Drink made her contrary. If I'd say the weather was fine, she'd tell me I was wrong. If I'd say it was raining, she'd say it was clearing. She'd correct me about everything I said, however small it was. She died in Bellevue Hospital one summer while I was working in Maine. She was the only family I had."

The directness with which Rosemary spoke had the effect on Amy of making her feel grown, and for once politeness came to her easily. "You must miss your sister a great deal," she said.

"I was just sitting here now thinking about her. She was in service, like me, and it's lonely work. You're always surrounded by a family, and yet you're never a part of it. Your pride is often hurt. The Madams seem condescending and inconsiderate. I'm not blaming the ladies I've worked for. It's just the nature of the relationship. They order chicken salad, and you get up before dawn to get ahead of yourself, and just as you've finished the chicken salad, they change their minds and want crab-meat soup."

"My mother changes her mind all the time," Amy said.

"Sometimes you're in a country place with nobody else in help. You're tired, but not too tired to feel lonely. You go out onto the servants' porch when the pots and pans are done, planning to enjoy God's creation, and although the front of the house may have a fine view of the lake or the mountains, the view from the back is never much. But there is the sky and the trees and the stars and the birds singing and the pleasure of resting your feet. But then you hear them in the front of the house, laughing and talking with their guests and their sons and daughters. If you're new and they whisper, you can be sure they're talking about you. That takes all the pleasure out of the evening."

"Oh," Amy said.

"I've worked all kinds of places—places where there were eight or nine in help and places where I was expected to burn the rubbish myself, on winter nights, and shovel the snow. In a house where there's a lot of help, there's usually some devil among them—some old butler or parlormaid—who tries to make your life miserable from the beginning. 'The Madam doesn't like it this way,' and 'The Madam doesn't like it that way,' and 'I've been with the Madam for twenty years,' they tell you. It takes a diplomat to get along. Then there is the rooms they give you, and every one of them I've ever seen is cheerless. If you have a bottle in your suitcase, it's a terrible temptation in the beginning not to take a drink to raise your spirits. But I have a strong character. It was different with my poor sister. She used to complain about nervousness, but, sitting here thinking about her tonight, I wonder if she suffered from nervousness at all. I wonder if she didn't make it all up. I wonder if she just wasn't meant to be in service. Toward the end, the only work she could get was out in the country, where nobody else would go, and she never lasted much more than a week or two. She'd take a little gin for her nervousness, then a little for her tiredness, and when she'd drunk her own bottle and everything she could steal, they'd hear about it in the front part of the house. There was usually a scene, and my poor sister always liked to have the last word. Oh, if I had had my way, they'd be a law against it! It's not my business to advise you to take anything from your father, but I'd be proud of you if you'd empty his gin bottle into the sink now and then—the filthy stuff! But it's made me feel better to talk with you, sweetheart. It's made me not miss my poor sister so much. Now I'll read a little more in my Bible, and then I'll get you some supper."

The Lawtons had had a bad year with cooks—there had been five of them. The arrival of Rosemary had made Marcia Lawton think back to a vague theory of dispensations; she had suffered, and now she was being rewarded. Rosemary was clean, industrious, and cheerful, and her table—as the Lawtons said—was just like the Chambord. On Wednesday night after dinner, she took the train to New York, promising to return on the evening train Thursday. Thursday morning, Marcia went into the cook's room. It was a distasteful but a habitual precaution. The absence of anything personal in the room—a package of cigarettes, a fountain pen, an alarm clock, a radio, or anything else that could tie the old woman to the place—gave her the uneasy feeling that she was being deceived, as she had so often been deceived by cooks in the past. She opened the closet door and saw a single uniform hanging there and, on the closet floor, Rosemary's old suitcase and the white shoes she wore in the kitchen. The suitcase was locked, but when Marcia lifted it, it seemed to be nearly empty.

Mr. Lawton and Amy drove to the station after dinner on Thursday to meet the eight-sixteen train. The top of the car was down, and the brisk air, the starlight, and the company of her father made the little girl feel kindly toward the world. The railroad station in Shady Hill resembled the railroad stations in old movies she had seen on television, where detectives and spies, bluebeards and their trusting victims, were met to be driven off to remote country estates. Amy liked the station, particularly toward dark. She imagined that the people who traveled on the locals were engaged on errands that were more urgent and sinister than commuting. Except when there was a heavy fog or a snowstorm, the club car that her father traveled on seemed to have the gloss and the monotony of the rest of his life. The locals that ran at odd hours belonged to a world of deeper contrasts, where she would like to live.

They were a few minutes early, and Amy got out of the car and stood on the platform. She wondered what the fringe of string that hung above the tracks at either end of the station was for, but she knew enough not to ask her father, because he wouldn't be able to tell her. She could hear the train before it came into view, and the noise excited her and made her happy. When the train drew in to the station and stopped, she looked in the lighted windows for Rosemary and didn't see her. Mr. Lawton got out of the car and joined Amy on the platform. They could see the conductor bending over someone in a seat, and finally the cook arose. She clung to the conductor as he led her out to the platform of the car, and she was crying. "Like peaches and cream," Amy heard her sob. "A lovely, lovely person." The conductor spoke to her kindly, put his arm around her shoulders, and eased her down the steps. Then the train pulled out, and she stood there drying her tears. "Don't say a word, Mr. Lawton," she said, "and I won't say anything." She held out a small paper bag. "Here's a present for you, little girl."

"Thank you, Rosemary," Amy said. She looked into the paper bag and saw that it contained several packets of Japanese water flowers.

Rosemary walked toward the car with the caution of someone who can hardly find her way in the dim light. A sour smell came from her. Her best coat was spotted with mud and ripped in the back. Mr. Lawton told Amy to get in the back seat of the car, and made the cook sit in front, beside him. He slammed the car door shut after her angrily, and then went around to the driver's seat and drove home. Rosemary reached into her handbag and took out a Coca-Cola bottle with a cork stopper and took a drink. Amy could tell by the smell that the Coca-Cola bottle was filled with gin.

"Rosemary!" Mr. Lawton said.

"I'm lonely," the cook said. "I'm lonely, and I'm afraid, and it's all I've got."

He said nothing more until he had turned into their drive and brought the car around to the back door. "Go and get your suitcase, Rosemary," he said. "I'll wait here in the car."

As soon as the cook had staggered into the house, he told Amy to go in by the front door. "Go upstairs to your room and get ready for bed."

Her mother called down the stairs when Amy came in, to ask if Rosemary had returned. Amy didn't answer. She went to the bar, took an open gin bottle, and emptied it into the pantry sink. She was nearly crying when she encountered her mother in the living room, and told her that her father was taking the cook back to the station.

When Amy came home from school the next day, she found a heavy, black-haired woman cleaning the living room. The car Mr. Lawton usually drove to the station was at the garage for a checkup, and Amy drove to the station with her mother to meet him. As he came across the station platform, she could tell by the lack of color in his face that he had had a hard day. He kissed her mother, touched Amy on the head, and got behind the wheel.

"You know," her mother said, "there's something terribly wrong with the guest-room shower."

"Damn it, Marcia," he said, 'I wish you wouldn't always greet me with bad news!"

His grating voice oppressed Amy, and she began to fiddle with the button that raised and lowered the window.

"Stop that, Amy!" he said.

"Oh, well, the shower isn't important," her mother said. She laughed weakly.

"When I got back from San Francisco last week," he said, "you couldn't wait to tell me that we need a new oil burner."

"Well, I've got a part-time cook. That's good news."

"Is she a lush?" her father asked.

"Don't be disagreeable, dear. She'll get us some dinner and wash the dishes and take the bus home. We're going to the Farquarsons'."

"I'm really too tired to go anywhere," he said.

"Who's going to take care of me?" Amy asked.

"You always have a good time at the Farquarsons'," her mother said.

"Well, let's leave early," he said.

"Who's going to take care of me?" Amy asked.

"Mrs. Henlein," her mother said.

When they got home, Amy went over to the piano.

Her father washed his hands in the bathroom off the hall and then went to the bar. He came into the living room holding the empty gin bottle. "What's her name?" he asked.

"Ruby," her mother said.

"She's exceptional She's drunk a quart of gin on her first day."

"Oh dear!" her mother said. "Well, let's not make any trouble now."

"Everybody is drinking my liquor," her father shouted, "and I am God-damned sick and tired of it!"

"There's plenty of gin in the closet," her mother said. "Open another bottle."

"We paid that gardener three dollars an hour and all he did was sneak in here and drink up my Scotch. The sitter we had before we got Mrs. Henlein used to water my bourbon, and I don't have to remind you about Rosemary The cook before Rosemary not only drank everything in my liquor cabinet but she drank all the rum, kirsch, sherry, and wine that we had in the kitchen for cooking. Then, there's that Polish woman we had last summer. Even that old laundress. *And* the painters. I think they must have put some kind of a mark on my door. I think the agency must have checked me off as an easy touch."

"Well, let's get through dinner, and then you can speak to her."

"The hell with that!" he said. "I'm not going to encourage people to rob me. *Ruby!*" He shouted her name several times, but she didn't answer. Then she appeared in the dining-room doorway anyway, wearing her hat and coat.

"I'm sick," she said. Amy could see that she was frightened.

"I should think that you would be," her father said.

"I'm sick," the cook mumbled, "and I can't find anything around here, and I'm going home."

"Good," he said. "Good! I'm through with paying people to come in here and drink my liquor."

The cook started out the front way, and Marcia Lawton followed her into the front hall to pay her something. Amy had watched this scene from the piano bench, a position that was withdrawn but that still gave her a good view. She saw her father get a fresh bottle of gin and make a shaker of martinis. He looked very unhappy.

"Well," her mother said when she came back into the room. "You know, she didn't look drunk."

"Please don't argue with me, Marcia," her father said. He poured two cocktails, said "Cheers," and drank a little. "We can get some dinner at Orpheo's," he said

"I suppose so," her mother said. "I'll rustle up something for Amy." She went into the kitchen, and Amy opened her music to "Reflets d'Automne." "COUNT," her music teacher had written. "COUNT and lightly, lightly. . . " Amy began to play. Whenever she made a mistake, she said "Darn it!" and started at the beginning again. In the middle of "Reflets d'Automne" it struck her that *she* was the one who had emptied the gin bottle. Her perplexity was intense, although she did not have the strength to continue playing the piano. Her mother relieved her. "Your supper's in the kitchen, dear," she said. "And you can take a popsicle out of the deep freeze for dessert. Just one."

Marcia Lawton held her empty glass toward her husband, who filled it from the shaker. Then she went upstairs. Mr. Lawton remained in the room, and studying her father closely, Amy saw that his tense look had begun to soften. He did not seem so unhappy any more, and as she passed him on her way to the kitchen, he smiled at her tenderly and patted her on the top of the head.

When Amy had finished her supper, eaten her popsicle, and exploded the bag it came in, she returned to the piano and played "Chopsticks" for a while. Her father came downstairs in his evening clothes, put his drink on the mantelpiece, and went to the French doors to look at his terrace and his garden. Amy noticed that the transformation that had begun with a softening of his features was even more advanced. At last, he seemed happy. Amy wondered if he was drunk, although his walk was not unsteady. If anything, it was more steady.

Her parents never achieved the kind of rolling, swinging gait that she saw impersonated by a tightrope walker in the circus each year while the band struck up "Show Me the Way to Go Home" and that she liked to imitate herself sometimes. She liked to turn round and round and round on the lawn, until, staggering and a little sick, she would whoop, "I'm drunk! I'm a drunken man!" and reel over the grass, righting herself as she was about to fall and finding herself not unhappy at having lost for a second her ability to see the world. But she had never seen her parents like that. She had never seen them hanging on to a lamppost and singing and reeling, but she had seen them fall down. They were never indecorous—they seemed to get more decorous and formal the more they drank—but sometimes her father would get up to fill everybody's glass and he would walk straight enough but his big shoes would seem to stick to the carpet. And sometimes, when he got to the dining-room door, he would miss it by a foot or more. Once, she had seen him walk into the wall with such force that he collapsed onto the floor and broke most of the glasses he was carrying. One or two people laughed, but the laughter was not general or hearty, and most of them pretended that he had not fallen down at all. When her father got to his feet, he went right on to the bar as if nothing had happened. Amy had once seen Mrs. Farquarson miss the chair she was about to sit in, by a foot, and thump down onto the floor, but nobody laughed then, and they pretended that Mrs. Farquarson hadn't fallen down at all. They seemed like actors in a play. In the school play, when you knocked over a paper tree you were supposed to pick it up without showing what you were doing, so that you would not spoil the illusion of being in a deep forest, and that was the way *they* were when somebody fell down.

Now her father had that stiff, funny walk that was so different from the way he tramped up and down the station platform in the morning, and she could see that he was looking for something. He was looking for his drink. It was right on the mantelpiece, but he didn't look there. He looked on all the tables in the living room. Then he went out onto the terrace and looked there, and then he came back into the living room and looked on all the tables again. Then he went back onto the terrace, and then back over the living-room tables, looking three times in the same place, although he was always telling her to look intelligently when she lost her sneakers or her raincoat. "Look for it, Amy," he was always saying. "Try and remember where you left it. I can't buy you a new raincoat every time it rains." Finally he gave up and poured himself a cocktail in another glass. I'm going to get Mrs. Henlein," he told Amy, as if this were an important piece of information.

Amy's only feeling for Mrs. Henlein was indifference, and when her father returned with the sitter, Amy thought of the nights, stretching into weeks—the years, almost—when she had been cooped up with Mrs. Henlein. Mrs. Henlein was very polite and she was always telling Amy what was ladylike and what was not. Mrs. Henlein also wanted to know where Amy's parents were going and what kind of a party it was, although it was none of her business. She always sat down on the sofa as if she owned the place, and talked about people she had never been introduced to, and asked Amy to bring her the newspaper, although she had no authority at all.

When Marcia Lawton came down, Mrs. Henlein wished her good evening. "Have a lovely party," she called after the Lawtons as they went out the door. Then she turned to Amy. "Where are your parents going, sweetheart?

"But you must know, sweetheart. Put on your thinking cap and try and remember. Are they going to the club?"

"No," Amy said.

"I wonder if they could be going to the Trenchers'," Mrs. Henlein said. "The Trenchers' house was lighted up when we came by."

"They're not going to the Trenchers'," Amy said. "They hate the Trenchers."

"Well, where are they going, sweetheart?" Mrs. Henlein asked.

"They're going to the Farquarsons'," Amy said.

"Well, that's all I wanted to know, sweetheart," Mrs. Henlein said. "Now get me the newspaper and hand it to me politely. *Politely,*" she said, as Amy approached her with the paper. "It doesn't mean anything when you do things for your elders unless you do them politely." She put on her glasses and began to read the paper.

Amy went upstairs to her room. In a glass on her table were the Japanese flowers that Rosemary had brought her, blooming stalely in water that was colored pink from the dyes. Amy went down the back stairs and through the kitchen into the dining room. Her father's cocktail things were spread over the bar. She emptied the gin bottle into the pantry sink and then put it back where she had found it. It was too late to ride her bicycle and too early to go to bed, and she knew that if she got anything interesting on the television, like a murder, Mrs. Henlein would make her turn it off. Then she remembered that her father had brought her home from his trip West a book about horses, and she ran cheerfully up the back stairs to read her new book.

It was after two when the Lawtons returned. Mrs. Henlein, asleep on the living-room sofa dreaming about a dusty attic, was awakened by their voices in the hall. Marcia Lawton paid her, and thanked her, and asked if anyone had called, and then went upstairs. Mr. Lawton was in the dining room, rattling the bottles around. Mrs. Henlein, anxious to get into her own bed and back to sleep, prayed that he wasn't going to pour himself another drink, as they so often did. She was driven home night after night by drunken gentlemen. He stood in the door of the dining room, holding an empty bottle in his hand. "You must be stinking, Mrs. Henlein," he said.

"Hmm," she said. She didn't understand.

"You drank a full quart of gin," he said.

The lackluster old woman—half between wakefulness and sleep—gathered together her bones and groped for her gray hair. It was in her nature to collect stray cats, pile the bathroom up to the ceiling with interesting and valuable newspapers, rouge, talk to herself, sleep in her underwear in case of fire, quarrel over the price of soup bones, and have it circulated around the neighborhood that when she finally died in her dusty junk heap, the mattress would be full of bankbooks and the pillow stuffed with hundred-dollar bills. She had resisted all these rich temptations in order to appear a lady, and she was repaid by being called a common thief. She began to scream at him.

"You take that back, Mr. Lawton! You take back every one of those words you just said! I never stole anything in my whole life, and nobody in my family ever stole anything, and I don't have to stand here and be insulted by a drunk man. Why, as for drinking, I haven't drunk enough to fill an eyeglass for twenty-five years. Mr. Henlein took me to a place of refreshment twenty-five years ago, and I drank two Manhattan cocktails that made me so sick and dizzy that I've never liked the stuff ever since. How dare you speak to me like this! Calling me a thief and a drunken woman! Oh, you disgust me—you disgust me in your ignorance of all the trouble I've had. Do you know what I had for Christ-

mas dinner last year? I had a bacon sandwich. Son of a bitch!" She began to weep. "I'm glad I said it!" she screamed. "It's the first time I've
used a dirty word in my whole life and I'm glad I said it. Son of a bitch!"
A sense of liberation, as if she stood at the bow of a great ship, came
over her. "I lived in this neighborhood my whole life. I can remember
when it was full of good farming people and there was fish in the rivers.
My father had four acres of sweet meadowland and a name that was
known far and wide, and on my mother's side I'm descended from
patroons, Dutch nobility. My mother was the spit and image of Queen
Wilhelmina. You think you can get away with insulting me, but you're
very, very, very much mistaken." She went to the telephone and, picking up the receiver, screamed, "Police! Police! Police! This is Mrs.
Henlein, and I'm over at the Lawtons'. He's drunk, and he's calling me
insulting names, and I want you to come over here and arrest him!"

The voices woke Amy, and, lying in her bed, she perceived vaguely
the pitiful corruption of the adult world; how crude and frail it was, like
a piece of worn burlap, patched with stupidities and mistakes, useless
and ugly, and yet they never saw its worthlessness, and when you
pointed it out to them, they were indignant. But as the voices went on
and she heard the cry "Police! Police!" she was frightened. She did not
see how they could arrest her, although they could find her fingerprints
on the empty bottle, but it was not her own danger that frightened her
but the collapse, in the middle of the night, of her father's house. It was
all her fault, and when she heard her father speaking into the extension
telephone in the library, she felt sunk in guilt. Her father tried to be
good and kind—and, remembering the expensive illustrated book
about horses that he had brought her from the West, she had to set her
teeth to keep from crying. She covered her head with a pillow and realized miserably that she would have to go away. She had plenty of friends
from the time when they used to live in New York, or she could spend
the night in the Park or hide in a museum. She would have to go away.

"Good morning," her father said at breakfast. "Ready for a good day!"
Cheered by the swelling light in the sky, by the recollection of the manner in which he had handled Mrs. Henlein and kept the police from

coming, refreshed by his sleep, and pleased at the thought of playing golf, Mr. Lawton spoke with feeling, but the words seemed to Amy offensive and fatuous; they took away her appetite, and she slumped over her cereal bowl, stirring it with a spoon. "Don't slump, Amy," he said. Then she remembered the night, the screaming, the resolve to go. His cheerfulness refreshed her memory. Her decision was settled. She had a ballet lesson at ten, and she was going to have lunch with Lillian Towele. Then she would leave.

Children prepare for a sea voyage with a toothbrush and a Teddy bear; they equip themselves for a trip around the world with a pair of odd socks, a conch shell, and a thermometer; books and stones and peacock feathers, candy bars, tennis balls, soiled handkerchiefs, and skeins of old string appear to them to be the necessities of travel, and Amy packed, that afternoon, with the impulsiveness of her kind. She was late coming home from lunch, and her getaway was delayed, but she didn't mind. She could catch one of the late-afternoon locals; one of the cooks' trains. Her father was playing golf and her mother was off somewhere. A part-time worker was cleaning the living room. When Amy had finished packing, she went into her parents' bedroom and flushed the toilet. While the water murmured, she took a twenty-dollar bill from her mother's desk. Then she went downstairs and left the house and walked around Blenhollow Circle and down Alewives Lane to the station. No regrets or goodbyes formed in her mind. She went over the names of the friends she had in the city, in case she decided not to spend the night in a museum. When she opened the door of the waiting room, Mr. Flanagan, the stationmaster, was poking his coal fire.

"I want to buy a ticket to New York," Amy said.

"One-way or round-trip?"

"One-way, please."

Mr. Flanagan went through the door into the ticket office and raised the glass window. "I'm afraid I haven't got a half-fare ticket for you, Amy," he said. "I'll have to write one."

"That's all right," she said. She put the twenty-dollar bill on the counter.

"And in order to change that," he said, "I'll have to go over to the other side. Here's the four-thirty-two coming in now, but you'll be able to get the five-ten." She didn't protest, and went and sat beside her cardboard suitcase, which was printed with European hotel and place names. When the local had come and gone, Mr. Flanagan shut his glass window and walked over the footbridge to the northbound platform and called the Lawtons'. Mr. Lawton had just come in from his game and was mixing himself a cocktail. "I think your daughter's planning to take some kind of a trip," Mr. Flanagan said.

It was dark by the time Mr. Lawton got down to the station. He saw his daughter through the station window. The girl sitting on the bench, the rich names on her paper suitcase, touched him as it was in her power to touch him only when she seemed helpless or when she was very sick. Someone had walked over his grave! He shivered with longing, he felt his skin coarsen as when, driving home late and alone, a shower of leaves on the wind crossed the beam of his headlights, liberating him for a second at the most from the literal symbols of his life—the buttonless shirts, the vouchers and bank statements, the order blanks, and the empty glasses. He seemed to listen—God knows for what. Commands, drums, the crackle of signal fires, the music of the glockenspiel—how sweet it sounds on the Alpine air—singing from a tavern in the pass, the honking of wild swans; he seemed to smell the salt air in the churches of Venice. Then, as it was with the leaves, the power of her figure to trouble him was ended; his gooseflesh vanished. He was himself. Oh, why should she want to run away? Travel—and who knew better than a man who spent three days of every fortnight on the road—was a world of overheated plane cabins and repetitious magazines, where even the coffee, even the champagne, tasted of plastics. How could he teach her that home sweet home was the best place of all?

Christmas Morning

I never really liked my brother, Sonny. From the time he was a baby
he was always the mother's pet and always chasing her to tell her
what mischief I was up to. Mind you, I was usually up to something. Until I was nine or ten I was never much good at school, and I really believe
it was to spite me that he was so smart at his books. He seemed to know
by instinct that this was what Mother had set her heart on, and you might
almost say he spelt himself into her favor.

"Mummy," he'd say, "will I call Larry in to his t-e-a?" or: "Mummy,
the K-e-t-e-l is boiling," and, of course, when he was wrong she'd correct him, and next time he'd have it right and there would be no standing
him. "Mummy," he'd say, "aren't I a good speller?" Cripes, we could
all be good spellers if we went on like that!

Mind you, it wasn't that I was stupid. Far from it. I was just restless
and not able to fix my mind for long on any one thing. I'd do the lessons
for the year before, or the lessons for the year after: what I couldn't stand
were the lessons we were supposed to be doing at the time. In the evenings I used to go out and play with the Doherty gang. Not, again, that I
was rough, but I liked the excitement, and for the life of me I couldn't
see what attracted Mother about education.

"Can't you do your lessons first and play after?" she'd say, getting
white with indignation. "You ought to be ashamed of yourself that your
baby brother can read better than you."

She didn't seem to understand that I wasn't, because there didn't seem to me to be anything particularly praiseworthy about reading, and it struck me as an occupation better suited to a sissy kid like Sonny.

"The dear knows what will become of you," she'd say. "If only you'd stick to your books you might be something good like a clerk or an engineer."

"I'll be a clerk, Mummy," Sonny would say smugly.

"Who wants to be an old clerk?" I'd say, just to annoy him. "I'm going to be a soldier."

"The dear knows, I'm afraid that's all you'll ever be fit for," she would add with a sigh.

I couldn't help feeling at times that she wasn't all there. As if there was anything better a fellow could be!

Coming on to Christmas, with the days getting shorter and the shopping crowds bigger, I began to think of all the things I might get from Santa Claus. The Dohertys said there was no Santa Claus, only what your father and mother gave you, but the Dohertys were a rough class of children you wouldn't expect Santa to come to anyway. I was rooting round for whatever information I could pick up about him, but there didn't seem to be much. I was no hand with a pen, but if a letter would do any good I was ready to chance writing to him. I had plenty of initiative and was always writing off for free samples and prospectuses.

"Ah, I don't know will he come at all this year," Mother said with a worried air. "He has enough to do looking after steady boys who mind their lessons without bothering about the rest."

"He only comes to good spellers, Mummy," said Sonny. "Isn't that right?"

"He comes to any little boy who does his best, whether he's a good speller or not," Mother said firmly.

Well, I did my best. God knows I did! It wasn't my fault if, four days before the holidays, Flogger Dawley gave us sums we couldn't do, and Peter Doherty and myself had to go on the lang. It wasn't for love of it, for, take it from me, December is no month for mitching, and we spent most of our time sheltering from the rain in a store on the quays. The only mistake we made was imagining we could keep it up till the holidays without being spotted. That showed real lack of foresight.

Of course, Flogger Dawley noticed and sent home word to know what was keeping me. When I came in on the third day the mother gave me a look I'll never forget, and said: "Your dinner is there." She was too full to talk. When I tried to explain to her about Flogger Dawley and the sums she brushed it aside and said: "You have no word." I saw then it wasn't the langing she minded but the lies, though I still didn't see how you could lang without lying. She didn't speak to me for days. And even then I couldn't make out what she saw in education, or why she wouldn't let me grow up naturally like anyone else.

To make things worse, it stuffed Sonny up more than ever. He had the air of one saying: "I don't know what they'd do without me in this blooming house." He stood at the front door, leaning against the jamb with his hands in his trouser pockets, trying to make himself look like Father, and shouted to the other kids so that he could be heard all over the road.

"Larry isn't left go out. He went on the lang with Peter Doherty and me mother isn't talking to him."

And at night, when we were in bed, he kept it up.

"Santa Claus won't bring you anything this year, aha!"

"Of course he will," I said.

"How do you know?"

"Why wouldn't he?"

"Because you went on the lang with Doherty. I wouldn't play with them Doherty fellows."

"You wouldn't be left."

"I wouldn't play with them. They're no class. They had the bobbies up at the house."

"And how would Santa know I was on the lang with Peter Doherty?" I growled, losing patience with the little prig.

"Of course he'd know. Mummy would tell him."

"And how could Mummy tell him and he up at the North Pole? Poor Ireland, she's rearing them yet! 'Tis easy seen you're only an old baby."

"I'm not a baby, and I can spell better than you, and Santa won't bring you anything."

"We'll see whether he will or not," I said sarcastically, doing the old man on him.

But, to tell the God's truth, the old man was only bluff. You could never tell what powers these superhuman chaps would have of knowing what you were up to. And I had a bad conscience about the langing because I'd never before seen the mother like that.

That was the night I decided that the only sensible thing to do was to see Santa myself and explain to him. Being a man, he'd probably understand. In those days I was a good-looking kid and had a way with me when I liked. I had only to smile nicely at one old gent on the North Mall to get a penny from him, and I felt if only I could get Santa by himself I could do the same with him and maybe get something worthwhile from him. I wanted a model railway: I was sick of Ludo and Snakes-and-Ladders.

I started to practice lying awake, counting five hundred and then a thousand, and trying to hear first eleven, then midnight, from Shandon. I felt sure Santa would be round by midnight, seeing that he'd be coming from the north, and would have the whole of the South Side to do afterwards. In some ways I was very farsighted. The only trouble was the things I was farsighted about.

I was so wrapped up in my own calculations that I had little attention to spare for Mother's difficulties. Sonny and I used to go to town with her, and while she was shopping we stood outside a toyshop in the North Main Street, arguing about what we'd like for Christmas.

On Christmas Eve when Father came home from work and gave her the housekeeping money, she stood looking at it doubtfully while her face grew white.

"Well?" he snapped, getting angry. "What's wrong with that?"

"What's wrong with it?" she muttered. "On Christmas Eve!"

"Well," he asked truculently, sticking his hands in his trouser pockets as though to guard what was left, "do you think I get more because it's Christmas?"

"Lord God," she muttered distractedly. "And not a bit of cake in the house, nor a candle, nor anything!"

"All right," he shouted, beginning to stamp. "How much will the candle be?"

"Ah, for pity's sake," she cried, "will you give me the money and not argue like that before the children? Do you think I'll leave them with nothing on the one day of the year?"

"Bad luck to you and your children!" he snarled. "Am I to be slaving from one year's end to another for you to be throwing it away on toys? Here," he added, tossing two half-crowns on the table, "that's all you're going to get, so make the most of it."

"I suppose the publicans will get the rest," she said bitterly.

Later she went into town, but did not bring us with her, and returned with a lot of parcels including the Christmas candle. We waited for Father to come home to his tea, but he didn't, so we had our own tea and a slice of Christmas cake each, and then Mother put Sonny on a chair with the holy-water stoup to sprinkle the candle, and when he lit it she said: "The light of Heaven to our souls." I could see she was upset because Father wasn't in—it should be the oldest and youngest. When we hung up our stockings at bedtime he was still out.

Then began the hardest couple of hours I ever put in. I was mad with sleep but afraid of losing the model railway, so I lay for a while, making up things to say to Santa when he came. They varied in tone from frivolous to grave, for some old gents like kids to be modest and well-spoken, while others prefer them with spirit. When I had rehearsed them all I tried to wake Sonny to keep me company, but that kid slept like the dead.

Eleven struck from Shandon, and soon after I heard the latch, but it was only Father coming home.

"Hello, little girl," he said letting on to be surprised at finding Mother waiting up for him, and then broke into a self-conscious giggle. "What have you up so late?"

"Do you want your supper?" she asked shortly.

"Ah, no, no," he replied. "I had a bit of pig's cheek at Daneen's on my way up." (Daneen was my uncle.) "I'm very fond of a bit of pig's cheek. . . . My goodness, is it that late?" he exclaimed, letting on to be astonished. "If I knew that I'd have gone to the North Chapel for midnight Mass. I'd like to hear the *Adeste* again. That's a hymn I'm very fond of—a most touching hymn."

Then he began to hum it falsetto.

"Adeste fideles
Solus domus dagus."

Father was very fond of Latin hymns, particularly when he had a drop in, but as he had no notion of the words he made them up as he went along, and this always drove Mother mad.

"Ah, you disgust me!" she said in a scalded voice, and closed the room door behind her. Father laughed as if he thought it a great joke; and he struck a match to light his pipe and for a while puffed at it noisily. The light under the door dimmed and went out but he continued to sing emotionally.

"Dixie medearo
Tutum tonum tantum
Venite adoremus."

He had it all wrong but the effect was the same on me. To save my life I couldn't keep awake.

Coming on to dawn, I woke with the feeling that something dreadful had happened. The whole house was quiet, and the little bedroom that looked out on the foot and a half of back yard was pitch-dark. It was only when I glanced at the window that I saw how all the silver had drained out of the sky. I jumped out of bed to feel my stocking, well knowing that the worst had happened. Santa had come while I was asleep, and gone away with an entirely false impression of me, because all he had left me was some sort of book, folded up, a pen and pencil, and a tuppenny bag of sweets. Not even Snakes-and-Ladders! For a while I was too stunned even to think. A fellow who was able to drive over rooftops and climb down chimneys without getting stuck—God, wouldn't you think he'd know better?

Then I began to wonder what that foxy boy, Sonny, had. I went to his side of the bed and felt his stocking. For all his spelling and sucking-up he hadn't done much better, because, apart from a bag of sweets like mine, all Santa had left him was a popgun, one that fired a cork on a piece of string and which you could get in any huxter's shop for sixpence.

All the same, the fact remained that it was a gun, and a gun was better than a book any day of the week. The Dohertys had a gang and the gang fought the Strawberry Lane kids who tried to play football on our road. That gun would be very useful to me in many ways, while it would be lost on Sonny who wouldn't be let play with the gang, even if he wanted to.

Then I got the inspiration, as it seemed to me, direct from Heaven. Suppose I took the gun and gave Sonny the book? Sonny would never be any good in the gang: he was fond of spelling, and a studious child like him could learn a lot of spellings from a book like mine. As he hadn't seen Santa any more than I had, what he hadn't seen wouldn't grieve him. I was doing no harm to anyone; in fact, if Sonny only knew, I was doing him a good turn which he might have cause to thank me for later. That was one thing I was always keen on; doing good turns. Perhaps this was Santa's intention the whole time and he had merely become confused between us. It was a mistake that might happen to anyone. So I put the book, the pencil, and the pen into Sonny's stocking and the popgun in my own and returned to bed and slept again. As I say, in those days I had plenty of initiative.

It was Sonny who woke me, shaking me to tell me that Santa had come and left me a gun. I let on to be surprised and rather disappointed in the gun, and to divert his mind from it made him show me his picture book, and cracked it up to the skies.

As I knew, that kid was prepared to believe anything, and nothing would do him then but to take the presents in to show Father and Mother. This was a bad moment for me. After the way she had behaved about the langing, I distrusted Mother, though I had the consolation of believing that the only person who could contradict me was now somewhere up by the North Pole. That gave me a certain confidence, so

Sonny and I burst in with our presents, shouting: "Look what Santa Claus brought!"

Father and Mother woke, and Mother smiled, but only for an instant. As she looked at me her face changed. I knew that look; I knew it only too well. It was the same she had worn the day I came home from langing when she said I had no word.

"Larry," she said in a low voice, "where did you get the gun?"

"Santa left it in my stocking, Mummy," I said, trying to put on an injured air, though it baffled me how she guessed that he hadn't. "He did, honest."

"You stole it from that poor child's stocking while he was asleep," she said, her voice quivering with indignation. "Larry, Larry, how could you be so mean?"

"Now, now, now," Father said deprecatingly, "'tis Christmas morning."

"Ah," she said with real passion, "it's easy it comes to you. Do you think I want my son to grow up a liar and a thief?"

"Ah, what thief, woman?" he said testily. "Have sense, can't you?" He was as cross if you interrupted him in his benevolent moods as if they were of the other sort, and this one was probably exacerbated by a feeling of guilt for his behavior of the night before. "Here, Larry," he said, reaching out for the money on the bedside table, "here's sixpence for you and one for Sonny. Mind you don't lose it now!"

But I looked at Mother and saw what was in her eyes. I burst out crying, threw the popgun on the floor, and ran bawling out of the house before anyone on the road was awake. I rushed up the lane behind the house and threw myself on the wet grass.

I understood it all, and it was almost more than I could bear; that there was no Santa Claus, as the Dohertys said, only Mother trying to scrape together a few coppers from the housekeeping; that Father was mean and common and a drunkard, and that she had been relying on me to raise her out of the misery of the life she was leading. And I knew that the look in her eyes was the fear that, like my father, I should turn out to be mean and common and a drunkard.

Blue Skies

In Hammonton, in upstate New York, where Sharon Richey's mother takes her to live after the divorce, they are always moving—one cheap rental after another. At first Sharon thinks this has something to do with her mother trying to keep ahead of, away from her father—whom she remembers, though vaguely, as an angry, impatient man—but gradually it becomes clear that Mum moves because she wants to move. "It's time."

There might be a spectacular quarrel with the landlord, or with another tenant, or a crude "misunderstanding." Mum's friendly, breezy, haphazard manner is frequently misunderstood, by men in particular. Or one of Mum's psychic friends might tell her that a profound change is imminent in her life and if she's shrewd she will take her destiny in her own hands. "I have my reasons," Mum says. Her reply is dignified, irrefutable.

How many times they move in Hammonton, how many household upsets, Sharon won't know, though years later, she will try to remember. These are the final years of Mum's life, though neither of them know it at the time.

Mum's name is Evelyn, Her maiden name Tharney, but officially she's Mrs. Tom Richey—wouldn't know how to go about changing her name back. The law frightens her. Lawyers, judges, courtrooms, even the look of the Hammonton courthouse give her the shivers. The one thing she knows, she says, is that the law isn't on her side. Meaning that though Tom Richey has been instructed to pay both child support and a modest amount of alimony per month, he pays precisely nothing and there's nothing to be done. If his paycheck is garnisheed, he'll just quit his job and move farther away, to Florida or Texas or someplace.

Only adults call Mum Evelyn, or Evvie; Sharon calls her a sequence of names over the years, never convinced that she has discovered the right, magical one. Mommy and Momma and Mom and finally Mum. "Mum," an embarrassed half-swallowed syllable.

It impresses Sharon, arouses her to envy, that, when she visits with them, her girlfriends call out so confidently, "Mom" or "Mommy" or even "Mother"—no embarrassment, absolutely direct and straightforward. They call their fathers Dad and Daddy, never Father, which is too formal. Sharon, who prides herself on being half an orphan, tries out the word "Daddy" under her breath and decides it's a silly, ugly sound she'd be incapable of saying aloud. Worse, even, than "Mum."

Sharon Richey's own name—her official name, on her birth certificate—is something truly preposterous: Rose-of-Sharon. Fortunately, Mum quickly settles on Sharon. Mum will call her "Rose-of-Sharon" only occasionally, when she's drunk, and then it doesn't quite count.

Sharon Richey is 13 years old when she first realizes that her mother is a person of subterfuge and deceit.

For instance: the increasingly scandalous matter of Mum's boyfriend(s).

For instance: Mum's new (mulatto) boyfriend.

For instance: deciding to move and then moving from the upstairs of a shabby wood-frame house on Pilaster Street, miles across town to the upstairs of a shabby wood-frame house on Holland Street in a single feverish day. Gerard, the "mulatto," as the neighbors call him behind Mum's back, takes Mum's possessions in his car, does most of the loading and unloading. The stairs in both houses are steep and poorly lighted.

Sharon is in a state of shock beyond tears—she will be starting classes on Monday in a new school where she doesn't know anyone. She will have to begin all over among strangers. And why are they moving? When Holland Street is no better than Pilaster Street, and the apartment just as cramped and tacky?

Mum says curtly, "I have my reasons."

Hammonton is a small city of fifteen thousand people midway between Buffalo and Rochester, about 20 miles south of Lake Ontario. Mum came back to Hammonton, her hometown, from Buffalo, when she was first separated from Sharon's father a very long time ago. Sharon complains maliciously that she can hardly remember her father at all—so many "boyfriends" and "uncles" have come between. Mum exhales smoke so luxuriant you'd think it was laughter, draws a languid hand through her shiny golden hair, says dryly, "Rejoice, then, baby— you've been spared."

Sharon does remember her father, in dreamy patches. Once, at the beach, he pretended to be lifting her into the sky—was going, he said, to set her atop a cloud. Another time, after he and Mum quarreled, he snatched her up, took her in the car with him, went on a wild, fast drive to Niagara Falls—Sharon was three years old at the time. It was winter and her father hadn't dressed her warmly enough, just a light jacket, no cap or mittens or boots. She remembers mainly being cold, the terrible wind off the Niagara River.

"Hammonton," says Mum. "Nowhere from nothing, as the crow flies."

Still, she acknowledges it is a place you can live, not like Buffalo. She grew up in Hammonton, went to school in Hammonton (until she dropped out, aged 17, to marry Tom Richey who was 22, so sweetly handsome in his Navy uniform). Both Mum's parents are dead but she has any number of relatives and friends here; Sharon is well-provided with girl and boy cousins, yet it happens to her bewilderment that, one by one, these people drop out of Mum's life. Mum can't tolerate people, no matter how well-intentioned, giving her advice, trying to tell her what to do. She much prefers new, casual friends, friends who don't make demands and who are fun, or interesting, or "characters."

Sharon has learned not to directly inquire after one or another relative of Mum's, or a women friend she hasn't seen in a while, since sometimes merely to inquire—innocently—is to provoke Mum's unpredictable wrath. And if Mum has been drinking, the wrath can continue for hours.

"Nothing better to do than spy on me!" Mum says. "Tell their filthy little tales about me to one another! I know! I know them all! *I know human nature!*"

Sharon cringes, Sharon is fascinated, observing Mum in one of Mum's spectacular fits of temper. At such times, Mum is beautiful, Sharon thinks, as beautiful as any movie actress: the color up in her cheeks as if she's been slapped, eyes shining with hurt and outrage, long, wavy bright blond hair disheveled. (Mum bleaches her hair, of course. It's just dishwater blond if she doesn't—but the very look of bleached hair, the very fakery of it, is part of Mum's style, like the penciled-in eyebrows, the red, red pouty mouth.)

If Mum has just returned home from work, it's likely she will still be wearing high heels, and what a racket they make on the floorboards, where the rug doesn't cover. But Mum, fierce and exultant in her rage, doesn't notice. No matter if the downstairs tenants bang on their ceiling with a broom handle and Sharon—poor jittery, embarrassed Sharon—covers her ears and runs off to hide in her room.

Mum's voice trails off. Sharon might hear her muttering to herself, or laughing, with a wry bitter knowledge. Then she's in the kitchen and the refrigerator door is opened (a bottle of beer) or it's the cupboard (wine, gin, bourbon or whiskey). Or maybe the telephone rings and it's a man, and in an instant Mum's tone changes and she's gentle, teasing, melodic, sweet.

Some of these incidents Sharon records meanly in her diary from Kresge's (red Leatherette cover, fake gold lock, tiny key she hides under the moldy old rug in her room where Mum would never trouble to look). She's sullen, vengeful, hurt. Unforgiving. *I hate her* and *She's crazy!* and *I wish we were both dead!* But only a few years later, after Mum is dead and Sharon makes an effort to read through her diary entries, she will be unable to remember which scenes, which rampages, she was writing about.

Mum has a succession of jobs, and each job has its own special glamour.

She is a salesgirl at Montgomery Ward's for a while. She can buy merchandise at a 20-percent discount, and unsold sale items very nearly for nothing—marred lipsticks, handbags whose simulated leather has begun to crack, pretty nylon or Orlon or "lambswool" sweaters with necks soiled by customers who'd tried them on and rejected them. (Sharon drifts through Montgomery Ward's after school, just to watch Mum when Mum is waiting on customers—so pretty and competent there behind the cosmetics counter.)

Then there's the Rexall Drugs on Dodge Street. And Fashions á la Mode on Main Street. And Sisley's Tearoom where for a season Mum is "hostess" and empowered to seat customers, lord it over the mere waitresses. While at Sisley's, Mum piles her golden hair elegantly atop her head, rouges her cheeks with care, wears a black silk dress with a prim neckline and tight-fitting sheath.

But the tearoom doesn't last; there is a misunderstanding with a customer, or a quarrel with the manager, or Mum is offered a better-paying job—with "lavish" tips—at the cocktail lounge in the Woolridge Hotel, or was it Lucky's Keyboard Lounge on the highway?

Sharon's diary isn't trustworthy about such matters of fact. *She's nicer these days* or *She hates me!* Or often, *I wish I could run away to live with my father!*

Never noted in Sharon's diary because these are the things you don't notice at the time: how Mum sings around the house, good mood or bad, "up" or "down," working in the kitchen or ironing or padding around barefoot in her champagne-colored negligee, her long hair drying, a cigarette burning in her fingers and sometimes a glass of beer, or bourbon and water, close by. "Blue Skies" is her favorite song. It's the one she's always singing, humming loudly when she's forgotten the words or her mind has drifted off.

Sometimes she sings it in a jolly, lilting manner (as it's meant to be sung? Sharon wonders), but sometimes in a slow dirge so that each syllable is drawn out and you can hear the silence between the words and see the terrible blue of the sky that's depthless and perfect and goes on forever and ever without end.

"Blue Skies," they say, but in school Sharon learns the sky isn't even blue and there isn't even any sky there actually, just an optical illusion. Listening to Mum going on and on, blue skies, blue skies smiling, smiling at me, nothing, nothing but, nothing but blue skies do I . . . Lying on the grass on your back, your head flat against the ground, and staring up into the sky and after a while, it might be five minutes, it might be five seconds, the terror grows in you that you can slip off the earth and fall. And fall and fall. For what's to stop you?

And when Mum sings "Blue Skies" in that slow, halting, sad way, as if she's about to cry, it's probably just because her mind is on other things. Like will the telephone ring tonight and should she answer or let it ring. Like should she make an appointment with a doctor because her stomach has been bad lately, she hasn't been able, as she says, to keep food "down."

"Get me some aspirin from the bathroom, Sharon, will you," she says in her bossy voice, and Sharon trots off, and as she opens the medicine cabinet door she can hear Mum singing in the other room: "Blue Skies."

Even if she doesn't feel so hot, Mum sings, it's her nature, she's upbeat, sunny, wisecracking, likes a good time 'cause life is short and you better believe it—the days flying by, as the song says, when you're in love and blue skies is all there is.

Mum does make an appointment to see a doctor, but on the very morning of the appointment she cancels out: Her logic is, she woke up feeling great, so why waste money? And doctors don't know anything anyway.

In a period of approximately four years, Mum will make dozens of appointments with doctors in Hammonton and, at the last minute, cancel out. Many of these times Sharon doesn't even know she has made the appointment, let alone that she has lost her nerve and canceled out. Nor will Sharon know how sick her mother is.

Here is Mum's "mulatto" boyfriend, Gerard—caramel-colored skin, mirthful dark brown eyes, trying to make conversation of a sort with Sharon while Mum, or Evvie as he calls her, is primping in the bathroom. But Sharon is staring at Gerard with narrowed watery eyes, can't smile except to bare her teeth.

He can barely hear her stingy little answers when he asks, How's school, What's she studying these days, Does she have a boyfriend, What kind of job does she want when she grows up?

When Sharon tells him "teacher" he looks sorry for her and says with a big smile, "Is that so!" Gerard is the scandal of Holland Street and of Mum's relatives generally. He's a flashy character. Good-looking and knows it. Mum is sweet on Gerard right now 'cause she hasn't had such a cheering-up kind of man in a long, long time.

Gerard sells clothes in a men's store in the black section of Hammonton and dresses with style himself—silky russet shirt worn tonight with a string tie, tight-fitting suede trousers, hand-tooled leather boots. A smooth operator, Mum calls him to his face. He's a good pal and a great drinking buddy and they've been going out for months, though (as Sharon gathers—wouldn't dare to ask Mum) there's a wife somewhere in the picture and children, too—but whose business is that? Not Mum's.

Sometimes Mum comes home at three or four in the morning and sometimes Mum doesn't make it home at all. Where she stays, those nights, Sharon doesn't know and Sharon doesn't ask. Nor will Mum make any excuses or apologies. The following day, mother and daughter simply try to avoid each other because, if Mum's hung over, the mere expression on Sharon's face (that pinched-asshole look as Mum crudely calls it) will trigger a scene. *I have to live, too, don't I! I have to have some fun in my goddamned fucking life, too, don't I!* And next thing

Sharon knows, Mum is splashing bourbon into a glass to, as she says, steady her nerves.

Mum has just quit her job, or maybe she was fired, the details aren't clear. Gerard, sweet Gerard, is lending her money to tide her over.

One night, driving back from Rochester, Gerard is flagged down by state highway patrolmen for no clear reason. He hasn't been speeding, or, in any case, he hasn't been speeding any more than other drivers— ten miles above the limit—and, though it's 2 A.M. and Gerard has been drinking, he isn't drunk but driving with his usual skill, so why have the police stopped him?

There's Mum beside him, golden-haired Mum squeezed in close. When the police pull up alongside Gerard's car, they shine their beacon into the front seat—blinding light like a kick in the gut. The patrolmen are white, of course.

Two of them, pistols drawn, a sight you don't quickly forget. Nor is Mum likely to forget how Gerard scrambles out of the car when he's ordered to, how he stands with his hands pressed against the hood of the car so he's leaning off balance. Legs awkwardly parted, he's forced to endure being frisked while the cops search him (for a concealed weapon? for dope?) and call him boy, buck, nigger, coon, meaning to provoke him. But he can't be provoked, he's too scared. Only after they see he's clean do they ask him for his driver's license, car registration.

Five minutes ago, Mum was a happy woman, cuddled in close beside her honey-man, not drunk but, as they say, feeling no pain. Now she's stone sober. It's part of their game that the cops pretend to be unaware of Mum. They're ignoring Mum, just concentrating on Gerard, asking Gerard questions in loud, insulting voices. And Mum can't help but hear, nor is she likely to forget, the quaver in Gerard's voice as he tries gamely to talk back, to defend himself, as you'd hope a man might do in such circumstances.

Gerard wants to know what law he broke, why he was stopped. The cops tell him there's a bulletin out for someone who resembles him. Meaning what, Gerard asks, meaning "nigger?" And what about his car? he asks. Are his license plates the ones they're after? But the cops say, for all they know the car could've been stolen a half-hour ago.

Driving home, Gerard is sweaty and agitated but not saying much; he knows he's lucky to get off with a speeding ticket and not a ticket for drunk driving or a beating or worse than a beating. Mum slides her arm around his neck and leans close against him, but she doesn't say much either, thinking what a damned shame—what a damned shame.

After Gerard, the men aren't so nice. How many men in the next two years, how many boyfriends, pals, drinking buddies? Sharon keeps track for a while, as if out of spite, then gives up. By the time Sharon is 16 years old and a junior in high school, Mum doesn't bring them home any longer.

Since they were asked to leave the Holland Street house and are living now on Market Street, almost downtown, Mum is on her good behavior. She's worried she'll be evicted again and the next street down from Market Street is maybe Tice Street, as she says with the dry, droll irony of a character in a movie. Tice is one of the trashiest streets in Hammonton, trailing out into the country, turning from cracked and potholed asphalt to gravel and from gravel to dirt, a road lined with tar-paper shacks, ending finally at the town dump.

Sharon discovers bottles hidden beneath the kitchen sink, beneath Mum's bed, inside a pile of sour-smelling laundry in a corner of Mum's closet. *She's an alcoholic. She won't stop drinking until she dies*, Sharon writes in her diary. When she reads what she's written, she gets frightened and tears out the page.

Sharon is 17 years old when Mum collapses for the first time in public, in the women's room of Covino's Bar & Grill where she has been working the 6 P.M.-to-2 A.M. shift in her cocktail-waitress's costume— short satiny black dress with a V neckline, no sleeves, black fishnet stockings, the usual spike-heeled shoes. Mum falls and strikes her forehead on the rim of the porcelain sink.

Fortunately, another waitress is with her and she's revived within minutes. Fortunately, the blackout isn't anything serious—the sort of thing that can happen to anyone. She's been on her feet for a long time, she's under a lot of strain—doesn't get along with the manager, for instance. And Mum isn't the only one—not by a long shot—who sips vodka back in the kitchen to keep going to get through those grinding after-midnight hours. Why should she be singled out for punishment? Humiliation? Paid off, driven home by old Covino himself and that's the end of it. Don't bother coming back. Sharon tells her, "Now you're going to have to stop drinking, Mum. Now you know that, don't you?" expecting a swift rejoinder or at least resistance, but Mum astonishes her by agreeing: "Yes, I guess so." Mum is repentant, guilty, rubs her bruised forehead and tries to joke but it isn't funny. Neither of them laughs. "I guess it's time, yes," she says.

Mum speaks with such sobriety, such chastened sincerity, it's clear she speaks the truth. She believes her own words. And Sharon believes them, too.

One day on the bus coming home from school, Sharon finds herself staring at a woman resembling Mum emerging from a Twelfth Street bar. She's wearing a coat like Mum's, black cloth with a fake-fur collar. But the woman isn't Mum because isn't Mum at work? And this woman is drunk at 5 P.M. in the company of a man Sharon has never seen before—tall, grinning, hollow-cheeked with a long nose—drunk, too, swaying on his feet—whispering something in the woman's ear and they're off in peals of laughter. It isn't Mum, though for a terrible instant Sharon believes it is. And she believes she knows who the man must be: The new one's named George, runs a jewelry store or maybe a pawnshop, gives Mum gifts and Mum says he's a sweetheart.

Blue skies.
    Glacial blue. Blue, and blue, and blue.
    Opening out forever, and there's nowhere for the eye to take
hold and you fall into it without resisting, without terror, simply falling,
falling . . .

In the clothes hamper. In the dirt-encrusted oven. In Mum's unmade bed where the bedspread's nubby material can be made to look accidentally bunched, so it's difficult to know if anything is hidden beneath it. Even, once, wrapped in newspaper secreted under the outside stairway in a place dangerously open to other tenants. A child's game of hide-and-seek played without mirth, and when Sharon confronts Mum with the evidence, Mum insists it means nothing: just a few bottles of wine, bourbon, vodka. Why the fuss? What is it to you?

She could stop if she wanted to. She just doesn't want to.

She does it on purpose—I hate her.

Sharon Richey seems to have stopped growing, has lost weight, has narrow hips, hard little breasts, face plain and sallow and pinched. Her eyes are bright with malice; the corners of her mouth turn downward in contempt for things others say. She has affected a lazy drawl. Oh, really? *Really?* In Mum's telephone style. One by one, her friends drop away, one by one, her teachers are offended. Sharon feels a thrill of satisfaction, thinking, *I am in control. I determine how people respond!* Though her grades slip considerably this final year, still she will manage to graduate tenth in her class of 86.

She boasts in her diary: *She can't ruin both our lives!*

Sharon begins to avoid the Market Street apartment. Mum is out with her new boyfriend, has gone away for a weekend (to the races, for instance). Sharon is loosed to the streets of Hammonton and walks and walks after school until she's groggy with fatigue. It's a sensation she comes to depend upon, bone-aching tired and her nerves steadied, and she goes to the public library and sits at the end of one of the long chill tables in the reference room, her back to the wall. She is happy here, doing her homework. Nearly always calm here, nearly always calm here.

The Hammonton Public Library is Sharon's secret place. Mum doesn't know. Impersonal as a church, rows of old leather-bound books and gilt-stamped encyclopedias, immense dictionaries and reference books no one ever consults. Heat comes in waves from the clanking radiators, and sometimes Sharon lays her head on her arms, and dreams, rapid as a snake's flicking tongue, dart through her skull and frighten her into wakefulness. And she looks up to see the librarians watching her, two women, middle-aged, frowning. They know who Sharon Richey is—of course—and they know the shameful circumstances of her life. They whisper about her, eyeing her curiously as if she's a freak, but Sharon cooly ignores them.

After the library closes, Sharon walks again, not knowing or caring where she goes. It's a way of clearing her head, getting calm again, working up an appetite when, like Mum, she has a general aversion to food and has to force herself, most days, to eat. Unlike Mum, though, Sharon can eat, does get hungry once she begins eating—ravenously hungry, in fact. She eats her supper in Kitty's Corner or in Garlock's Bar-B-Q or in the Greyhound Terminal restaurant where she's enraptured by so many faces she's never seen before, travelers with unknown destinations. She stares at them, takes note of their clothing, suitcases, conversations. There's a dreamy scene she imagines and has elaborated in her diary: She buys a bus ticket, gets on one of the buses (to Chicago? New York City?), takes her seat, and. . .

But no, she's still in the terminal restaurant, eating a tuna-fish-salad sandwich or a hamburger and French fries. Sugary cole slaw. Giant-sized Coke.

Here is Mum vomiting into a basin Sharon holds for her in shaking hands. Mum's eyes bulging with the strain, ghastly wracking heaves. She gasps and chokes even when there's nothing left to throw up. Afterward she swears she'll never "touch a drop again"—her exact words—but this time Sharon knows better, isn't greatly surprised when she returns from school the following week to find a scribbled note on the kitchen table. *Don't wait up for me honey. I'll call before bedtime. Love ya!*

And here is Mum raising a fork to her mouth, then lowering it to her plate, raising it as if it were precious, or mysteriously heavy—then low-

ering it again to her plate. Sharon isn't watching, but she sees the sweat
beading on Mum's forehead, tiny glittering droplets. Sharon has cooked
them up some scrambled eggs and toast. It's a meal that might be called
supper, though served at an odd time, 1:15 A.M. Mum is trying
valiantly but not succeeding and it's spectacular, it's memorable, her
failure to succeed. Sharon counts four, five times that Mum lifts the fork
before giving up. Then Mum reaches for her pack of cigarettes, lights
one and sucks in a deep, grateful breath as if it's fresh, reviving air, precious to life.

Sharon says nothing, head bowed over her plate. She has worked up
an appetite and she's going to eat.

Mum starts chattering, sweat riding her upper lip. She has pushed
away her plate of eggs, there's a bottle of ale at her elbow and she's sipping from it casually, even daintily. The strongest thing she's had all
day, she swears.

Merely by chance, Sharon sights Mum—surely it *is* Mum this time,
glamorous in her new raincoat, dark maroon shot with iridescent
threads—on lower Main Street about to enter the Cloverleaf Grill in the
company of a man. A stranger—tall, thickset. Coarse bulldog look to
him. *Mean*. And she's standing there so that Mum can't help but see.
Liar, tramp, whore, hag, Sharon thinks. Look at me! Do you dare not to
look at me! Do you dare! Sharon has eaten her supper at the Greyhound
restaurant, the greasy, salty food is compacted in her stomach, she's
wired tight, spoiling for trouble. And there's Mum (who insists she has
given up on men, only goes out with girls from work) with her arm linked
tight through her boyfriend's. Mum staring at Sharon, astonished, as if
she's never seen this wild-eyed girl before in her life.

"Sharon... Hon? What are you doing here? Why aren't—?"

Sharon doesn't answer, Sharon stands her ground, that wide, bright
smile and her eyes flashing with malice.

Mum tries to bring the scene off, not knowing what else to do, says,
"Roy—this is my daughter, Sharon. Sharon, this is my friend Roy."
Roy does nothing more than grunt hello, gives Sharon a grudging smile.
He has an alcoholic's red venous nose and close-set eyes that remind

Sharon of her own. Sharon says nothing. Just that look of hers, knowing, accusing, brimming with spite.

Mum suggest they all have a bite to eat somewhere, but neither Sharon nor Roy responds. Roy looks distinctly unhappy with the idea.

Then Mum says, turning to Roy, half-angry, half-pleading, "Look— I'd better go with her. Okay? I'd better go with her. Can I call you tomorrow?" Roy looks yet more unhappy, draws Mum off to the side. He's clearly a man accustomed to having his way with women.

"Listen. . . " he says, and Mum says sharply, "*You* listen. . . " and Roy pulls at Mum's arm, and Mum tries to shove him away, poor Mum staggering in her high heels, wisps of hair in her face. He's angry and so is she, but she still wants to placate him, charm him. It's what Mum knows best, no matter that flush-faced Roy is gripping her hard by the arm, shaking her. Sharon knows she is witnessing something she shouldn't see. She has made a terrible mistake. She's sick with apprehension—wants to be gone.

She turns and runs. Mum calls after her, "Sharon! Sharon!" But she doesn't hear, just runs, runs.

She spends the hours from approximately 8 P.M. to 2 A.M. in the Palace Theater where she sees, or sits through, a double feature, and in the waiting room of the Greyhound terminal. Then, frightened (of men who are eyeing her, of policemen making their rounds), she goes home, a mile and a half along dimly-lighted city streets, and when she unlocks the door to their apartment, she sees a light burning and Mum's raincoat thrown down on the sofa—meaning Mum is home already. Mum came home before she did. She knows that Roy isn't here because there's no sign of him, not a whiff of him.

Her teeth are chattering and she's so apprehensive or so happy, being home—and Mum, too, is home—and Sharon moves stealthily through the rooms switching off lights. She undresses in her room and uses the bathroom quietly, then stands by Mum's door for a while—the door is closed but not tightly—her head inclined as she listens for Mum's heavy, hoarse breathing, scarcely breathing herself. She's in her flannel nightgown, bare toes curling on the cold linoleum floor.

She pushes the door open. "Mum?" The familiar smells of unwanted laundry, sharp perfume, whiskey. Mum is in bed asleep or seemingly so, breathing quietly and rhythmically. There's a faint ghostly light filtering through the curtains and Sharon whispers, "Mum?" And again Mum makes no response.

Sharon tiptoes to the bed, lies down outside the covers. She swings her feet up with care, crosses her ankles. Mum's heat, so close, and Mum's deep rhythmic breathing. Is she asleep, or only pretending? As, often, she'd pretend, when Sharon crept into her room as a very little girl, wanting to slide between the covers with her, wanting to hug and cuddle. And it was nicest when Mum wasn't fully awake but would just turn to her, sleepy, smiling, and gather her in her arms, and not a word.

Now Mum doesn't offer to share the bedclothes with her, but Sharon is so grateful to be here she could cry, stinging, embarrassing baby-tears she'd be ashamed to show Mum by daylight. She's still, shivering, but it's with excitement, not with cold. Oh, yes.

They lie like that, side by side, until morning.

And a week later Mum is dying.

Though Sharon notes in her diary merely: *March 22. Aunt Lil and I took Mum to the hospital today, in her car.*

Afterward—though it isn't to be until years afterward—she will understand it was an old story: an alcoholic's slow, then rapid, death. Dizzying rapidity at the end. An old story, but new to Sharon.

It happens that, that night, Mum is vomiting—sick, and within a few hours raving sick.

Sharon is terrified, and calls her mother's cousin Lillian, and it's only through Lillian's astonished eyes that Sharon sees, yes, Mum *is* sick, her face gone a queer orangish yellow, like rancid butter; the whites of her eyes eerily yellowed; her breath foul. A film of grainy white powder has collected at the corners of her mouth. As Aunt Lil draws the bedclothes out of Mum's clutching fingers and down—something Sharon never could have done!—she sees that Mum's body has become wasted, skeletal, except for her belly which is oddly swollen, almost like a man's beer paunch. Mum's collar-bones and ribs jut out with a look of pain, her breasts are collapsed and flaccid as empty balloons. Her lovely breasts! In a gesture of dazed shame, Mum tries to cover herself with her bony arms.

No. No. No. No. No.

March 23. Mum is in Hammonton General, intensive care. The doctor says it will be a while before she can come back home.

Sharon's thinking is initially optimistic—now that Mum is in the hospital at last, she'll receive the treatment she needs. No more making appointments with doctors and breaking them at the last minute. Now that Mum is in the hospital she can't drink and she'll be so badly scared that, when she gets out, she *won't* drink.

And when it's explained to Sharon that Mum has something called "cirrhosis of the liver"—among other medical problems—her first response is childlike relief. It isn't anything serious, then, like cancer or heart disease.

Those days, weeks—late winter into a cold, drizzly spring— accelerating toward the end like water as it nears a falls. The roaring deepens so gradually you can't hear it.

Mum in intensive care, kept alive by IV fluids dripping into her veins. Her few visitors are shocked by her appearance, and claim they wouldn't recognize her: discolored skin, eyes swollen nearly shut, a look of fatigue, age. And that queer puffed-up little belly, not so big, really, except in proportion to the rest of her. Sharon no longer attends classes but sits at Mum's bedside waiting for Mum, her Mum, the real Mum, to emerge from this sick woman. She's waiting for Mum to wake fully, to look at her and say she's sorry.

Mostly Mum is unconscious, or too exhausted to open her eyes. Sharon learns that it can demand a terrible effort, to open your eyes. But once, a few days before the end, Mum jerks herself awake, and her eyes shift into focus and she reaches out for Sharon's hand, gripping it with a child's quick, vehement strength. Her lips are scabby with sores. Her hair, now a dull faded brown, has been skimmed back severely from her face. She whispers, "Hon?—why are we here?"

Sharon tells her it's the hospital, she's getting medical treatment, she has to rest, lie still. But Mum is agitated, looking around, says wildly, "Help me out of here! This coffin!"

And Sharon says, "I will, Mum.' Says brightly, "I will, Mum, when the doctor says you're well."

Mum's body is nervy, coiled tight—Sharon feels the trembling deep inside her bones. but in a minute, Mum goes limp again. "No, that's all right, hon," she says, relenting. "It's where they want me. It's their plan. I'm in one place now."

Progression

• • • • • • • •

JULIE HAYDEN

• • • • • • •

Day-Old Baby Rats

D own near the river a door slams; somebody wakes up, immediately flips over onto her back. She dreamt she went fishing, which is odd because she's never fished in her life. She thought someone was calling her "baby."

There's a lot of January light crawling from beneath room-darkener shades, casting mobile shadows on walls and ceiling. The mobile is composed of hundreds of white plastic circles the size of Communion wafers. As they spin they wax and wane, swell and vanish like little moons. Their shadows are like summer, like leaves, the leaves of the plane tree at the window, which hasn't any, right now, being in hibernation.

Through the crack between window and sill, air that tomorrow's papers will designate Unsatisfactory flows over one exposed arm, making the hairs stand up like sentries. Long trailer trucks continue to grind along the one-way street, tag end of a procession that began at 4 A.M. with the clank and whistle of trains on dead-end sidings, as melancholy as though they were the victims they had carried across the Hudson. The trucks carry meat for the Village butcher shops, the city's restaurants—pink sides of prime beef that you cannot purchase at the supermarket, U.S.D.A. choice, or commercial, pigs, lambs, chickens, rabbits, helped off the trucks by shivering men who warm their hands over trash-basket fires.

In the apartment across the hall the baby is bawling, "I want my milk."

It's cold and bloody in the refrigerated warehouses where the meat is stored prior to distribution. It's pretty cold in here, too. On her feet now, naked, she looks under the shade, which snaps smartly to the top of the window, disclosing a day: very clear for January. And colorful: stained-glass sky over a row of nineteenth-century houses painted pink and lime and lilac and beige, topped by clusters of chimney stacks, one of which emits a tornado of oily black smoke, fast dispersing. She ought to report it.

"I am sorry. The Office of Air Resources is closed till Monday. Please state the nature of the offense and the name and address of the violator and we will take action upon it when the office is open. This is a recording."

A pair of eyes on the fire escape, the golden gaze of the fat seven-toed tom from the next apartment; she hasn't a stitch on, backs away. Next thing, she's in the middle of the kitchen, bare and green as a guppy, trembling from head to toe, so much that it is difficult to open the door to the lower cabinet, which turns out to house a sizable bottle collection. On her knees she pours into a glass an ounce of Scotch, part of which sloshes over the linoleum in an amber puddle, fast dispersing. She gets the glass between her teeth. One, two, three, wait—the tremor peaks, subsides. She yawns and wipes the sleep from her eyes.

Getting dressed now, the radio going, the listener-sponsored radio. *Don't speak his name. He is everywhere, like spring. His eyes are leaves.*

She can find only one shoe and digs desperately in the welter of foot-wear like a retreat of mercenaries in the bottom of the closet; how did she get so many shoes? She tends to lose things that go in pairs. "Where's my other glove? My new earring—who took it?" she will wonder helplessly, too old to pray to St. Anthony, patron of lost objects.

His eyes are leaves, the birds his messengers.

Certainly somebody took her wallet last week while she was shopping for pants on Eighth Street. It *was* lifted, rather than absentmindedly abandoned in a restaurant, or on top of a cigarette machine. Later that evening a thin, limping man showed up on the doorstep with one half of her driver's license. He explained he had found it in a litter basket in Washington Square.

Look, flickering in the thicket, at the heart of the thorn tree. Cold as wind—Half shod, she switches to an all-news program: It is after ten o'clock; utilities are unchanged. The other shoe is in the bathroom; she spies it—spitting out a mouthful of toothpaste—under the radiator.

The shadow of a black man, the ripple of a war.

She wraps herself in a white rabbit-fur coat and goes out without locking the door, fumbling for her huge polarized sunglasses in her leather shoulder pouch, down two flights of stairs and onto the sidewalk. Now, here is the big brown United Parcel Service truck lumbering illegally up on to the curb and halting just short of the plane tree, which bears two deep gouges where the same truck wounded it last Monday morning. The driver hustles out and starts up the steps with a brown parcel, whistling.

In the vestibule he rings her bell, which of course nobody answers, since the apartment occupant is beside the truck, copying the license-plate and other relevant numbers into a little spiral notebook.

Still whistling, the young man with the brown uniform and small brown mustache comes back out with his parcel. The woman in the furry coat leans against the tree, glaring through her dark lenses.

"Lady." He stops in mid-trill. "Be nice. I can't go through this again. Just sign the little slip, I give you the package, and everybody's happy."

Through clenched teeth she says, "This time I am really going to report you. Really. Do you know that tree cost one hundred dollars to plant? And people like you, people like you—" But the last words emerge with difficulty, and tears fuzz the sharp outlines, her polarized vision of the sunny world. He cannot see the tears.

She's dying to know what is in the package. With rage the driver throws it back into the truck, THIS SIDE UP down. "You're bad news, lady," he yells, hurtling into the driver's seat; revs the motor. Afraid he's going to take out his temper on the tree, she gets in front of it, and now he cannot move the truck. "If you Don't. Get. Out. Of my. Way. I'm. Going. To Run. You. Down." His voice changes. "What do you want from me, lady?" he implores, unanswerably.

He gets his truck away without a mishap after all.

On the next block the drunk man starts out of the doorway where he has lain all night, stumbling toward her, clawing at his stained clothes. "Hey, don't I know you from somewheres?" His eyes look like pebbles, yellow and veined. "I know you. I know you a nice lady. Won'tcha gimme something, please? Fourteen cents, all I needs' like fourteen cents." Smiling brilliantly, dancing around her: "I know you, I watches you comings and you goings."

Finally she digs up from the depths of her pocketbook some change, which falls to the sidewalk; he goes after it, fumbling and muttering in the gutter. All fall he was a worry to her, sleeping so still in his doorway, a crumpled overcoat, and a bottle still in its paper bag at his head like a candle. He has lost the overcoat but acquired some mittens. How does he know her? How has he managed to fight the cold this long, into January?

Back in the apartment with the newspaper and their interesting headlines:

4 **CHAIN-STORES
FIRE-BOMBED**

7 **L.I. CHILDREN
DIE IN BUS CRASH**

**FEAR TEN SLAIN
IN RACKETS WAR**

**GRAVEDIGGERS
CALL STRIKE**

**Drug Girl, 12, Tells of Freakout
A HUNGRY BABY
DIES: JAIL MOM**

**Army Dismisses Charge of
War Crimes by General**

FOE ATTACKS . . .

POPE BLESSES . . .

**Actual Tests Used to Prepare
Pupils for Reading Exams**

At the table, with a cup of tea and a cigarette, she gets the gist of the day's news and what the department stores are featuring, since she has errands to run, things to buy. Fidgeting, tongue between her teeth. ("Don't *do* that," her mother used to say watchfully, "you'll ruin your occlusion.") Reaching the weather report (occluded front), she looks warily around, as though she were being watched. But there is nobody in the house, which is suddenly so quiet the only sound is her own, her heartbeat.

There are no clocks in the apartment. What time has it gotten to be? She rushes to the telephone to dial the time, and when she lifts the receiver a voice is immediately in her ear. "Washington operator here. I have a person-to-person call for Mmm. Blur. Hello, New York, will you accept the call, please, New York?" Superimposed on the operator's voice is another, tinny and distant—a woman's?—but she cannot make out the words.

Who does she know in Washington?

No, she will not accept the call, she will not accept the charges. It must be past noon; the sun will be setting before too long. Before 4:37, according to the newspaper.

She has not lost her wristwatch, but she cannot seem to extricate it from the repair shop; it's been there for three weeks with a shattered crystal and a broken hand that she suspects they're keeping in traction. She turns her own hands palms up; the creases gleam with sweat—snail tracks.

Steadier now, tongue emergent, she's refilling a pocket flask from the kitchen liquor supply. It's a four-ounce hip-hugger model with a cute red leather jacket that can be unbuttoned for cleaning; she carries it everywhere in case of emergency, of entrapment in subway or elevator. Its predecessor fell on the floor of the ladies room at the Art Students League, where she was waiting for a perennial art student to finish his life-studies class so they could go out to dinner and drinks or vice-versa; how sorry she was to lose it! But she quickly replaced it with an identical model from Hoffritz.

With him she went to an island remote from the city and from everything else. Ten miles out in the Atlantic, off the coast of Maine, where the foghorn cries all night long, once a minute, "It *hurts*," warning ships off the rocks where lobsters lie low (skittering anyway into the baited traps) and the brightest thing by night is the eye of the lighthouse since the island is without community electricity. The wind blew constantly on the headlands several hundred feet over the sea. When the fog lifted, the ocean was the color of melted blue wax. Way down on the rocks, seals grazed, polychromatic as pigeons: blue, grey, brown, and spotted. Once, they thought they saw far out the spout of a whale.

Some sportsmen that week harpooned a small whale, a blackfish, and towed it into the harbor, stranding it on Fish Beach. All afternoon they worked to extract their three spearheads, up to the arms in blubber, till the sand was red and sticky and thick with flies.

She and he walked in the woods when he wasn't painting, watched birds and the sunset, ate lobster with slippery fingers. Then she had an appetite, and used to collect leftover oranges or bananas from other tables to devour thoughtfully at night while the light house spun and the foghorn ached. Having gone through her fruit and her library books, she got into bed at last; he sighed, set on by his own bad dreams. It wasn't a success, that holiday. Making love in a blueberry patch, they reached up for berries and ate them where they lay. The days seemed very long. On the rocky cliffs they fought, wind whipping their barbed words out to sea. Back on the mainland, at the bus terminal, early in the morning: "You'll be all right?" he asked, peering into her face as though it were a steamed-up mirror.

On the river, a ship leaving for Valparaiso when the shipping page said it would sound its plangent departure whistle-music for bones. Three times, as if it would never end, then ends for that particular voyage. It makes her eyes water.

Tropical fish in the living room move around in their tank, weaving gaudily through the underwater foliage, striped golden angelfish, jewel-like neon tetras, gouramis, a fat black molly. The one-eyed catfish oozes along the bottom of the aquarium as though vacuuming a rug. As she bends over them they rise, expecting a shower of ant eggs, frantically kissing the surface. She has forgotten to feed them. Again.

Somebody leaves the house for the second and final time that day. A fire siren evokes the noise of every dog on the block. There has been a fire in the Chinese laundry. An old Italian lady in a greasy black dress giggles at the snakes in the pet-shop window, her week's groceries piled in her grocery cart, and her cat on top of them. *He spreads like fire—don't smile.*

The Goodwill Exterminators have a new exhibit: among the pickled bugs and childishly hand-lettered signs, a jar of milk-white shrimps with tails, labelled "Day-old baby Rats, caught in a Volkswagen on Perry Street by Myron." She digs her nails into her gloveless palms. *Don't smile; he hates it. Pretend not to tremble.* She checks her left wrist to see what time it is.

The sign over the bank spells out time and temperature in yellow dots:

12:57

79°

Very warm for January.

Near the subway entrance she buys the afternoon paper, and a man pushes her change over the papers with his hook.

The train stops just outside of the Fourteenth Street station and refuses to budge for several minutes. At Twenty-third Street, for some reason, a mob storms the cars, hustling for seats. A very small woman gets jammed in the half-open door—a midget, really, but still an ordinary-looking middle-aged woman in an out-of-style tweed coat and an out-of-town hat with a little veil, which is looped rakishly, accidentally, over one ear. She appears so helpless that somebody offers her a seat. "Hurry up, Daddy! Over here!" The other half of the door shuts, and she screams. The door opens. Her husband, who is taller, but only by an inch, rushes in, swinging a tiny child over the edge of the platform. They plop him onto the seat she gave up and stand guard, protectively.

"I need a lollipop," the baby shouts over the shriek of the train; no larger than a year-old infant, an achondroplastic dwarf without his parents' good proportions, with very short plump baby arms, and no legs to speak of. His forehead bulges above a big, perplexed face, mouth turned down at the corners. Like any child he squirms petulantly in his seat, under a sign which reads "Little enough to ride for free? Little enough to ride your knee!" Daddy midget gives him a lemon lollipop.

She has to cook dinner for eight people next Thursday. She picks out a five-quart casserole in Macy's basement, tries to charge it, discovers that all her credit cards are missing, buys it anyway, orders it sent. "Jeez, Miss, didn't you inform Credit yet?" The elevator to Credit is suffocatingly hot and reeks of fur and perfume. It stops at every floor, and by the eighth she has recalled that she has no charge account with Macy's.

(The U.P.S. man will make a real effort to deliver the dish in time, nicking off more of the bark of the plane tree; ringing and ringing but nobody's home.)

Sweating in her fur coat, she proceeds down the maze that leads to the subway platform, through a crowd of people eating ice-cream cones and asking which way to the Port Authority Bus Terminal; nearly bumps into a soldier who has taken a post by a gum machine. Not an ordinary G.I. but someone on his way to a revolution. Leaf-patterned trousers tucked into combat boots, combat jacket of a different green, green beret pulled down nearly over his eyebrows—even his canteen is in camouflage. Only his gun is not. He holds his rifle butt end down between his boots like a walking stick. He stares impassively over the crowd, as though he thinks he is invisible. And perhaps he is.

She has reached the last staircase when there is a voice at her back, whisper: "Hey lady, you need help with your packages?" But her hands are empty.

She is holding very tightly to the railing. Another voice: Middle-aged lady who inquires kindly, "Are you sick, Miss? Do you need some help!"

She shakes her head no, but the lady helps her down anyway, talking cozily. "You know, I had a friend once who was so scared of the subway she'd get nauseous when the train came in. It's called claustrophobia?

Well, finally the husband made her see the doctor. Well, it turned out that her brother had locked her in a closet once, when she was a bitty thing, and she'd forgotten all about it. But her heart remembered." A leap of the heart. "You know, it was a funny thing. After she got well and rode subways without thinking twice about it, she had one of those freak accidents and almost lost an arm on a Flushing train. I bet the operations cost her more than the psychiatrist did. Well, honey, here's your train."

Tottering onto the lit car, she supports herself against a post, breathes easier until the doors have closed and the train starts down the dark passage. With a felt-tip pen, someone has lettered on the L&M ad, "God is a Sadist."

Quickly tiring of her own reflection in the dressing-room mirrors, she buys the first dress she tried on, a silky blue Ban-Lon number that makes her look thin as a doll. There is a delay when she tries to charge it. Shifting from foot to foot with impatience, says yes, she will report the loss.

(She will be extremely surprised when next tenth of the month a bill arrives from this department store for $600 worth of merchandise she never purchased. But perhaps she will have notified Credit Service in time to avoid the liability.)

A very young girl with a face like an angel's sits in an armchair in the ladies' lounge, breast bare to her infant daughter; the baby nurses with an expression of concentration, pink palm closing and unclosing rhythmically like a sea anemone. The mother's knees are spread in fatigue. Assorted clothes, diapers, bottles, and magazines are falling out of the department-store shopping bags beside her chair. She looks as though she has been travelling a long time. She has just gone to sleep; eyelashes hover like black spiders over her cheekbones. She snores.

Baby loses the soda fountain and wails angrily. Her mother automatically readjusts the small head and closes her eyes upon the world once more, breathing onto it the syllables, like prayer, "Goddamn son of a bitch bastards."

"Breathe in," the nurse instructed. "Pant. Harder." She tried to, like a good girl, sobbing obediently. "It won't hurt so much this way." Actually it hurt very little. "It works like a vacuum cleaner." Nature, she said, abhors a vacuum. "I usually have a cleaning woman," she told the fluorescent ceiling lights.

A sip from the red flask in the toilet, followed by a rush of acid.

Outside on Fifth Avenue, asbestos flakes eddy in spiral air currents like snow, the carcinogenic emission from a new skyscraper. Something blows into her eye before she can get out her dark glasses. She blinks to tear it away.

Bells jangle. The saffron robes, the shaven-head Buddhists chanting "Hare Krishna" surround her, offering their literature with gentle words. Under their sleazy peach-tinted rayon saris they wear sweaters and sweatshirts and sneakers instead of sandals. Surely they're in the wrong climate. They sing, "Hare Krishna, Hare Krishna, Krishna Krishna, Hare Hare," snapping their belled fingers and jouncing to ward off the cold.

The literature is called "Back to Godhead," and shows a circle of girls with pleated skirts like fans dancing beneath stylized Indian flowers, a round moon. "Hare Rama, Hare Rama, Rama Rama, Hare Hare," the hectic singers chant.

"Oh my God, isn't that Al Silberstang from Fire Island?" says a passerby, nudging her companion to a halt. Al Silberstang does not cease from his dance. His eyes dwell on inner secrets. She searches for money so she can escape their circle. "Peace, peace, lady," says Al Silberstang, whirling away with her money. But there is no peace from the Buddhists, no peace from the chestnut and pretzel sellers, one at each corner, warming their hands over the braziers and reiterating their spiel.

Here she is, the rival sect's headquarters, St. Patrick's Cathedral. A man on the steps brandishes a sign, "ANNOYING SICK H-BOMB DIC-TATOR WILL BE PUNISHED," at an old lady in an old mink, in a walker, going up the steps with the aid of a younger female, daughter or niece, who looks put-upon and cold in her short cloth coat. The old lady's arm is grasped on the other side by a nun. You can tell it is a nun from the navy-blue tailored outfit, like an airline stewardess's, and the truncated veil, revealing a steel-grey curly bang. Nuns never used to have grey hair. Or calves. The nuns of her youth floated like blackbirds. Step. By step. By step, the old lady is guided through a small door set into the heavily ornamented bronze ones. Around the corner is the aftermath of a Filipino wedding, the small white bride shivering and smiling for the photographers.

The nuns with their pale faces taught them myths about eternity and how to walk in processions. "'Tis the month of our Mother, the blessed and beautiful days," the parochial school-children sang in May, carrying their sheaves of wheat down suburban sidewalks, under the magnolias. A pretty sight. Though *she'd* never really cottoned to Our Lady; she much preferred the Holy Ghost, perhaps because he was a bird.

Heaven, hell, purgatory, limbo, where little unbaptized children lived pleasantly in a garden, crawling on the green grass, and it never snowed. Purgatory was where they melted your sins away; hell was very hot. (A little boy died and a saint revived him. "Oh Mother," he cried, "I have been in such a terrible place!") She is cold. And hungry: the smell of burning chestnuts rises like incense. "Getcha hot chestnuts! Getcha pretzels!"

He scatters a handful of raw nuts over the coals, extends a bagful with a hand that is like a burnt pretzel, grins brilliantly. "I bet you're hungry, pretty lady; I know you—"

Tugging at the door to the Cathedral, where she's never been. *He eats terror, gulps tears, and spits catastrophes.* The smell of incense, dazzling banks of red votive candles, the purple light from high stained-glass windows decorated with suffering saints. Tourists move chattily around the gloom of the nave; in the side aisles kneel the reverent few. She looks dizzily at the vaulted ceiling, light-years away. She steadies herself on a granite basin. Then, to show she's all right, dabbles holy water from the font and blesses herself like the tourists just ahead. The basin has specks floating in it and a layer of silt.

Her heart beats as though it were trying to get out. Looking for a place to sit down, she travels along an enormous aisle, toward where she sees people as at the small end of the telescope her father gave her once when she was thirteen and infatuated with science. It has been years since she was in a church. And what a church! Are you supposed to cover your head these days? She has no cover, not even a handkerchief to pin to her hair.

At a side pew occupied mostly by women her knees signal *no farther*, and she slides in. Her uncovered scalp prickles dangerously. She thinks, with longing, of her flask.

As she plans about getting down the aisle, or at least behind a stone pillar, the women begin trickling out the other side of the pew. An elbow in the ribs: it is the niece or daughter of the woman in the walker. "Miss, could you please move along, or are you asleep, dope?"

Unable to reply, she shies into the aisle, abandoning (she will remember later, in a crowded room) a brown-and-white box from Saks Fifth Avenue to the niece or the H-bomb man or St. Patrick. Or him, the god of fear. There's a convenient pillar, and—what is this?—a curtained cubicle behind a brass gate, private, hidden, a good place to take stock and think her way out, back to the right door. Sneaking a backward glance, she parts the white curtain, ducks in, groping for familiar leathery corners. Just as she has the cap off and is tilting the flask back, there is a hair-raising creak. Somebody else is only a breath away. And listening. And murmuring, through a grille, *"Ja, mein Kind?"* Fallen into the hands of the Nazis. "Yes, my child," he says impatiently.

Good heavens, somebody is answering. It is her own high parochial-school voice, her very tongue snapping out the appropriate response. "Bless me, Father, for I have sinned. It has been fifteen years since my last confession." At last she gets the bottleneck in her mouth. Alcohol is instantly absorbed through the stomach lining into the bloodstream. At once the molecules are joined up, spreading the cheerful news.

Anticipatory silence. Perhaps he only understands German. She racks her brain—she has no wish to go spilling the secrets of her life to a stranger. First you confessed sins against the Church, then against God. She remembers a sin against the Church: "I have missed Mass."

"How many times?"

"Every time." Quick swallow. A rush of confidence. "I used God's name in vain five times. I disobeyed my parents three times. I was rude to a nun once. I slapped my little sister. I was untruthful—" Running out of sins, she adds, desperately, "I smoked marijuana."

"On how many occasions?"

"I don't remember."

He clears his throat, beginning to sound like a Viennese psychiatrist. "So, is that all that you wish to tell me?"

"Well, not quite," she stalls (once more should do the trick.) Then she realizes that now there are three of them in the confessional; someone else is waiting on the other side, behind the priest, making a priest sandwich, getting restless. She shifts heavily to assert her presence— probably the niece woman who called her "dope."

"Oh no, Father," she says, tilting the flask back for another round. Not all of it reaches her mouth, there's spillage; the booth fills with the odor of alcohol in addition to that of Listerine. She is tempted to offer him a nip through the grill, for his stomach's sake. "But it's been such a long time." A weak giggle. Her time, and the jig, is up.

The Big Ear is no longer fooled. "My daughter, I suspect you are spoofing me. There are penitents waiting; you are wasting my time. Why are you here? What do you want?" No answer. "Do you want absolution? If you are in some kind of trouble, we shall discuss it in the rectory at two-forty next Wednesday. Father Kleinhardt is the name."

"Father Kleinhardt, I am frightened."

"For your penance say three Hail Marys. Now make an Act of Contrition." Switching tongues, he begins to absolve her in Latin.

"I am frightened to death, Father." But he chooses not to hear.

She begins, "Oh my God, I am heartily sorry," and slips out, leaving him committed to the end of his Latin prayer, noticing a sign taped to the side altar: "Father Kleinhardt: English—Deutsche." At the altar of St. Anthony a prayer is posted in mock parchment, promising the reciter forty days' indulgence. She has got away with it, she is outside, she is free.

The morning she left the northern island a young deer escaped from it, the only one of the herd imported from Boothbay Harbor who couldn't settle down but rampaged through the woods like a crazy thing and ate roses out of village gardens. After they found hoofprints on the beach, they put out salt for him in the woods. He passed her boat swimming like a small horned seal in a mainland direction; it was too late and too foggy for the lobster smacks to find him. By the time she reached the city he was fathoms deep, and the fish were grazing off his antlers. "Taxi, lady?" said a cabdriver outside the Port Authority Bus Terminal. The man drove demonically, hunched like a jockey over the wheel; only when they reached her apartment did she observe that it was because he couldn't straighten his back. In the full glare of the street lamp his features leapt at her; the thrust chin, the snub nose, the furrowed forehead with its huge wen, the maimed, cleft, two-fingered hoof of a congenitally deformed right hand. Smiling hilariously, he scratched at the wen. "Take it easy now, lady," he told her.

(The dead deer lies among the rocks, nibbled bare by sea worms and crustaceans, far from home; barnacles have attached themselves to his skeleton; when spring comes a fisherman will draw up with his catch its alien skull, and think it is something new.)

Once you have seen him he will never let you get away with anything.

Now it is time, definitely time, to start uptown, taking it easy and crossing with the lights. The sun has gone down, leaving a stain in the west. At a store window she acknowledges with a slight smile her reflection: a thin woman in a white coat and big black glasses, soon to be middle-aged, puzzled because the years went so fast and the days so slowly. And someday, old.

Killing time, she stops to light a cigarette and is nearly swept over by an energetic group of tiny children, chattering in the half-light by Central Park. There are about eight of them, fat as chickadees in their snow-suits. Isn't it late for them to be out? "I'm *cold*," complains one grumpy mite with thick glasses and a circle of mustard around his mouth to one of the two teachers, long-haired girls in furry coats like her own. They seem to have lassoed her. Then she realizes it's a rope; they're clinging to a rope, with a teacher at each end, and she has got in the middle. What a good idea; little children will hold on if you tell them to.

The teachers untangle her and say, "Come along now," jerking the children briskly down the sidewalk. A small spectacled girl has a pink balloon floating from the end of her little finger. There are a lot of pairs of spectacles for such a small group of kindergarten-aged children.

The children are blind. These are blind children, with their teachers, sightless among the seeing, though she can't see any too well herself, in her dark glasses with the sun gone down, hurrying toward an uptown appointment.

The hot light. An egg, a shiny egg dancing in a glass. (Sunday morning she will burn the bacon and spill the scrambled eggs on the floor trying to stamp out the fire in her bedroom slippers.) Lying on a table, somebody cried, "Hey that hurts, it hurts," and yet it didn't hurt that much.

"Relax. Don't fight it," said the nurse. "Would you care for a cigarette? I'm afraid all I've got is Salems"—putting it between dry lips.

An involvement of the inner space, a truly savage pain. Slurp, water whizzing in the basin. Will it travel down the sewers like an abandoned pet, eyeless, lost to the gene pool, never to breed?

Doctor having left the room, his assistant matter-of-factly sprinkled water over what was in the basin, saying, "I baptize thee in the name of the Father and of the Son and of the Holy Ghost."

"You are baptizing a newt," she said reproachfully.

The nurse looked ashamed. "Sorry, but I just have to do this. Say, you know, I keep newts?"

"I have tropical fish, myself."

Let's go to bed and tell lies—almost there now. *Committing our murders decently in private.* Punching the moon-white elevator button. The elevator boxes her into a private space; she rises with it, shaking in silence. *I don't know the enemy's you. You haven't heard he is me.*

He greets her at the door, waving a Martini glass, reeling her into the party. "Oh my God, am I glad to see you," she says.

The Cure

He always told his dream at the breakfast table, and this one was not unlike the others.

"Maw came back to me last night," he began, his lids fluttering over watery eyes marred by cataracts. "She was standing on the piazza with a long stick in her hand and she was calling me so loud I could still hear her voice after it woke me up. Then I knew it wasn't a piazza she was standing on because we haven't got a piazza here like we had down home in Louisiana. She was standing out there in the yard by the pump and shaking one of them willow switches at me."

My grandmother didn't want to hear any more. She rose abruptly and walked over to the kitchen window with cup and saucer in her hands.

"That old whiskey you been drinking—that's all."

Buddy Joe Ward wasn't offended. He took her remark not as a reproach, but simply as a statement—and not a very enlightened one. When he looked at me, his smile showed an indulgence for his older sister that he expected me to understand.

"She was aiming to beat me, Maw was. One thing about Maw: she believed in the rod. Didn't make no difference how old you was, Maw would lay it on if you needed it. I was a grown man, talking about getting married, last time Maw whipped me."

Grandma kept her eyes fixed on the sugar beet fields behind our house on Almeda Road and the cattail swamps beyond.

"You was grown, but you wasn't no man," she corrected.

Again Buddy gave me his smile and nod. This older sister had been looking after him since before Maw died; she was still looking after him, and he owed her a certain deference, but this did not require him to answer all her nonsense. He waited a moment and then went on as if he had not been interrupted.

"I came in the house kind of late that time. I'd been drinking and maybe my clothes was mussed up."

"No such thing." Grandma lost her patience. "It was the next day. You'd been in jail. The police picked you up, and Mr. O'Shea had to go down in the morning to get you out. When four o'clock came and you wasn't in the bakery getting the bread started, he knew right where to go. It was after breakfast when you came home to change up for work. That's why Maw beat you. Pity she ain't here now."

Buddy sighed. He put his cup down, pushed his chair away from the table, got up, and began fumbling for pipe and tobacco in the pockets of his disreputable old coat.

"All right, Sarah." He let his voice drop. A moment later he mashed an old hat down on his head and went out the back door. I noticed that his pants had been rolled up at the bottoms because they were too long and his shoes were unlaced.

"He's started in again," my grandmother told me after he wavered past the window, pipe smoke curling around his head. "I got to do something about Joe Ward's drinking."

"What *can* you do?"

"There's ways," she assured me. "Seems like a man that's been through all he has would learn a lesson by the time he's sixty years old."

"I like to hear him tell his dreams," I confessed.

"You just a young boy, Arna, not eleven yet. You wouldn't think they was all that amusing if you'd heard them many times as I have. Joe Ward's been fighting whiskey since he wasn't much older'n you. It's about got the best of him."

A few moments later Buddy was back again, his elbows resting on the window sill as he peered at us through the screen.

"Don't let your grandma turn you against me," he said with a wink.

"You out of your mind, Joe Ward."

"I might be crazy," he argued, "but I got more sense than you have. You don't believe in dreams and you don't believe in ghosts. Anybody knows that's pure crazy. I seen more ghosts than I got fingers and toes. One stopped me on the road the other night."

"Time for you to find something to do now. Get on away from that window. Go pump some water and fill the trough for the heifers. I noticed it was empty when I was milking this morning. You'll have this boy afraid to leave the house alone—you and your ghosts."

"I wasn't drunk when I seen it neither," he insisted.

"That's *your* opinion. Get busy now."

We heard him singing in a gay, half-falsetto voice as he drew the water and tottered back and forth between the two wooden buckets from the barnyard to the pump. Meanwhile, my grandmother opened the kitchen safe and brought out a fifth of whiskey. Knowing what I did about Buddy, I couldn't help being surprised. Nobody had ever left liquor any place in the house where he could be tempted by it.

"Has that been there all the time?"

"Since day before yesterday," she smiled. "He's seen it too. That's why he's singing so loud. I was looking at him out of the corner of my eye when he helped me set the table this morning. He came across it up there amongst the dishes, and he must of thought Doug forgot and left it when he and Rose were here the other day. Anyhow I saw him pushing it back a little further and trying to hide it so I wouldn't take it away before he could get to it."

My grandmother wasn't given to pranks. She was never cruel, and I wondered why her eyes twinkled as she recalled his sly discovery and the quick-witted maneuver with which he followed it.

"You going to hide it now?"

"No, I'm going to put it back where he can find it—after I fix it."

The "fixing" of which she spoke involved pouring the whiskey into a bowl and putting several tiny fish in it.

"They say this will turn him against whiskey," she explained confidently.

We stayed in the kitchen the rest of the morning, and Buddy did not return. Several times I saw him come suspiciously near, whistling or singing with a casual air, and throw a quick glance through the screen door or the window. On each occasion he retreated promptly—either toward the front gate or in the direction of the fields behind the barn. Later he moved the grindstone to a position under the willow tree where he could keep an eye on us while working the pedal and grinding the dull blades he found lying about the place.

This pleased my grandmother. Obviously a part of her plan was to keep him waiting, but after a while I went out to watch the fidgety old fellow put new edges on the ax, the garden hoes, the beet knives, and the long scythe. It was a tedious chore, and I knew he was working under a strain.

"Sarah keeps awful busy," he observed, stuffing a handful of tobacco in his cheek.

"She's nearly through," I said.

"That's where you're wrong. You don't know your grandma." His irritation could no longer be concealed. "She'll horse around in that one room all day, sweeping first one way and then the other. She gets on my nerves doing that. I wish she'd go in the front of the house and sit down a while."

She did go soon afterwards, and Buddy touched his moistened thumb against the blade he had been grinding and suddenly discovered that it had a completely satisfactory edge.

"Guess that'll do the business now," he said, stepping gingerly around the grindstone and gathering up the sharpened tools. "Reckon you can hang this scythe in the barn for me?"

I could see through his scheme, but I didn't object.

"I'll take the beet knives too," I said. "I know where they go."

My back was turned, and I had taken a few steps on the path when I heard Buddy muttering behind me.

"Goddamn my unhardlucky soul."

"What's happened?"

He looked flustered when I faced him.

"Nothing—nothing much. Thought I'd cut myself on this old ax, but I guess not."

His real concern, of course, was that Grandma was standing in the screen door again trying hard to hold her mouth straight.

"I s'pose you all don't want no lunch today," she taunted.

Buddy made this the excuse for an explosion.

"Who said so? I work round here all morning and end up by almost cutting the blood out of myself on this devilish ax, and you come talking about no lunch. Goddamit, I'm sick and tired."

"Hush, Joe Ward. Come on in and eat when you get ready. I'll have something waiting."

When I came in to help with the table, I discovered the whiskey in the safe. She had poured it from the bowl back into the bottle, and she had been careful to place it exactly where Buddy had previously hidden it.

Buddy was sullen and dull as he sank into his chair. There was no light behind the cataracts that dimmed his eyes. He had run his hands through his thinning black hair so many times it now looked as it had when he first crawled out of bed in the morning. His mustache had a skimpy, plucked look; his head was bowed; his mouth turned downward.

"I'm going to leave you with it," my grandmother announced suddenly. "Never mind the dishes. I'll do them later."

Buddy perked up a little.

"Where you going?"

"Just out in the front yard. I got a basket of socks to darn. Why don't you come read to me when you get through, Arna?"

I promised I would, and a few moments later I got up and left Buddy with his cold meat and his fantasies. In the living room I stopped at the bookcase and found the copy of *Treasure Island* which we had started. There was a carpet-covered stool in the corner and I took this out too, for there were so many ants you couldn't sit on the ground and read. Grandma was rocking under the pepper tree, the basket of socks beside her, with a lump like an egg bulging from the toe of the one she was working on. When I set the stool directly in front of her, she shook her head.

"Not there. Move it over to the side a little so you can see when he goes out."

"He's leaving now," I noticed.

Buddy was already on the path and headed toward the barn.

"You think it'll cure him, Grandma?"

"They say it will. He won't know anything's wrong with the whiskey. He'll think it's just hisself turning against the taste of the stuff."

It sounded to me like a reasonable idea.

"We tried everything else we knew before we came out here. Sent him down to Keeley's in New Orleans twice. He'd stop drinking for a little while, but not long. After the rest of us came to California, he got so bad he couldn't even hold his job in the bakery. They said he cried like a baby. Promised me faithful he'd never taste another drop if I'd just send for him. Well, I did, and now look at him. Which way did he go?"

"Behind the barn," I said.

"Don't you ever be like him, Arna."

Suddenly a question that intrigued me as much as his drinking popped out, and I found myself asking, "Is that why he never got married and had a family of his own like other men?"

"Well—in a way."

"Didn't he ever act like he wanted to—wasn't there anybody he liked when he was young?"

She slipped the artificial egg out of the sock she was darning and put it in the heel of another. She waited so long to answer I began to think she was going to ignore me. She bit off another strand of yarn.

"No reason why you shouldn't know," she said finally. "Joe Ward went with a girl once. Maw and the rest of us was hoping he'd get married and settle down. He never did."

"Why?"

"They broke up."

She may have been sorry she had opened the subject at all. I have always been a relentless question asker. As far back as I can remember, people have tried to curb my curiosity. Grandma was no exception, but she didn't seem to blame me too much for wanting to know about Buddy. He was fond of me, and I seemed to have more sympathy for him than most others had.

"Well, he's your uncle—your own great uncle, that is—and if I tell you about him, you got to keep it to yourself. Understand?"

"Yes'm, I understand."

"Elvire was a mighty pretty girl," she recalled softly. "Color of a apricot. Hair hanging down her back in two big ropes. Her father was white, of course. Alexandria was full of fine-looking colored people in those days. Elvire was as pretty as Adah Isaacs Menken."

I didn't know who Menken was, but the comparison was impressive as my grandmother pronounced the three names. I could tell she was quoting.

"Who said that, Grandma?"

"Mr. Silas Boatman—he was a business man that came to Alexandria off and on. He'd seen Adah on the stage and off, and he said she'd never known the day when she was any better looking than Elvire Du Plaz. I told him if that was the case then Alexandria had at least a dozen that was Adah's equal in looks. Anyhow, it was this Elvire that Joe Ward started out to keeping company with. That was back—let me see—"

"Before I was born," I supplied.

Grandma smiled.

"Before your mother was born. Let me see, Joe Ward was born during the Rebellion. That would make him about—well, this was in the early eighties. Reconstruction was still on. When him and Elvire danced together at parties, folks gave them plenty room. They was something to see. She had a lot of pretty silk clothes and lace parasols and the like. Joe Ward was a dresser too. Sometimes his hat, his suit, and the strap on his umbrella handle all matched perfect. He could have things like that because he was making good money."

Suddenly I caught a glimpse of Buddy going across the sugar beet fields behind our one-acre plot. The tiny, battered, but still strangely flamboyant old man was nearing the edge of a dark clump beyond.

"There he goes." I interrupted. "He's almost to the swamp."

She didn't even look up from her darning.

"Let him go. Joe Ward always liked to slip off by himself. It was like that when he was a little boy. We'd miss him now and then and find him afterwards back on the shady side of a fence or under a hedge—reading. That's what he liked. You remind me of him sometimes. One thing though: he could spell better'n you. People came from miles around to give him words to spell. He never went to school much either. This was just what Mr. George Kelsey taught him. He learned to be a fancy pastry baker the same way, and he was doing fine by the time him and Elvire started talking about getting married."

"But they never did," I reminded her.

"This Mr. Silas Boatman kept coming around and talking about how Elvire was the prettiest thing he ever saw. He got so he wanted people to see her. Next he was wondering how she would look in a dress he saw in New Orleans, so he brought it back to her with matching beads and earrings. Then nothing would do but she had to put it on and let some of his friends see her wearing it.

"This went on a good while, but Elvire and Joe Ward didn't stop dancing together. On Sundays they'd row on the river in a boat. Sometimes Joe Ward would get Maw to let him take the horse and buggy, and the two would drive across the river and out around Pineville. They was getting on so nice together it surprised me when he commenced drinking too much. But he had his reasons.

"Once I said something about it—I forget what it was—but he looked at me so sad-like I had to turn my face. So he waited a minute and then said, 'You ask me that, Sarah? *You ask me that question?*' There wasn't nothing left for me to say to him about his drinking after that. It wouldn't have been so bad if another colored man had wanted to marry Elvire and tried to win her away from Joe Ward. Then it would of been just who shall and who sha'n't. But with a rich white man like Mr. Boatman, a family man in business down in New Orleans, and things being like they are down home, and the Reconstruction going on and the Klan riding and all, what was a young man like Joe Ward going to do?

"Well, he started doing just what he's doing now—slipping away by hisself with a bottle. He quit seeing Elvire. He quit seeing any women.

All he did with his time when he wasn't working was to read magazines and dime novels and drink whiskey. Later he went on to gambling. At his work he behaved peculiar. He made birthday cakes like none you ever heard about. He put funny little decorations on wedding cakes. You could see he didn't know whether to laugh or cry. When Mr. Boatman carried Elvire away to Shreveport and lived with her a while, Joe Ward didn't even hear about it till she was back in town. Nobody would mention it, and he wasn't trying to find out anything.

"Once after that they met. She'd been crying a lot, and folks said she was pretty broken up. Love matches between white and colored were not as popular down home then as they'd been before the Rebellion, and Mr. Boatman couldn't see hisself setting her up in a fine house and all. Some of his friends might criticize him. Maybe they'd started doing it already. On the other hand, there was Joe Ward, acting more like a child than ever in Mr. O'Shea's pastry shop and hiding away with his bottle and his books when he wasn't at work. When she couldn't stand it no longer, Elvire got all dressed up in one of her prettiest silks, put on her best jewelry and a few touches of perfume, and hired a hack to drive her to our house.

"She didn't get out. Instead she sent the driver to call Joe Ward. It was evening. The moon was out, and the leaves of the pecan tree in the yard were just barely moving. When I called Joe Ward, he came out of his room, and I followed him to the front door and stood there and watched him weaving on the path. He wasn't mad with Elvire, so far as I could see. He talked almost like he was glad to see her. 'You look pretty, gal,' he said, 'just as shiny as a star back in the dark there. I'm glad you come by.' That was about as far as he went. She was in favor of letting old things be new again with them—starting over and making up. But by then Joe Ward's liquor had commenced talking, and he wouldn't give her nothing that would make sense. When she started crying and asked the hackman to drive on, he didn't know what to make of it. I was waiting when Joe Ward came back down the path, and I opened the door for him. 'Wonder how come she acted like that?' he asked, child-like. I told him to go on to bed and maybe he'd find out later."

"Did he?" I asked.

"I don't think so," she said.

She rocked a little longer under the tree. Then the breeze from the ocean became cooler, and she suggested that we move inside. This reminded me of the book I hadn't opened yet, and I mentioned it to her.

"Never mind that," she said. "We can read it tonight."

She didn't mention Buddy again that afternoon, and I interested myself in other things. Neither of us expected him to show up for supper, and we were not disappointed. In fact, I think we were both surprised at twilight when we saw him crossing the beet fields with his arms loaded with white flowers. We had gone to the barn to put out some alfalfa and close the chicken coops. It was almost dark enough for a lantern, but it was much too early for Buddy to be getting back from one of his lonely excursions. We walked to the house and waited on the back steps.

Buddy struggled along like a man walking in quicksand. When he reached the yard, we could see the mud still clinging to his clothes. He seemed to be weighted down by it. The masses of white flowers were being crushed in his arms, but they grew more and more vivid in the shadows under the trees. He saw us finally and stood swaying dimly before the steps.

"Well—" Grandma said.

"I'm back, Sarah."

"So I see."

"I found something I thought you and Arna would like."

"You must of found something else too."

"I did," he confessed. "Did you miss it?"

"Was it good?" she asked eagerly.

"Can't you tell?" he asked with a lilt.

"I mean how'd it taste?"

He thought a moment.

"Taste? Don't believe I know. I helt my breath when I drank it. Never did like the *taste* of whiskey."

My grandmother uttered a deep moan. "Put the flowers by the pump," she said. "Go in and get out of them muddy clothes. I don't know what to do with you, Joe Ward."

He seemed ready to cry.

"Don't abuse me, Sarah," he pleaded. "I brought you these flowers."

She took my hand, and I could feel the sternness coming back into her bones as she opened the door.

"Nobody's abusing you, Joe Ward. Do as I say."

"All right, Sarah," he whispered.

He hadn't moved when she closed the door.

Hey Sailor, What Ship?

1

The grimy light; the congealing smell of cigarettes that had been smoked long ago and of liquor that had been drunk long ago; the boasting, cursing, wheedling cringing voices, and the greasy feel of the bar as he gropes for his glass.

Hey Sailor, what ship?

His face flaring in the smoky mirror. The veined gnawing. Wha's it so quiet for? Hey, hit the tune-box. (*Lennie and Helen and the kids.*) Wha time's it anyway? Gotta. . .

Gotta something. Stand watch? No, din't show last night, ain't gonna show tonight, gonna sign off. Out loud: Hell with ship. You got any friends, ship? then hell with your friends. That right Deeck? And he turns to Deeck for approval, but Deeck is gone. Where's Deeck? Givim five bucks and he blows.

All right, says a nameless one, you're loaded. How's about a buck? Less one buck. Company. But he too is gone.

And he digs into his pockets to see how much he has left.

Right breast pocket, a crumpled five. Left pants pocket, three, no, four collapsed one-ers. Left jacket pocket, pawn ticket, Manila; card, "When in Managua it's Marie's for Hospitality"; union book; I.D. stuff;

trip card; two ones, one five, accordion-pleated together. Right pants pocket, jingle money. Seventeen bucks. And the hands tremble.

Where'd it all go? and he lurches through the past. One hundred and fifty draw yesterday. No, day before, maybe even day 'fore that. Seven for a bottle when cashed the check, twenty to Blackie, thirty-three back to Goldballs, cab to Frisco, thirty-eight, thirty-nine for the jacket and the kicks (new jacket, new kicks, look good to see Lennie and Helen and the kids), twenty-four smackers dues and ten-dollar fine. That fine...

Hey, to the barkeep, one comin' up. And he swizzles it down, pronto. Twenty and seven and thirty-three and thirty-nine. Ten-dollar fine and five to Frenchy at the hall and drinkin' all night with Johnson, don't know how much, and on the way to the paymaster. . . .

The PAYmaster. Out loud, in angry mimicry, with a slight scandihoovian accent, to nobody, nobody at all: Whaddaya think of that? Hafta be able to sign your name or we can't give you your check. Too stewed to sign your name, he says, no check.

Only seventeen bucks. Hey, to the barkeep, how 'bout advancing me fifty? Hunching over the bar, confidential, so he sees the bottles glistening in the depths. See? and he ruffles in his pockets for the voucher, P.F.E., Michael Jackson, thass me, five hundred and twenty-seven and eleven cents. You don' know me? Been here all night, all day. Bell knows me. Get Bell, Been drinkin' here twenty-three years, every time hit Frisco. Ask Bell.

But Bell sold. Forgot, forgot. Took his cushion and moved to Petaluma to raise chickens. Well hell with you. Got any friends? then hell with your friends. Go to Pearl's. (*Not Lennie and Helen and the kids?*) See what's new, or old. Got 'nuf lettuce for *them* babies. But the idea is visual, not physical. Get a bottle first. And he waits for the feeling good that should be there, but there is none, only a sickness lurking.

The Bulkhead sign bile green in the rain. Rain and the street clogged with cars, going-home-from-work cars. Screw 'em all. He starts across. Screech, screech, screech. Brakes jammed on for a block back. M. Norbert Jacklebaum makes 'em stop; said without glee. On to Pearl's.

But someone is calling. Whitey, Whitey, get in here you stumblebum. And it is Lennie, a worn likeness of Lennie, so changed he gets in all right, but does not ask questions or answer them. (Are you on a ship or on the beach? How long was the trip? You sick, man, or just stewed? Only three or four days and you're feeling like this? *No,* no stopping for a bottle or to buy presents.)

He only sits while the sickness crouches underneath, waiting to spring, and it muddles in his head, *going to see Lennie and Helen and the kids, no presents for 'em, an' don't even feel good.*

Hey Sailor, what ship?

2

And so he gets there after all, four days and everything else too late. It is an old peaked house on a hill and he has imaged and entered it over and over again, in a thousand various places a thousand various times: on watch and over chow, lying on his bunk or breezing with the guys; from sidewalk beds and doorway shelters, in flophouses and jails; sitting silent at union meetings or waiting in the places one waits, or listening to the Come to Jesus boys.

The stairs are innumerable and he barely makes it to the top. Helen (Helen? so... grayed?), Carol, Allie, surging upon him. A fever of hugging and kissing. 'Sabout time, shrills Carol over and over again. 'Sabout time.

Who is real and who is not? Jeannie, taller than Helen suddenly, just standing there, watching. I'm in first grade now, yells Allie, now you can fix my dolly crib, Whitey, it's smashted.

You hit it just right. We've got stew, pressure cooker stuff, but your favorite anyway. How long since you've eaten? And Helen looks at him, kisses him again, and begins to cry.

Mother! orders Jeannie, and marches her into the kitchen.

Whassamatter Helen? One look at me, she begins to cry.

She's glad to see you, you S.O.B.

Whassamatter her? She don't look so good.

You don't look so good either, Lennie says grimly. Better sit for a while.

Mommy oughta quit work, volunteers Carol; she's tired. All the time.

Whirl me round like you always do, Whitey, whirl me round, begs Allie.

Where did you go this time, Whitey? asks Carol. Thought you were going to send me stamps for my collection. Why didn't you come Christmas? Can you help me make a puppet stage?

Cut it, kids, not so many questions, orders Lennie, going to the stairs to wash. Whitey's got to take it easy. We'll hear about everything after dinner.

Your shoes are shiny, says Allie. Becky in my class got new shoes too, Mary Janes, but they're fuzzy. And she kneels down to pat his shoes.

Forgotten, how big the living room was. (And is he really here?) Carol reads the funnies on the floor, her can up in the air. Allie inspects him gravely. You got a new hurt on your face, Whitey. Sing a song, or say Thou Crown 'n Deep. And after dinner can I bounce on you?

Not so many questions, repeats Carol.

Whitey's gonna sit here. . . . Should go in the kitchen. Help your mommy.

Angry from the kitchen: Well, I don't care. I'm calling Marilyn and tell her not to come; we'll do our homework over there. I'm certainly not going to take a chance and let her come over here.

Shhh, Jeannie, shhh. He beg that, or Helen? The windows are blind with steam, all hidden behind them the city, the bay, the ships. And is it chow time already? He starts up to go, but it seems he lurched and fell, for the sickness springs at last and consumes him. And now Allie is sitting with him. C'mon, sit up and eat, Whitey, Mommy says you have to eat; I'll eat too. Perched beside him, pretty as you please. I'll take a forkful and you take a forkful. You're sloppy. Whitey—for it trickles down his chin. It does not taste; the inside of him burns. She chatters and then the plate is gone and now the city sparkles at him through the windows. Helen and Lennie are sitting there and somebody who looks like somebody he knows.

Chris, reminds Lennie. Don't you remember Chris, the grocery boy when we lived on Aerial Way? We told you he's a M.D. now. Fat and a poppa and smug; aren't you smug, Chris?

I almost shipped with you once, Whitey. Don't you remember?

(Long ago. Oh yes, oh yes, but there was no permit to be had; and even if there had been, by that time I didn't have no drag.) Aloud: I remember. You still got the itch? That's why you came round, to get fixed up with a trip card?

I came around to look at you. But that was all he was doing, just sitting there and looking.

Whassmatter? Don't like my looks? Get too beautiful since you last saw me? Handsome new nose 'n everything.

You got too beautiful. Where can I take him, Helen?

Can't take me no place. M. Norbert Jacklebaum's fine.

You've got to get up anyhow, Whitey, so I can make up the couch. Go on, go upstairs with Chris. You're in luck, I even found a clean sheet.

He settles back down on the couch, the lean scarred arms bent under his head for a pillow, the muscles ridged like rope.

He's a lousy doc. Affectionately. Gives me a shot of B-1, sleeping pills, and some bum advice. . . . Whaddaya think of that, he remembered me. Thirteen years and he remembers me.

How could he help remembering you with all the hell his father used to raise cause he'd forget his deliveries listening to your lousy stories? You were his hero. . . . How do you like the fire?

Your wood, Whitey, says Helen. Still the stuff you chopped three years back. Needs restacking though.

Get right up and do it. . . Whadja call him for?

You scared us. Don't forget, your last trip up here was for five weeks in Marine Hospital.

We never saw it hit you like this before, says Lennie. After a five-, six-week tear maybe, but you say this was a couple days. You were really out.

Just catching up on my sleep, tha's all.

There is a new picture over the lamp. Bleached hills, a fresh-ploughed field, red horses and a blue-overalled figure.

I got a draw coming. More'n five hundred. How's financial situation round here?

We're eating.

Allie say she want me to fix something? Or was it Carol? Those kids are sure. . . . A year'n a half. . . . An effort to talk, for the sleeping pills are already gripping him, and the languid fire, and the rain that has started up again and cannot pierce the windows. How *you* feeling, Helen? She looks more like Helen now.

Keeping my head above water. She would tell him later. She always told him later, when he would be helping in the kitchen maybe, and suddenly it would come out, how she really was and what was really happening, sometimes things she wouldn't even tell Lennie. And this time, the way she looked, the way Lennie looked. . . .

Allie is on the stairs: I had a bad dream, Mommy. Let me stay here till Jeannie comes to bed with me, Mommy. By Whitey.

What was your bad dream, sweetheart?

Lovingly she puts her arms around his neck, curls up. I was losted, she whispers, and instantly is asleep.

He starts as if he has been burned, and quick lest he wake her, begins stroking her soft hair. It is destroying, dissolving him utterly, this helpless warmth against him, this feel of a child—lost country to him and unattainable.

Sure were a lot of kids begging, he says aloud. I think it's worse.

Korea? asks Len.

Never got ashore in Korea. Yokohama, Cebu, Manila. (The begging children and the lost, the thieving children and the children who were sold.) And he strokes, strokes Allie's soft hair as if the strokes would solidify, dense into a protection.

We lay around Pusan six weeks. Forty-three days on that tub no big-ger'n this house and they wouldn't give us no leave ashore. Forty-three days. Len, I never had a drop, you believe me, Len?

Felt good most of this trip, Len, just glad to be sailing again, after

Pedro. Always a argument. Somebody says, Christ it's cold, colder'n a whore's heart, and somebody jumps right in and says, colder'n a whore's heart, hell, you ever in Kobe and broke and Kumi didn't give you five yen? And then it starts. Both sides.

Len and Helen like those stories. Tell another. Effort.

You should hear this Stover. Ask him, was you ever in England? and he claps his hands to his head and says, was I ever in England, Oh boy, was I ever in England, those limeys, they beat you with bottles. Ask him, was you ever in Marseilles and he claps his hands to his head and says, was I ever in Marseilles, Oh boy, was I ever in Marseilles, them frogs, they kick you with spikes in their shoes. Ask him, was you ever in Shanghai, and he says, was I ever in Shanghai, was I ever in Shanghai, man, they throw the crockery and the stools at you. Thass everyplace you mention, a different kind of beating.

There was this kid on board, Howie Adams. Gotta bring him up here. Told him 'bout you. Best people in the world, I says, always open house. Best kid. Not like those scenery bums and cherry pickers we got sailing nowadays. Guess what, they made me ship's delegate.

Well, why not? asks Helen; you were probably the best man on board.

A tide of peaceful drowsiness washes over the tumult in him; he is almost asleep, though the veined brown hand still tremblingly strokes, strokes Allie's soft pale hair.

Is that Helen? No, it is Jeannie, so much like Helen of years ago, suddenly there under the hall light, looking in at them all, her cheeks glistening from the rain.

Never saw so many peaceful wrecks in my life. Her look is loving. That's what I want to be when I grow up, just a peaceful wreck holding hands with other peaceful wrecks (For Len and Helen are holding hands). We really fixed Mr. Nickerson. Marilyn did my English, I did her algebra, and her brother Tommy wrote for us "I will not" five hundred times; then we just tagged on "talk in class, talk in class, talk in class."

She drops her books, kneels down beside Whitey, and using his long ago greeting asks softly, Hey Sailor, what ship?, then turns to her parents. Study in contrasts, Allie's face and Whitey's, where's my camera? Did you tell Whitey I'm graduating in three weeks, do you think you'll be here then, Whitey, and be. . . all right? I'll give you my diploma and write in your name so you can pretend you got through junior high, too. Allie's sure glad you came.

And without warning, with a touch so light, so faint, it seems to breathe against his cheek, she traces a scar. That's a new one, isn't it? Allie noticed. She asked me, does it hurt? Does it?

He stops stroking Allie's hair a moment, starts up again desperately, looks so ill, Helen says sharply: It's late. Better go to bed, Jeannie, there's school tomorrow.

It's late, it's early. Kissing him, Helen, Lennie. Good night. Shall I take my stinky little sister upstairs to bed with me whatever she's doing down here, or shall I leave her for one of you strong men to carry?

Leaning from the middle stair: didn't know you were sick, Whitey, thought you were like. . . some of the other times. From the top stair: see you later, alligators.

Most he wants alone now, alone and a drink, perhaps sleep. And they know. We're going to bed now too. Six comes awful early.

So he endures Helen's kiss too, and Len's affectionate poke. And as Len carries Allie up the stairs, the fire leaps up, kindles Len's shadow so that it seems a dozen bent men cradle a child up endless stairs, while the rain traces on the windows, beseechingly, ceaselessly, like seeking fingers of the blind.

Hey Sailor, what ship? Hey Sailor, what ship?

3

In his sleep he speaks often and loudly, sometimes moans, and toward morning begins the trembling. He wakes into an unshared silence he does not recognize, accustomed so to the various voices of the sea, the multi-pitch of those with whom sleep as well as work and food is shared, the throb of engines, churn of the propeller; or hazed through drink, the noises of the street, or the thin walls like ears—magnifying into lives as senseless as one's own.

Here there is only the whisper of the clock (motor by which this house runs now) and the sounds of oneself.

The trembling will not cease. In the kitchen there is a note:

> *Bacon and eggs in the icebox and coffee's made. The kids are coming straight home from school to be with you. DON'T go down to the front, Lennie'll take you tomorrow. Love.*

Love.

The row of cans on the cupboard shelves is thin. So things are still bad, he thinks, no money for stocking up. He opens all the doors hopefully, but if there is a bottle, it is hidden. A long time he stares at the floor, goes out into the yard where fallen rain beads the grasses that will be weeds soon enough, comes back, stares at his dampened feet, stares at the floor some more (needs scrubbing, and the woodwork can stand some too; well, maybe after I feel better), but there are no dishes in the sink, it is all cleaner than he expected.

Upstairs, incredibly, the beds are made, no clothes crumpled on the floor. Except in Jeannie's and Allie's room: there, as remembered, the dust feathers in the corners and dolls sprawl with books, records, and underwear. Guess she'll never get it clean. And up rises his old vision, of how he will return here, laden with groceries, no one in the littered house, and quickly, before they come, straighten the upstairs (the grime in the washbasin), clean the downstairs, scrub the kitchen floor, wash the hills of dishes, put potatoes in and light the oven, and when they finally troop in say, calmly, Helen, the house is clean, and there's steak for dinner.

Whether it is this that hurts in his stomach or the burning chill that will not stop, he dresses himself hastily, arguing with the new shoes that glint with a life all their own. On his way out, he stops for a minute to gloss his hand over the bookcase. Damn good paint job, he says out loud, if I say so myself. Still stands up after fourteen years. Real good that red backing Helen liked so much 'cause it shows above the books.

Hey Sailor, what ship?

4

It is five days before he comes again. A cabbie precedes him up the stairs, loaded with bundles. Right through, right into the kitchen, man, directs Whitey, feeling good, oh quite obviously feeling good. The shoes are spotted now, he wears a torn Melton in place of the new jacket. Groceries, he announces heavily, indicating the packages plopped down. Steak. Whatever you're eating, throw it out.

Didn't I tell you they're a good-looking bunch? triumphantly indicating around the table. 'Cept that Lennie hyena over there. Go on, man, take the whole five smackers.

Don't let him go, Whitey, I wanta ride in the cab, screams Allie.

To the top of the next hill and back, it's a windy curly round and round road, yells Carol.

I'll go too, says Jeannie.

Shut up, Lennie explodes, let the man go, he's working. Sit down, kids. Sit down, Whitey.

Set another plate, Jeannie, says Helen.

An' bring glasses. Got coke for the kids. We gonna have a drink.

I want a cab ride, Allie insists.

Wait till your mean old bastard father's not lookin'. Then we'll go.

Watch the language, Whitey, there's a gentleman present, says Helen. Finish your plate, Allie.

Thass right. Know who the gen'lmun is? I'm the gen'lmun. The world, says Marx, is divided into two classes. . . .

Seafaring gen'lmun and shoreside bastards, choruses Lennie with him.

Why, Daddy! says Jeannie.

You're a mean ole bassard father, says Allie.

Thass right, tell him off, urges Whitey. Hell with waitin' for glasses. Down the ol' hatch.

My class is divided by marks, says Carol, giggling helpless at her own joke, and anyway what about ladies? Where's *my* drink? Down the hatch.

I got presents, kids. In the kitchen.

Where they'll stay, warns Helen, till after dinner. Just keep sitting.

Course Jeannie over there doesn't care 'bout a present. She's too grown up. Royal highness doesn't even kiss old Whitey, just slams a plate at him.

Fork, knife, spoon too, says Jeannie, why don't you use them?

Good chow, Helen. But he hardly eats, and as they clear the table, he lays down a tenner.

All right, sailor, says Lennie, put your money back.

I'll take it, says Carol, if it's an orphan.

If you get into the front room quick, says Lennie, you won't have to do the dishes.

Who gives a shit about the dishes?

Watch it, says Helen.

Whenja start doin' dishes in this house after dinner anyway?

Since we got organized, says Lennie, always get things done when they're supposed to be. Organized the life out of ourselves. That's what's the matter with Helen.

Well, when you work, Helen starts to explain.

Lookit Daddy kiss Mommy.

Give me my present and whirl me, Whitey, whirl me, demands Allie.

No whirling. Jus' sat down, honey. How'd it be if I bounce you? Lef' my ol' lady in New Orleans with twenny-four kids and a can of beans.

Guess you think 'cause I'm ten I'm too big to bounce any more, says Carol.

Bounce everybody. Jeannie, Your mom. Even Lennie.

> *What is life*
> *Without a wife* (bounce)
> *And a home* (bounce bounce)
> *Without a baby?*

Hey, Helen, bring in those presents. Tell Jeannie, don't come in here, don't get a present. Jeannie, play those marimba records. Want marimba. Feel good, sure feel good. Hey, Lennie, get your wild ass in here, got things to tell you. Leave the women do the work.

Wild ass, giggles Allie.

Jeannie gets mad when you talk like that, says Carol. Give us our presents and let's have a cab ride and tell us about the time you were torpedoed.

Tell us Crown 'n Deep.

Go tell yourself. I'm gonner have a drink.

Down the hatch, Whitey.

Down the hatch.

Better taper off, guy, says Lennie, coming in. We want to have an evening.

Tell Helen bring the presents. She don't hafta be jealous. I got money for her. Helen likes money.

Upstairs, says Helen, they'll get their presents upstairs. After they're ready for bed. There's school tomorrow.

First we'll get them after dinner and now after we're ready for bed. That's not fair, wails Allie.

I never showed him my album yet, says Carol. He never said Crown n' Deep yet.

It isn't fair. We never had our cab ride.

Whitey'll be here tomorrow, says Helen.

Maybe he won't, says Carol. He's got a room rented, he told me. Six weeks' rent in advance and furnished with eighteen cans of beans and thirty-six cans of sardines. All shored up, says Whitey. Somebody called Deeck stays there too.

Lef' my wile ass in New Orleans, twenty-four kids and a present of beans, chants Allie, bounding herself up and down on the couch. And it's not *fair*.

Say good night to them, Whitey, they'll come down in their nightgowns for a good-night kiss later.

Go on, kids. Mind your momma, don't be like me. An' here's a dollar for you an' a dollar for you. An' a drink for me.

But Lennie has taken the bottle. Whass matter, doncha like to see me feelin' good? Well, screw you, brother, I'm supplied, and he pulls a pint out of his pocket.

Listen, Whitey, says Jeannie, I've got some friends coming over and. . . Whitey, please, they're not used to your kind of language.

That so? Scuse me, your royal highness. Here's ten dollars, your royal highness. Help you forgive?

Please go sit in the kitchen. Please, Daddy, take him in the kitchen with you.

Jeannie, says Lennie, give him back the money.

He gave it to me, it's mine.

Give it back.

All right. Flinging it down, running up the stairs.

Quit it, Whitey, says Lennie.

Quit what?

Throwing your goddam money around. Where do you think you are, down on the front?

'S better down on the front. You're gettin' holier than the dago pope.

I mean it, guy. And tone down that language. Let's have the bottle.

No. Into the pocket. Do *you* good to feel good for a change. You 'n Helen look like you been through the meat grinder.

Silence.

Gently: Tell me about the trip, Whitey.

Good trip. Most of the time. 'Lected me ship's delegate.

You told us.

Tell you 'bout that kid, Howie? Best kid. Got my gear off the ship and lef' it down at the hall for me. Whaddaya think of that?

(Oh feeling good, come back, come back.)

Jeannie in her hat and coat. Stiffly. Thank you for the earrings, Whitey.

Real crystals. Best. . . Lennie, 'm gonna give her ten dollars. For treat her friends. After all, ain't she my wife?

Whitey, do I have to hear that story again? I was four years old.

Again? (He had told the story so often, as often as anyone would listen, whenever he felt good, and always as he told it, the same shy happiness would wing through him, how when she was four, she had crawled into bed beside him one morning, announcing triumphantly to her mother: I'm married to Whitey now, I don't have to sleep by myself any more.) Sorry, royal highness won't mention it. How's watch I gave you, remember?

(Not what he means to say at all. Remember the love I gave you, the worship offered, the toys I mended and made, the questions answered, the care for you, the pride in you.)

I lost the watch, remember? 'I was too young for such expensive presents.' You keep talking about it because that's the only reason you give presents, to buy people to be nice to you and to yak about the presents when you're drunk. Here's your earrings too. I'm going outside to wait for my friends.

Jeannie! It is Helen, back down with kids. Jeannie, come into the kitchen with me.

Jeannie's gonna get heck, says Carol. Geeeee, down the hatch. Wish *I* could swallow so long. Is my dresser set solid gold like it looks?

Kiss the dolly you gave me, says Allie. She's your grandchild now. You kiss her too, Daddy. I bet she was the biggest dolly in the store.

Your dolly can't talk. Thass good, honey, that she can't talk.

Here's my album, Whitey. It's got a picture of you. Is that really you, Whitey? It don't look like. . . .

Don't look, he says to himself, closing his eyes. Don't look. But it is indelible. Under the joyful sun, proud sea, proud ship as background, the proud young man, glistening hair and eyes, joyful body, face open to life, unlined. Sixteen? Seventeen? Close it up, he says, M. Norbert Jacklebaum never saw the guy. Quit punchin' me.

Nobody's punchin' you Whitey, says Allie. You're feeling your face.

Tracing the scars, the pits and lines, the battered nose; seeking to find .

Your name's Michael Jackson, Whitey, why do you always say Jacklebaum? marvels Allie.

Tell Crown 'n Deep. I try to remember it and I never can, Carol says, softly. Neither can Jeannie. Tell Crown 'n Deep, tell how you learnt it. If you feel like. Please.

Oh yes, he feels like. *When there is November in my soul*, he begins.
No, wrong one.

Taking the old proud stance. The Valedictory, written the dawn 'fore
he was executed by Jose Rizal, national hero of the Philippines. Taught
me by Li'l Joe Roco, not much taller'n you, Jeannie, my first shipmate.

I'm Carol, not Jeannie.

Li'l Joe. Never got back home, they were puttin' the hatch covers on
and. . . I only say it when it's special. Jose Rizal: El Ultimo Adiós.
Known as The Valedictory, 1896.

> *Land I adore, farewell. . . .*
> *Our forfeited garden of Eden,*
> *Joyous I yield up for thee my sad life*
> *And were it far brighter,*
> *Young or rose-strewn, still would I give it.*
>
> *Vision I followed from afar,*
> *Desire that spurred on and consumed me,*
> *Beautiful it is to fall,*
> *That the vision may rise to fulfillment.*

Go on, Whitey.

> *Little will matter, my country,*
> *That thou shouldst forget me.*
> *I shall be speech in thy ears, fragrance and color,*
> *Light and shout and loved song. . . .*

Inaudible.

> *O crown and deep of my sorrows,*
> *I am leaving all with thee, my friends, my love,*
> *Where I go are no tyrants. . . .*

He stands there, swaying. Say good night, says Lennie. Whitey'll tell
it all some other time. . . . Here, guy, sit down.

And in the kitchen.

You know how he talks. How can you let him? In front of the little kids.

They don't hear the words, they hear what's behind them. There are worse words than cuss words, there are words that hurt. When Whitey talks like that, it's everday words; the men he lives with talk like that, that's all.

Well, not the kind of men I want to know. I don't go over to anybody's house and hear words like that.

Jeanie, who are you kidding? You kids use them all.

That's different, that's being grown-up, like smoking. And he's so drunk. Why didn't Daddy let me keep the ten dollars? It would mean a lot to me, and it doesn't mean anything to him.

It's his money. He worked for it, it's the only power he has. We don't take Whitey's money.

Oh no. Except when he gives it to you.

When he was staying with us, when they were rocking chair, unemployment checks, it was different. He was sober. It was his share.

He's just a Howard Street wino now—why don't you and Daddy kick him out of the house? He doesn't belong here.

Of course he belongs here, he's a part of us, like family. . . . Jeannie, this is the only house in the world he can come into and be around people without having to pay.

Somebody who brings presents and whirls you around and expects you to jump for his old money.

Remember how good he's been to you. To us. Jeannie, he was only a few years older than you when he started going to sea.

Now you're going to tell me the one about how he saved Daddy's life in the strike in 1934.

He knows more about people and places than almost anyone I've ever known. You can learn from him.

When's he like that anymore? He's just a Howard Street wino, that's all.

Jeannie, I care you should understand. You think Mr. Norris is a tragedy, you feel sorry for him because he talks intelligent and lives in a nice house and has quiet drunks. You've got to understand.

Just a wino. Even if it's whisky when he's got the money. Which isn't for long.

To understand.

In the beginning there had been youth and the joy of raising hell and that curious inability to take a whore unless he were high with drink.

And later there were memories to forget, dreams to be stifled, hopes to be murdered.

Know who was the ol' man on the ship? Blackie Karns, Kissass Karns hisself.

Started right when you did, Whitey.

Oh yes. (A few had nimbly, limberly clambered up.) Remember in the war he was the only one of us would wear his braid uptown? That one year I made mate? Know how to deal with you, Jackson, he says. No place for you on the ships any more, he says. My asshole still knows more than all of you put together, I says.

What was it all about, Whitey?

Don't remember. Rotten feed. Bring him up a plate and say, eat it yourself. Nobody gonna do much till we get better. We got better.

This kid, overtime comin' to him. Didn't even wanta beef about it. I did it anyway. Got fined by the union for takin' it up. M. Norbert Jacklebaum fined by the union, "conduct unbefittin' ship's delegate" says the Patrolman, "not taking it up through proper channels." (His old fine talent for mimicry jutting through the slurred-together words.)

These kids, these cherry pickers, they don't realize how we got what we got. Beginnin' to lose it, too. Think anybody backed me up, Len? Just this Howie and a scenery bum, Goldballs, gonna write a book. Have you in it, Jackson, he says, you're a real salt.

Understand. The death of the brotherhood. Once, once an injury to one is an injury to all. Once, once they had to live for each other. And whoever came off the ship fat shared, because that was the only way of survival for all of them, the easy sharing, the knowing that when you needed, waiting for a trip card to come up, you'd be staked.

Now it was a dwindling few, and more and more of them winos, who shipped sometimes or had long ago irrevocably lost their book for nonpayment of dues.

Hey, came here to feel good. Down the hatch. Hell with you. You got any friends? Hell with your friends.

Helen is back. So you still remember El Ultimo, Whitey. Remember when we first heard Joe recite it?

I remember.

Remember too much, too goddam much. For twenty-three years, the water shifting: many faces, many places.

But more and more, certain things the same. The gin mills and the cathouses. The calabozas and jails and stockades. More and more New York and Norfolk and New Orleans and Pedro and Frisco and Seattle like the foreign ports: docks, clip joints, hockshops, cathouses, skid rows, the Law and the Wall: only so far shall you go and no further, uptown forbidden, not your language, not your people, not your country.

Added sometimes now, the hospital.

What's going to happen with you, Whitey?

What I care? Nobody hasta care what happens to M. Jacklebaum.

How can we help caring, Whitey? Jesus, man, you're a chunk of our lives.

Shove it, Lennie. So you're a chunk of my life. So?

Understand. Once they had been young together.

To Lennie he remained a tie to adventure and a world in which men had not eaten each other; and the pleasure, when the mind was clear, of chewing over with that tough mind the happenings of the times or the queernesses of people, or laughing over the mimicry.

To Helen he was the compound of much help given, much support: the ear to hear, the hand that understands how much a scrubbed floor, or a washed dish, or a child taken care of for a while, can mean.

They had believed in his salvation, once. Get him away from the front where he has to drink for company and for a woman. The torn-out-of-him confession, the drunken end of his eight-months-sober try to make a go of it on the beach—don't you see, I can't go near a whore unless I'm lit?

If they could know what it is like now, so casual as if it were after thirty years of marriage.

*Later, the times he had left money with them for plans: fix his teeth,
buy a car, get into the Ship Painters, go see his family in Chi. But soon
enough the demands for the money when the drunken need was on him,
so that after a few tries they gave up trying to keep it for him.*

*Later still, the first time it became too much and Lennie forbade the
house to him unless he were "O.K."—"because of the children."*

*Now the decaying body, the body that was betraying him. And the
memories to forget, the dreams to be stifled, the hopeless hopes to be murdered.*

What's going to happen with you, Whitey? Helen repeats. I never
know if you'll be back. If you'll be able to be back.

He tips the bottle to the end. Thirstily he thinks: Deeck and his room
where he can yell or sing or pound and Deeck will look on without
reproach or pity or anguish.

I'm goin' now.

Wait, Whitey. We'll drive you. Want to know where you're shacked,
anyway.

Go own steam. Send you a card.

By Jeannie, silent and shrunken into her coat. He passes no one in
the streets. They are inside, each in his slab of house, watching the
flickering light of television. The sullen fog is on his face, but by the
time he has walked to the third hill, it has lifted so he can see the city
below him, wave after wave, and there at the crest, the tiny house he has
left, its eyes unshaded. After a while they blur with the myriad others
that stare at him so blindly.

Then he goes down.

Hey Sailor, what ship?
Hey Marinero, what ship?

SAN FRANCISCO   1953, 1955
For Jack Eggan, Seaman. (1915–1938)
Killed in the retreat across the Ebro, Spain.

Delusions

. . . .

WILLIAM GOYEN

• • • • • • •

Where's Esther?

How could we know *that* was what it was? That we were losing a whole person? We were having a ball. While before our eyes Esther Haverton was having a downward plunge to—I don't know what to call it. It began in the Fall, lasted most of the season, Easter saw it over and Esther at Greenfarm.

Well, she always bent the old elbow a *lot*—who doesn't? But I mean *lots* when the onset of this started—whatever it is—coming last Fall (now, looking back, we know). Starting at 11 A.M., *onze heures*, that bejeweled hand went right for the Vodka Martini with a deadly grip, oh my dear!

Why didn't somebody stop her? But how could they *know?* That she was on her way to—*this?* Anyway, what would things have been like if we'd stopped Esther? Dreary. Morbid. Too glum to think about. But once Esther Haverton started, you just couldn't stop her. A whole party stopped for *her*. She was a real entertainer, you know; a natural performer. Oh she danced and she switched her bottom and just made everyone roar with laughter. She was here, there and everywhere, like a bird in a room. If she fell, she was up on her feet before you could help her up; and not one scratch! She was at all the parties, no one could wait until she got there and when she got there they wished she hadn't come, within ten minutes. There were some who cursed her and accused her of insulting them, including the very host and hostess, who were finally upon *each other* like dog and cat. Because of Esther! *She* caused it, turned the closest friends and most devoted lovers upon each other. And how had she done it? No one could guess, could even notice signs of rupture—until suddenly there were these two intimates at each other's throat.

Nevertheless, when Esther left, all followed. The night was young! Into a restaurant, which Esther at once commanded. She was at the waiters as if they had done something personal to her, and they had only asked for her order; called them names of rankest insult, which somehow prompted all her friends to beat on the table, stomp the floor with delight, screaming "Esther!"; and even the waiters liked it.

What *made* Esther? Well, she had the laugh of all times, to begin with. It was so *verbal*. The things that laugh said! Then she just plain had the face for it: a huggable face, sweet-featured, like somebody feeding a baby—so sentimental but with the chic-est hairdo over it my dear, to let you know she meant business. What wrong could a face like that do? Until those lips started curling. They were preparing to emit foul cries, oh my dear! She had a body that rivaled the best, curving tight in various simple but exclusive creations—by somebody she had on West 55th Street, a personal designer—and topped off by a real pair of breasts. *That* I envied, considering my personal limitations. Still, as I told her, I come from a line of humble-breasted women of the Midwest. Never tell Esther Haverton anything. She'll use it back on you literally as if she'd memorized it, at the most unscrupulous time. *Why* did she have to be so unscrupulous? But she was gay-hearted and didn't mean it, I guess. Besides, as we know now, she was losing her poor— marbles? More coffee, please. I love this coffee shop. Never heard of Irish coffee in *here*, thank God! Black's best, anyway.

Thirdly, Esther had the carelessness for it! Why she didn't give a hoot. Why should she? She had all the money in the world. She just sawed her wood, and let it fall where it would, to use an old Midwestern expression. Still, nobody could care *that* little. I think the pills did it— made her tell the world to go peddle its apples. Sawed a lot of timber those pills—whatever they were—some were of colors not even in the rainbow. I got flashes of them when she opened her bag, glowing like a

Tiffany lamp, my dear. Yet I never saw her take one as long as I went around with her. End with a dimpled shoulder, and a behind that went with her and not against her—you know, not fighting her—and there you have Esther!

How could anybody know that Esther was—well, I still can't believe it. She was go gay—such a character, and just the best person in the world, would give you her right arm if you asked for it and with her diamond bracelet on it—that's Esther! Yet, here she was, going rockers. We thought it was her natural wit. Anyway, her demeanor in public grew to such infamous proportions and resounded to such acclaim that she was the most vaunted guest. Her profanity increased to dazzling proportions. Esther would slap out a nasty word that would spatter all over a place like she'd thrown a messy pie. It was generally against somebody in our bunch—somebody she had apparently been good friends with, and then this—"You—!" That person would storm out. A phone call the next day got the whole thing aright. People were so forgiving of Esther. Thank goodness, now that I think about it, sober, and see that she was going bonkers. But I don't know how she got by with it, I swear. Anybody else would have had their heads knocked off, but not Esther. Of course they were all drunk, but even then! But thank goodness, we were all forgiving of her, knowing what we do now.

The next day on the phone: "Sugar, I don't remember a word of it. If I said it, forget it. Come for a hair at six." You'd be there at six. By eight you'd had your head knocked off again. Why was that? Why did we sanction that?

Oh, Esther! Racing at night through the streets of gold and laughter, drink here, run on there, drink yonder; and suddenly they were telling you it was 4 A.M. Who cared? Heaven could wait! On to somebody's place. Dawn! and Esther absolutely incandescent. At those times she was like a blazing serpent, flashing and striking. She caused people to surpass themselves beyond their wildest dreams. It was the *responses* to Esther that held people to her. What you heard yourself say to her was magnificent. What would we have been without her? She made us— *marvelous!* Why she could have led us to the terrace and told us to jump out and fly, and we'd have flown—*somehow*. Esther put wings on you!

Once I did a whole soft-shoe routine—complete with ride-out—it was at somebody's penthouse—on an open terrace nineteen flights up—and I'd never soft-shoed in my life, couldn't again. Because of Esther! She made wonders out of us. Isn't that weird? Like she had some kind of— you know—*power* over us.

Esther, lying there drab in that room at Greenfarm and not herself at all. If I didn't know her so well, I'd say she was a changeling—that somebody kidnapped Esther and replaced her with a blah stranger. Who wants that nothing person lying there? Another person, that's all, could be anybody, why that's an ordinary person lying there, not Esther. Where's Esther? This calm person lying there is not Esther. As though she existed out of booze. Vodka made Esther! Pour several drinks into this person and out develops who we call Esther! Don't pour the booze, you get *this*. I'm beginning to see. A sober view of Esther, you might say. The most boring conversations—Unity pamphlets strewn around. Why Esther doesn't know Unity from Simplicity—the patterns, I mean. Sweetie, she's an *agnostic*. Only two things she cares about are Dior and Majorska, and she'd cut that in half if she could wear a Vodka bottle designed by Dior; just *dress* in it, my dear. Well, they can have whoever *that* is. That's not Esther! "Where's Esther?" I kept wanting to say. "Who are *you*?" I kept wanting to say. "I don't believe we've met." You zombie! Oh, I need a laugh. Some drinks and a laugh. But with *Esther*.

Well, the whole thing has rather sobered me up. A week on the wagon, without Esther, during which time I've done me some thinking over coffee, as I am right now, and a change is coming over my mind. I'm going to say it. I don't even feel like going back to Greenfarm to visit Esther. She's beginning to shape up in my mind's eye as something I can do without. Why, I've been thinking of some of the things she said about me in public. They're beginning to come back to me, over coffee. I'm beginning to take them seriously (I mean *I* can be serious, too). God damn it. I mean, I'm not a fat-ass, like she called me several times, and once at a seated dinner. And perhaps I am a little flat—you know, like I said—but why did Esther bring *that* to the public eye by shouting it out at lunch at *Maude Chez Elle?* I feel like disliking Esther now. I feel like she *wanted* to hurt me. *In vino veritas,* my dear. All the terrible things she did to us and said to us are dawning back over me after a week of black coffee, and now I'm going to say it: Who needs Esther Haverton? Screw her! Isn't that right? I mean, to hell with Esther! I mean, good riddance.

Well, I guess I'm taking too sober a view. Thinking too much. A stiff drink *does*—may I add—keep you from taking *too* sober a view towards things, keeps you from thinking too much. Maybe I should just go on with the bunch. Heaven can wait. You only come around this way once. I mean, life is hard enough. This isn't *church!* Why should I go on worrying about Esther Haverton! Maybe I should just go on with the bunch. But why go on with that bunch without Esther. Those creeps. I'm mixed up! Let's face it: we need her. In the absence of Esther we are nothing— just about like what *she* is now, without booze. Jesus, it's like we drank Esther. Oh I'm going crazy. When I go into a place where we used to go, with everybody calling, "Where's Esther? Where's Esther?" I feel like a damned ghost. As if nobody saw *me*. And I hear myself asking the same question. "Where's Esther?"

I must admit that the other night, before I went on an alcohol-free diet, on one of our sans-Esther sprees, I found myself, in the absence of Esther, imitating her. Well, I was knocked on my backside within one minute! Do you know what? Only Esther can do it. I feel so drab, so dull, so dead, so plain. And I'm feeling crazy. Nerves jumping out of my skin; rattling the coffee cup. And who sleeps? Just can't find that spot in the bed—and when I think I have, guess who's in it? Old Sleeping Beauty, dozing sweet as a choirboy—which he definitely is *not*. I flee from *that*. Esther knows.

Last night I dreamt I went into the most beautiful bar, dark and cool, deep cushions, soft music: and who do you think was there, elbow on bar, Martini hoisted? Yep, Miss You-know-who: divine Esther! Tongue like a serpent's, poised to strike. Life began! All afternoon we laughed and drank. We drank and we drank. And I was my old self again. Because of Esther. The bar was ours. We never fought, not once. We drank the world away, laughing and laughing. "I want Esther!" I cried when I woke up in the dark. "Esther, Esther! Come back!"

Who wants this life, without the old days? But I tell you they are surely gone. I can see that a mile a minute, now. All those good times, all that laughing—gone. Oh I think I need some help. I don't know what to do. If I drink I'm like a bad Esther—and anyway, what's a drink without her? If I don't drink, I'm like Esther now, drab, dull, dead, plain. Will somebody please tell me what to do? Now that you've heard a little of it? To get over what's happened to Esther?

Minnie Again

Y ou know I wish my Cousin Minnie would leave New York and go on back down home to Virginia where she come from," allowed Simple. "Even if she did come North looking for freedom, Harlem is too much for her."

"Why? What's happened now?" I asked.

"Last week Minnie got behind in her rent and was about to be evicted from the house where she rooms at," said Simple. "So she come calling *me* up from a pay phone to ask me am I going to let her get put out in the street."

"What did you say?"

"I told Minnie I has nothing to do with the matter, being as I'm neither her landlord, her husband, her father, nor her brother. I am just an off-cousin—not even by marriage."

"Minnie said, 'Jess, I did not waste my time and my dime to call you up to listen to no such talk as that concerning our cousinship, which is by blood, if not by law. I needs me some money.'

"Now, I hate to get too plain-spoken with anybody, least of all a woman. But I had to tell Minnie what I thought she was. After which I told her what I thought she wasn't—which is that she ain't right bright. Minnie ought to could look at me by now and tell I never have no money. I also told Minnie that she is not stable, as the Relief folks says, because to my knowledge Minnie has had four jobs in three weeks and kept none of them.

"'Furthermore, Minnie,' I says, 'you are not sober. I can tell right now the way you talk on this phone you are not sober. Tomorrow, you will have a hang-over, and cannot go to work again, even if you have a job. Don't bother me about money,' I said and I started to hang up. But before I got the hook from my ear, Minnie called me a name which no man can take on the phone. In fact, Minnie were so indignant she called me *out of my name*. So I was forced to reply. Just then Central said, 'Five cents more, please,' which Minnie did not have. So our conversation were cut off on an unpleasant note with the last word being Minnie's. Boy, did you ever have a begging relative?"

"Who hasn't had such kinfolks?" I asked.

"Just when Joyce and me get a phone in our room, after being married almost two years without a phone of our own, who should come to New York and start phoning us but Cousin Minnie! I got a good mind to take my phone out of its socket."

"Then Minnie would probably come to your house and worry you in person," I said.

"Not if my wife put the evil eye on her," said Simple. "Joyce is a good girl, but she can look *so-ooo-oo-o* mean at times that even me, her lawful wedded husband, am scared to look back at her. Joyce can keep Minnie out of our house. Only reason she has not done so up to now is because Joyce tries to treat the woman right since Minnie is my kinfolks. But Minnie is driving kinship in the ground. Minnie loves money more than she does me, else she would not bug me with that word so much. From the first time I laid eyes on Cousin Minnie she needed money. First, money to stay in town after she got here, then money to buy something to eat (which is what she calls drink), then money to pay for a job at the employment office, then money to get out to her new job in the subway, then money to get another job after she quit the first job because the lady who hired her did not like frozen food, and Minnie said she did not intend to shell no fresh peas when peas come already shelled frozen. Now Minnie wants money to keep from getting put out in the street because she is three weeks behind on her rent. Minnie thinks I am a Relief Station, else God—and I ain't nothing but a man, a working man, and a colored man at that. Do you believe Minnie's in her right mind?"

"I think she is simply uninformed as to our habitual state of impecunity in Harlem," I said, "Many newly arrived immigrants from the South think all New Yorkers are rich. they don't realize that most of us live from day to day, from hand to mouth."

"I have tried to break that sad news to Minnie," said Simple, "but it does not seem to penetrate. I have put my hand in my pocket and turned it inside out to show her that my pockets are empty. I have told Minnie that my wife and me runs on a budget and that the budget runs out before the week does. But I want to tell you one thing, cousin or not, the next time Minnie asks me for money, I am going to sic Joyce on her, and I bet you Minnie will understand then!"

"Why would you bring Joyce into your family affairs?" I asked.

"Joyce is my loving wife," said Simple, "and from her I hides only a few secrets. You know it is nice to have a nice wife. And, so far, Joyce treats all my relatives polite. When Joyce first met Cousin Minnie, newly come to our town from Virginia, to tell the truth I thought my wife might snob Minnie. But Joyce did not snob her. My wife is as nice to Cousin Minnie as if Minnie was cultured—which Minnie is not. In fact, as you know, Minnie drinks. But Minnie had sense enough to come to my house last night almost sober. But she come, as usual, with a purpose. The first thing Minnie said last night was 'Jess, I been caught in the toils of the law.'

"I said, 'Minnie, don't toil me up in no law, because I will have nothing to do with what you been doing. What have you done?'

"'Well,' said Cousin Minnie, 'I were caught in an afterhours spot when it got raided Saturday, and they took everybody down, including me.'

"'What was a lady like you doing out so late in a speakeasy?' I inquired.

"'Ain't you never been out late yourself?' said Minnie.

"'I admit I were.'

"'And in an after-hours spot?' asked Minnie.

"'I have been in such,' I said, 'but I did not allow myself to get caught. Nobody has caught me in a speak-easy, except folks like me that was in there themselves, and they were not polices.'

"'You been lucky,' says Minnie. 'I been caught two or three times in raids—twice in Virginia where they catch so many Negroes they let us all off easy. But up here in the North, I been remaindered for a hearing. And it is not prejudice, because that joint was integrated. There was white folks in the place, too, drinking, and they got remaindered also. Remaindered means I might have to pay a fine, and I has no money, which is why I turn to you, Jess, my only cousin in New York City.'

"'I wish you was no relation to me,' I says, 'because I has no money, neither and I hate to turn a relative down.'

"'If you are just temporarily out of cash,' says Minnie, 'can't you borrow some?'

"'My credit is not good,' I said. 'And were I borrowing for myself, it would be hard. For you, that is another story. Minnie, I don't hardly know you, even if you do be Uncle Willie's child. We was not raised up together at no time?'

"As easy as I can, I says, 'I has no money, never have had no money and if you looking to borrow what money I get, *I never will have none* . Do you not remember our Aunt Lucy who used to say, "Neither a borrower nor a lender be?" That was her motto. It is also mine.'

"'That,' says Minnie, 'is a very old corny motto. You ain't hep to the jive. The new motto now is, "Beg, borrow, and ball till you get it all—a bird in the hand ain't nothing but a man."'

"'I ain't coming on that,' I said, 'You sound like a woman I used to know named Zarita in my far-distant past. But, Minnie, I'm a married man now. I need my money for my home.'

"'For lack of five simoleons you would let me maybe go to jail, your own blood-cousin, here all alone by herself in Harlem where I don't know nobody. The reason I were in that joint that got raided was, I was trying to get acquainted. I met a right nice colored man in there who bought me a drink and seemed really interested in me until we all got hauled down to the Precinct. Then I asked that man if he would help me to get out. He said, "Baby, I got to get myself out, I can't be bothered with you." Peoples is hardhearted in New York City. You are hard-hearted, too, Jesse B. Semple.'

"'Hard as that rock in the St. Louis-Blues that were cast into the sea! Minnie, I regrets this is what big-town life does to peoples. Girl, you had ought to stayed down yonder where you was in Virginia.'

"'I'll say no more,' said Minnie. 'Have you got some beer in the icebox?'

"'Not with me around the house.' I says. About that time Joyce comes back out of the kitchenette where she was peeling potatoes and says, 'Miss Minnie, could I offer you a nice fresh glass of Kool-Aid?'

"So you know what Minnie says? She says, 'Thank you, I never drinks a drop of no kind of ade, neither nothing else clear colored such as water. I thank you just the same, Cousin-in-law, married as you is to my favorite cousin, Jesse B., I thank you just the same. And good night.'

"The very word Kool-Aid run Minnie out of the house. When she left Joyce laughed and said, 'I knowed that would get rid of her—Kool-Aid! I would never let Minnie drink up that nice cold pint of beer I just bought for you on my ways home from work out of our budget.'

"'Joyce, I don't know which I love the most,' I said, 'you or your bud-get!'"

Crown of Thorns

A month after June died Gordie took the first drink, and then the
need was on him like a hook in his jaw, tipping his wrist, sending
him out with needles piercing his hairline, his aching hands. From the
beginning it was his hands that made him drink. They remembered
things his mind could not—curve of hip and taut breast. They remembered farther back, to the times he spent with June when the two were
young. They had always been together, like brother and sister, stealing
duck eggs, blowing crabgrass between their thumbs, chasing cows.
They got in trouble together. They fought but always made up easy and
quick, until they were married.

His hands remembered things he forced his mind away from—how
they flew out from his sides in rage so sudden that he could not control
the force and the speed of their striking. He'd been a boxer in the
Golden Gloves. But what his hands remembered now were the times
they struck June.

They remembered this while they curled around the gold-colored can
of beer he had begged down the road at Eli's.

"You gone too far now." Eli said. Gordie knew he was sitting at his
Uncle Eli's table again because the orange spots in the oilcloth were
there beneath his eyes. Eli's voice came from the soft pure blackness
that stretched out in all directions from the lighted area around the beer
can. Gordie's hands felt unclean. The can felt cold and pure. It was as

though his hands were soiling something never touched before. The way the light fell it was as though the can were lit on a special altar.

"I'm contaminated," Gordie said.

"You sure are." Eli spoke somewhere beyond sight. "You're going to land up in the hospital."

That wasn't what he'd meant, Gordie struggled to say, but he was distracted suddenly by the size of his hands. So big. Strong.

"Look at that," said Gordie wonderingly, opening and closing his fist. "If only they'd let me fight the big one, huh? If only they'd gave me a chance."

"You did fight the big one," said Eli. "You got beat."

"That's right," said Gordie. "It wasn't even no contest. I wasn't even any good."

"You forget those things," said Eli. He was moving back and forth behind the chair.

"Eat this egg. I fixed it over easy."

"I couldn't," said Gordie, "or this bun either. I'm too sick."

His hands would not stay still. He had noticed this. They managed to do an alarming variety of things while he was not looking. Now they had somehow crushed the beer can into a shape. He took his hands away and studied the can in its glowing spotlight. The can was bent at the waist and twisted at the hips like the torso of a woman. It rocked slightly side to side in the breeze from the window.

"She's empty!" he realized suddenly, repossessing the can. "I don't think it was full to begin with. I coundn't've."

"What?" asked Eli. Patiently, his face calm, he spooned the egg and fork-toasted bread into his mouth. His head was brown and showed through the thin gray stubble of his crew cut. A pale light lifted and fell into the room. It was six A.M.

"Want some?" Eli offered steaming coffee in a green plastic mug, warped and stained. It was the same color as his work clothes.

Gordie shook his head and turned away. Eli drank from the cup himself.

"You wouldn't have another someplace that you forgot?" said Gordie sadly.

"No," said Eli.

"I've got to make a raise then," said Gordie.

The two men sat quietly, then Gordie shook the can, put it down, and walked out of the door. Once outside, he was hit by such a burst of determination that he almost walked normally, balanced in one wheel rut, down Eli's little road. Some of his thick hair stuck straight up in a peak, and some was crushed flat. His face sagged. He'd hardly eaten that week, and his pants flapped beneath his jacket, cinched tight, the zipper shamefully unzipped.

Eli watched from his chair, sipping the coffee to warm his blood. He liked the window halfway open although the mornings were still cold. When June lived with him she'd slept on the cot beside the stove, a lump beneath the quilts and army blankets when he came in to get her up for the government school bus. Sometimes they'd sat together looking out the same window into cold blue dark. He'd hated to send her off at that lonely hour. Her coat was red. All her clothes were from the nuns. Once he'd bought June a plastic dish of bright bath-oil beads. Before he could stop her she had put one in her mouth, not understanding what it was. She'd swallowed it down, too. Then, when she'd started crying out of disappointment and shame, bubbles had popped from her lips and nose.

Eli laughed out loud, then stopped. He saw her face and the shocked look. He sat there thinking of her without smiling and watched Gordie disappear.

Two cars passed Gordie on the road but neither stopped. it was too early to get anything in town, but he would have appreciated a ride to his house. It was a mile to his turnoff, and his need grew worse with each step he took. He shook with the cold, with the lack. The world had narrowed to this strip of frozen mud. The trees were slung to either side in a dense mist, and the crackle his feet made breaking ice crystals was bad to hear. From time to time he stopped to let the crackle die down. He put his hands to his mouth to breathe on them. He touched his cold cheeks. The skin felt rubbery and dead. Finally the turnoff came and he went down to the lake where his house was. Somehow he gained the stairs and door then crawled across the carpet to the phone. He even looked the number up in the book.

"Royce there?" he asked the woman's voice. She put her husband on without a word.

"You still drinking?" said Royce.

"Could you bring me some quarts? Three, four, last me out. I'll pay you when I get my check."

"I don't make house calls or give no credit."

"Cousin. . . you know I work."

There was a pause.

"All right then. Credit's one dollar on the bottle, and house call's two."

Gordie babbled his thanks. The phone clicked. Knowing it would come, Gordie felt much stronger, clearer in the brain. He knew he would sleep once he got the wine. He noticed he'd landed underneath the table, that he'd brought the phone down. He lay back restfully. It was a good place to stay.

A lot of time went by, hours or days, and the quarts were gone. More wine appeared. One quart helped and the next didn't. Nothing happened. He'd gone too far. He found himself sitting at the kitchen table in a litter of dried bread, dishes he must have eaten something from, bottles and stubbed cigarettes. Either the sun was rising or the sun was going down, and although he did not feel that he could wait to find out which it was, he knew he had no choice. He was trapped there with himself. He didn't know how long since he had slept.

Gordie's house was simple and very small. It was a rectangle divided in half. The kitchen and the living room were in one half and the bedroom and the bathroom were in the other. A family of eight had lived here once, but that was long ago in the old days before government housing. Gordie bought the place after June left. He'd fixed it up with shag carpeting, linoleum tile, paint and Sheetrock and new combination windows looking out on the lake. He had always wanted to live by a lake, and now he did. All the time he had been living there he both missed June and was relieved to be without her. Now he couldn't believe that she would not return. He had been together with her all his life. There was nothing she did not know about him. When they ran away from everybody and got married across the border in South Dakota, it was just a formality for the records. They already knew each other better than most people who were married a lifetime. They knew the good things, but they knew how to hurt each other, too.

"I was a bastard, but so were you," he insisted to the room. "We were even."

The sun was setting, he decided. The air was darker. The waves rustled and the twigs scraped together outside.

"I love you, little cousin!" he said loudly. "June!" Her name burst from him. He wanted to take it back as soon as he said it. Never, never, ever call the dead by their names, Grandma said. They might answer. Gordie knew this. Now he felt very uneasy. Worse than before.

The sounds from the lake and trees bothered him, so he switched on the television. He turned the volume up as loud as possible. There was a program on with sirens and shooting. He kept that channel. Still he could not forget that he'd called June. He felt as though a bad thing was pushing against the walls from outside. The windows quivered. He stood in the middle of the room, unsteady, listening to everything too closely. He turned on the lights. He locked each window and door. Still he heard things. The waves rustled against each other like a woman's stockinged legs. Acorns dropping on the roof clicked like heels. There was a low murmur in the breeze.

An old vacuum cleaner was plugged in the corner. He switched that on and the vibrations scrambled the sounds in the air. That was better. Along with the television and the buzz of the lights, the vacuum cleaner was a definite help. He thought of other noises he might produce indoors. He remembered about the radio in the bedroom and lurched through the doorway to turn that on too. Full blast, a satisfying loud music poured from it, adding to the din. He went into the bathroom and turned on his electric shaver. There were no curtains in the bathroom, and something made him look at the window.

Her face. June's face was there. Wild and pale with a bloody mouth. She raised her hand, thin bones, and scratched sadly on the glass.

When he ran from the bathroom she got angry and began to pound. The glass shattered. He heard it falling like music to the bathroom floor. Everything was on, even the oven. He stood in the humming light of the refrigerator, believing the cold radiance would protect him. Nothing could stop her though. There was nothing he could do, and then he did the wrong thing. He plugged the toaster into the wall.

There was a loud crack. Darkness. A ball of red light fell in his hands. Everything went utterly silent, and she squeezed through the window in that instant.

Now she was in the bedroom pulling the sheets off the bed and arranging her perfume bottles. She was coming for him. He lurched for the door. His car key. Where was it? Pants pocket. He slipped through the door and fell down the stairs somehow pitching onto the hood of the Malibu parked below. He scrambled in, locked up tight, then roared the ignition. He switched the headlamps on and swung blindly from the yard, moving fast, hitting the potholes and bottoming out until he met the gravel road.

At first he was so relieved to escape that he forgot how sick he was. He drove competently for a while, and then the surge of fear that had gotten him from the house wore off and he slumped forward, half sightless, on the wheel. A car approached, white light that blinded. He pulled over to catch his senses. His mind lit in warped hope on another bottle. He'd get to town. Another bottle would straighten him out. The road was five miles of bending curves and the night was moonless, but he would make it. He dropped his head a few moments and slept to gain his strength.

He came to when the light roared by, dazzling him with noise and its closeness. He'd turned his own lights off, and the car had swerved to avoid him. Blackness closed over the other car's red taillights, and Gordie started driving. He drove with slowness and utter drunken care, craning close to the windshield, one eye shut so that the road would not branch into two before him. Gaining confidence, he rolled down his window and gathered speed. He knew the road to town by heart. The gravel clattered the wheel wells and the wind blew cold, sweet in his mouth, eager and watery. He felt better. So much better. The turn came so quickly he almost missed it. But he spun the wheel and swerved, catching himself halfway across the concrete road.

Just there, as he concentrated on controlling the speed of the turn, he hit the deer. It floated into the shadow of his headbeams. The lamps blazed stark upon it. A sudden ghost, it vanished. Gordie felt the jolt somewhat after he actually must have hit it, because, when he finally stopped the car, he had to walk back perhaps twenty yards before he found it sprawled oddly on its belly, legs splayed.

He stood over the carcass, nudged it here and there with his foot. someone would trade it for a bottle, even if it was a tough old doe. It was surprising, Gordie thought, to find one like this, barren from the looks of her, unless her fawn was hidden in the ditch. He looked around, saw nothing but then the brush was tall, the air black as ink.

Bending slowly, he gripped the delicate fetlocks and pulled her down the road.

When he reached the car, he dropped the deer and fumbled with his pocket. He found the only key he had was the square-headed one for the ignition. He tried to open the trunk, but the key did not fit. The trunk unlocked only with the rounded key he'd left at home.

"Damn their hides," he shouted. Everything worked against him. He could not remember when this had started to happen. Probably from the first, always and ever afterward, things had worked against him. He leaned over the slope of the trunk then turned onto his back. He was shaking hard all over, and his jaw had locked shut. The sky was an impenetrable liquid, starless and grim. He had never really understood before but now, because two keys were made to open his one car, he saw clearly that the setup of life was rigged and he was trapped.

He was shaking dead sick, locked out of his car trunk, with a doe bleeding slowly at his feet.

"I'll throw her in the back then," he said, before confusion smashed down. The seat was vinyl. It was important that he get a bottle, several bottles, to stop the rattling. Once the shaking got a good start on him nothing would help. It would whip him back and forth in its jaws like a dog breaks the spine of a gopher.

He opened the rear door and then, holding the deer under the front legs and cradled with its back against him, ducked into the back seat and pulled her through. She fits nicely, legs curled as if to run, still slightly warm. Gordie opened the opposite door and climbed out. Then he walked around the front and sat down in the driver's seat. He started the car and moved onto the highway. It was harder now to see the road. The night had grown darker or the shaking had obscured his vision. Or maybe the deer had knocked out a headlight. Clearly, he was sure of it, there was less light. He tried to accommodate the shaking. To keep it under control he took deep shuddering breaths that seemed to temporarily loosen its hold, but then it would be back, fiercely jolting him from side to side in his seat, so that the wheel twisted in his hands. He drove with impossible slowness now, hardly able to keep his course. A mile passed slowly. Perhaps another. Then he came to the big settlement of the Fortiers. Their yard blazed with light. He drove a few yards past their gate, and then something made him even more uncomfortable than the shaking. He sensed someone behind him and glanced in the rearview mirror.

What he saw made him stamp the brake in panic and shock. The deer was up. She'd only been stunned.

Ears pricked, gravely alert, she gazed into the rearview and met Gordie's eyes.

Her look was black and endless and melting pure. She looked through him. She saw into the troubling thrashing woods of him, a rattling thicket of bones. She saw how he'd woven his own crown of thorns. She saw how although he was not worthy he'd jammed this relief on his brow. Her eyes stared into some hidden place but blocked him out. Flat black. He did not understand what he was going to do. He bent, out of her gaze, and groped beneath the front seat for the tire iron, a flat-edged crowbar thick as a child's wrist.

Then he raised it. As he turned he brought it smashing down between her eyes. She sagged back into the seat again. Gordie began to drive.

This time, when the shaking started, there was no limit to the depth. It was in the bones, then the marrow of the bones. It ran all through him.

His head snapped back. He stopped the car. The crowbar was in his lap in case she came to life again. He held it, fusing his hands to the iron to keep them still.

He sat there in the front seat, holding tight to the bar, shaking violently all around it. He heard loud voices. The windshield cracked into a spider's nest. The dash fell open and the radio shrieked. The crowbar fell, silencing that too.

The shaking stopped, a sudden lull that surprised him.

In that clear moment it came to his attention that he'd just killed June.

She was in the back seat, sprawled, her short skirt hiked up over her hips. The sheer white panties glowed. Her hair was tossed in a dead black swirl. What had he done this time? Had he used the bar? It was in his hands.

"Get rid of the evidence," he said, but his fingers locked shut around the iron, as if frozen to it. He would never be able to open his hands again. He was cracking, giving way. Control was caving like weathered ground. The blood roared in his ears. He could not see where he was falling, but he knew, at length, that he'd landed in an area of terrible vastness where nothing was familiar.

Sister Mary Martin de Porres played the clarinet and sometimes, when she was troubled or sleep was elusive, wrote her own music. Tonight she woke, staring, from an odd dream. For a long moment she vaguely believed she was at home in Lincoln. She had been drawing a cool bath for herself, filling the clawed tub, stirring the water with her hands. The water smelled sharp, of indestructible metals. The cicadas buzzed outside, and the pods were blackening on the catalpas. She thought that once she stripped herself and crawled into the tub, she would change, she would be able to breathe under water. But she woke first. She turned on her side, found she was in her room at Sacred Heart, and reached for her eyeglasses. Her clock said one. She watched the glowing minute hand glide forward and knew, without even attempting to close her eyes again, that it was another of "her nights," as the others put it on those days when she was unusually out of sorts. "Sister Mary Martin's had one of her nights again."

Her nights were enjoyable while she was having them, which was part of the problem. Once she woke in a certain mood and thought of the clarinet, sleep seemed dull, unnecessary even, although she knew for a fact that she was not a person who could go sleepless without becoming irritable. She rolled out of bed. She was a short, limber, hardworking woman, who looked much younger than she was, that is, she looked thirtyish instead of forty-two. Most of the others, people noticed, looked younger than their true ages, also.

"It's no darn use anyway," she mumbled, slipping on her old green robe. Already she felt excited about rising alone, seeing no one. Her own youthfulness surprised her on nights like this. Her legs felt springy and lean, her body taut like a girl's. She raised her arms over her head, stretched hard, and brought them down. Then she eased through her door. It was the one at the end of the halls, the quietest room of all. She walked soundlessly along the tiles, down the stairs, through another corridor, and back around the chapel into a small sitting room impossibly cluttered with afghans and pillows.

She turned on the floor lamp and pulled her instrument case from beneath the sofa. Kneeling with it, she lifted the pieces from the crushed and molded velvet and fit them together. She took a small, lined music notebook from a shelf of books. A sharpened pencil was already attached to the spine with a string. Last of all, before she sat down, she draped an enormous bee-yellow afghan around her shoulders. Then she settled herself, hooked her cold feet in the bottom of the knit blanket, wet the reed, and began to play.

Sometimes it put her to sleep in half an hour. Other times she hit on a tune and scribbled, wherever it took her, until dawn. The sitting room was newly attached to the main convent and insulated heavily, so her music disturbed no one. On warm nights she even opened windows and let the noises drift in, clear in the dry air, from the town below. They were wild noises—hoarse wails, reeling fiddle music, rumble of unmuffled motors, and squeals of panicked acceleration. Then after three or four in the morning a kind of dazed blue silence fell, and there was nothing but her own music and the black crickets in the wall.

Tonight, perhaps because of her dream, which was both familiar and something she did not understand, the music was both faintly menacing and full of wonder. It took her in circles of memories. A shape rose in her mind, a tree that was fully branched like the main candelabrum on the altar of the Blessed Virgin. It had been her favorite tree to climb on as a child, but at night she had feared the rasp of its branches.

She stopped, particularly struck by a chance phrase, and played it over with slight variations until it seemed too lovely to discard. Then she wrote it down. She worked in silence for a while after, seeing something that might become a pattern, approaching and retreating from the strength of her own design.

An hour or perhaps two hours passed. The air was still. Sister Mary Martin heard nothing but the music, even when she stopped playing to write down the notes. A slim gravel path led around the back of the convent, but perhaps, she thought later, the man had walked through the wet grass, for she did not hear him approaching and only realized his presence at the window when the sill rattled. He'd tried to knock, but had fallen instead against the frame. Mary Martin froze in her chair and laid the clarinet across her lap.

"Who's there?" she said firmly. There was no answer. She was annoyed, first to have her night invaded and then with herself for not having drawn the blinds, because the sky was black and she could not see even the shadow of the prowler's shape while she herself was perfectly exposed, as on a stage.

"What do you want?" There was still no answer, and her heart sped, although the windows were screened and secure. She could always rouse the others if she had to. But she was consistently the one called upon to lift heavy boxes and jumpstart the community's car. Probably it would be up to her to scare off this intruder herself, even if the others came downstairs.

She reached up and switched the lamp off. The room went utterly dark. Now she heard his breath rasp, his shudder lightly ring the screen. Her eyes adjusted, and she saw the blunt outline of him, hang-dog, slumped hard against the window.

"What do you want?" she repeated, rising from the chair. She began to lower the clarinet to the carpet, then held it. If he came through the screen she could poke him with the playing end. She walked over to the dense shadow of the bookshelf, near the window and against the wall, where she thought it would be impossible for him to see her.

A breeze blew through the screen and she smelled the sour reek of him. Drunk. Probably half conscious.

But now he roused himself with a sudden jerk and spoke.

"I come to take confession. I need to confess it."

She stood against the wall, next to the window, arms folded against her chest.

"I'm not a priest."

"Bless me Father for I have sinned. . . . "

The voice was blurred, stupidly childish.

"I'll go get a priest for you," she said.

"It's been, shit, ten years since my last confession." He laughed, then he coughed.

The wind blew up, suddenly, a cold gust from the garden, and a different, specifically evil, smell came from his clothes, along with the smell of something undefinably worse.

"What do you want?" she said for the third time.

He banged the screen with his elbow. He turned, hugging himself, pounding his arms with his fists, and threw his forehead against the window frame. He was weeping, she recognized at last. This was the soundless violent way that this particular man wept.

"All right," she said, knowing and not wanting to know. It would be a very bad thing that he had to say. "Tell me."

And then he tried to tell her, stumbling and stuttering, about the car and the crowbar and how he'd killed June.

A low humming tension collected in the dark around Mary Martin as she sorted through his jumbled story. He could not stop talking. He went on and on. Finally it became real for her also. He had just now killed his wife. Her throat went dry. She held the clarinet across her chest with both hands, fingers pressed on the warm valves and ebony. She listened. Clarity. She could not think. The word fell into her mind, but her mind was not clear. The metal valve caps were silky smooth. She thought she smelled the blood on him. A knot of sickness formed in her stomach and uncurled, rising in her throat, burning. She wanted urgently to get away from him and sleep. She needed to lie down.

"*Stop,*" she begged. Her throat closed. He fell silent on her word. But it was too late. She saw the woman clubbed, distinctly heard the bar smash down, saw the vivid blood.

Her fists were tight knobs. Tears had filled the slight cup where her glasses frames touched her cheeks, and they leaked straight down from there along the corners of her mouth. The tears dropped on her hands. She had to say something.

"Are you sure that she's dead?"

His silence told her that he was. He seemed to have relaxed, breathing easier, as if telling her had removed some of the burden from him already. She heard him fumble through his clothes. A match snicked. There was a brief glare of light, and then tobacco curled faintly through the window and disappeared in the black room. Something lit furiously in Mary Martin when she heard him take the smoke in with a grateful sigh. Light pinwheeled behind her eyes, red and jagged, giving off a tide of heat that swept her to the window. For what she did not know.

Now she stood, trembling, inches from him and spoke into the shadow of his face.

"Where is she?"

"Outside in my car."

"Take me to see her then," said Mary Martin.

To get to the portico of the back entryway, she had to pass through the dark chapel. A candle burned, soft orange in its jar, before the small wooden sacristy where the host was kept. She walked by without genuflecting or making the sign of the cross, then made herself stop and go back. The calm of the orange glow reproached her. But after she had bent her knee and crossed herself she felt no different. She left her clarinet on one of the stairs and walked out to unlatch the back door. She stepped into the cool night air. He had gone before her and was already part way down the path walking bowlegged for balance. She stamped out the glowing cigarette stub he flipped in the grass. He stopped twice, giving in to a spasm of rolling shivers against a drainpipe then again where the gate opened out to the front yard. His car was parked in the lot, askew. She saw it right off—a long, low-slung green car directly lit by the yard light. He stopped at the edge of the gravel lot, swaying slightly, and put his hand to his mouth.

She had not seen his face yet, and now, as she stood beside him, forced herself to look, to find something, before she went to the car, that would make it impossible to hate him.

But his face was the puckered, dull mask of a drunk, and she turned quickly away. She walked over to the car, leaving him where he stood. The back seat was lit from one side, she saw, and so she walked up to it, taking deep breaths before she bent and gazed through the window.

Mary Martin had prepared herself so strictly for the sight of a woman's body that the animal jolted her perhaps more than if the woman had been there. At the first sight of it, so strange and awful, a loud cackle came from her mouth. Her legs sagged, suddenly old, and a fainting surge of weakness spread through her. She managed to open the door. There was no mistake—dun flanks, flag tail, curled legs, and lolling head. The yard light showed it clearly. But she had to believe. She bent into the car, put her hands straight out, and lowered them carefully onto the deer. The flesh was stiff, but the short hair seemed warm and alive. The smell hit her—the same frightening smell that had been on the man—some death musk that deer give off, acrid and burning and final. Suddenly and without warning, like her chest were cracking, the weeping broke her. It came out of her with hard violence, loud in her ears, a wild burst of sounds that emptied her.

When it was over, she found herself in the back seat wedged against the animal's body.

Night was lifting. The sky was blue gray. She thought she could smell the dew in the dust and silence. Then, almost dreamily, she shook her head toward the light, blank for a moment as a waking child. She heard the wailing voice, an echo of hers, and remembered the man at the edge of the gravel lot.

She crawled from the car, shook the cramps from her legs, and started toward him. Her hands made gestures in the air, but no sound came from her mouth. When he saw that she was coming at him he stopped in the middle of a bawl. He stiffened, windmilled his arms, and stumbled backward in a cardboard fright. Lights were on behind him in the convent. Mary Martin began to run. He whirled to all sides, darting glances, then fled with incredible quickness back along the sides of the building to the long yard where there were orchards, planted pines, then the reservation grass and woods.

She followed him, calling now, into the apple trees but lost him there, and all that morning, while they waited for the orderlies and the tribal police to come with cuffs and litters and a court order, they heard him crying like a drowned person, howling in the open fields.

Trying to Stop

· · · · · · · ·

Where I'm Calling From

J.P. and I are on the front porch at Frank Martin's drying-out facility. Like the rest of us at Frank Martin's, J.P. is first and foremost a drunk. But he's also a chimney sweep. It's his first time here and he's scared. I've been here once before. What's to say? I'm back. J.P.'s real name is Joe Penny, but he says I should call him J.P. He's about thirty years old. Younger than I am. Not much younger, but a little. He's telling me how he decided to go into his line of work, and he wants to use his hands when he talks. But his hands tremble. I mean, they won't keep still. "This has never happened to me before," he says. He means the trembling. I tell him I sympathize. I tell him the shakes will idle down. And they will. But it takes time.

We've only been in here a couple of days. We're not out of the woods yet. J.P. has these shakes, and every so often a nerve—maybe it isn't a nerve, but it's something—begins to jerk in my shoulder. Sometimes it's at the side of my neck. When this happens, my mouth dries up. It's an effort just to swallow then. I know something's about to happen and I want to head it off. I want to hide from it, that's what I want to do. Just close my eyes and let it pass by, let it take the next man. J.P. can wait a minute.

I saw a seizure yesterday morning. A guy they call Tiny. A big fat guy, an electrician from Santa Rosa. They said he'd been in here for nearly two weeks and that he was over the hump. He was going home in a day or two and would spend New Year's Eve with his wife in front of the TV. On New Year's Eve, Tiny planned to drink hot chocolate and eat cookies. Yesterday morning he seemed just fine when he came down for breakfast. He was letting out with quacking noises, showing some guy how he called ducks right down onto his head. "Blam. Blam," said Tiny, picking off a couple. Tiny's hair was damp and was slicked back along the sides of his head. He'd just come out of the shower. He'd also nicked himself on the chin with his razor. But so what? Just about everybody at Frank Martin's has nicks on his face. It's something that happens. Tiny edged in at the head of the table and began telling about something that had happened on one of his drinking bouts. People at the table laughed and shook their heads as they shoveled up their eggs. Tiny would say something, grin, then look around the table for a sign of recognition. We'd all done things just as bad and crazy, so, sure, that's why we laughed. Tiny had scrambled eggs on his plate, and some biscuits and honey. I was at the table, but I wasn't hungry. I had some coffee in front of me. Suddenly, Tiny wasn't there anymore. He'd gone over in his chair with a big clatter. He was on his back on the floor with his eyes closed, his heels drumming the linoleum. People hollered for Frank Martin. But he was right there. A couple of guys got down on the floor beside Tiny. One of the guys put his fingers inside Tiny's mouth and tried to hold his tongue. Frank Martin yelled, "Everybody stand back!" Then I noticed that the bunch of us were leaning over Tiny, just looking at him, not able to take our eyes off him. "Give him air!" Frank Martin said. Then he ran into the office and called the ambulance.

Tiny is on board again today. Talk about bouncing back. This morning Frank Martin drove the station wagon to the hospital to get him. Tiny got back too late for his eggs, but he took some coffee into the dining room and sat down at the table anyway. Somebody in the kitchen made toast for him, but Tiny didn't eat it. He just sat with his coffee and looked into his cup. Every now and then he moved his cup back and forth in front of him.

I'd like to ask him if he had any signal just before it happened. I'd like to know if he felt his ticker skip a beat, or else begin to race. Did his eyelid twitch? But I'm not about to say anything. He doesn't look like he's hot to talk about it, anyway. But what happened to Tiny is something I won't ever forget. Old Tiny flat on the floor, kicking his heels. So every time this little flitter starts up anywhere, I draw some breath and wait to find myself on my back, looking up, somebody's fingers in my mouth.

In his chair on the front porch, J.P. keeps his hands in his lap. I smoke cigarettes and use an old coal bucket for an ashtray. I listen to J.P. ramble on. It's eleven o'clock in the morning—an hour and a half until lunch. Neither one of us is hungry. But just the same we look forward to going inside and sitting down at the table. Maybe we'll get hungry.

What's J.P. talking about, anyway? He's saying how when he was twelve years old he fell into a well in the vicinity of the farm he grew up on. It was a dry well, lucky for him. "Or unlucky," he says, looking around him and shaking his head. He says how late that afternoon, after he'd been located, his dad hauled him out with a rope. J.P. had wet his pants down there. He'd suffered all kinds of terror in that well, hollering for help, waiting, and then hollering some more. He hollered himself hoarse before it was over But he told me that being at the bottom of that well had made a lasting impression. He'd sat there and looked up at the well mouth. Way up at the top, he could see a circle of blue sky. Every once in a while a white cloud passed over. A flock of birds flew across, and it seemed to J.P. their wingbeats set up this odd commotion. He heard other things. He heard tiny rustlings above him in the well, which made him wonder if things might fall down into his hair. He was thinking of insects. He heard wind blow over the well mouth, and that sound made an impression on him, too. In short, everything about his life was different for him at the bottom of that well. But nothing fell on him and nothing closed off that little circle of blue. Then his dad came along with the rope, and it wasn't long before J.P. was back in the world he'd always lived in.

"Keep talking, J.P. Then what?" I say.

When he was eighteen or nineteen years old and out of high school and had nothing whatsoever he wanted to do with his life, he went across town one afternoon to visit a friend. This friend lived in a house with a fireplace. J.P. and his friend sat around drinking beer and batting the breeze. They played some records. Then the doorbell rings. The friend goes to the door. This young woman chimney sweep is there with her cleaning things. She's wearing a top hat, the sight of which knocked J.P. for a loop. She tells J.P.'s friend that she has an appointment to clean the fireplace. The friend lets her in and bows. The young woman doesn't pay him any mind. She spreads a blanket on the hearth and lays out her gear. She's wearing these black pants, black shirt, black shoes and socks. Of course, by now she's taken her hat off. J.P. says it nearly drove him nuts to look at her. She does the works, she cleans the chimney, while J.P. and his friend play records and drink beer. But they watch her and they watch what she does. Now and then J.P. and his friend look at each other and grin, or else they wink. They raise their eyebrows when the upper half of the young woman disappears into the chimney. She was all-right-looking, too, J.P. said.

When she'd finished her work, she rolled her things up in the blanket. From J.P.'s friend, she took a check that had been made out to her by his parents. And then she asks the friend if he wants to kiss her. It's supposed to bring good luck," she says. That does it for J.P. The friend rolls his eyes. He clowns some more. Then, probably blushing, he kisses her on the cheek. At this minute, J.P. made his mind up about something. He put his beer down. He got up from the sofa. He went over to the young woman as she was starting to go out the door.

"Me, too?" J.P. said to her.

She swept her eyes over him. J.P. says he could feel his heart knocking. The young woman's name, it turns out, was Roxy.

"Sure," Roxy says. "Why not? I've got some extra kisses." And she kissed him a good one right on the lips and then turned to go.

Like that, quick as a wink, J.P. followed her onto the porch. He held the porch screen door for her. He went down the steps with her and out to the drive, where she'd parked her panel truck. It was something that was out of his hands. Nothing else in the world counted for anything. He knew he'd met somebody who could set his legs atremble. He could feel her kiss still burning on his lips, etc. J.P. couldn't begin to sort an thing out. He was filled with sensations that were carrying him every which way.

He opened the rear door of the panel truck for her. He helped her store her things inside. "Thanks," she told him. Then he blurted it out—that he'd like to see her again. Would she go to a movie with him sometime? He'd realized, too, what he wanted to do with his life. He wanted to do what she did. He wanted to be a chimney sweep. But he didn't tell her that then.

J.P. says she put her hands on her hips and looked him over. Then she found a business card in the front seat of her truck. She gave it to him. She said, "Call this number after ten tonight. We can talk. I have to go now." She put the top hat on and then took it off. She looked at J.P. once more. She must have liked what she saw, because this time she grinned. He told her there was a smudge near her mouth. Then she got into her truck, tooted the horn, and drove away.

"Then what?" I say. "Don't stop now, J.P."

I was interested. But I would have listened if he'd been going on about how one day he'd decided to start pitching horseshoes.

It rained last night. The clouds are banked up against the hills across the valley. J.P. clears his throat and looks at the hills and the clouds. He pulls his chin. Then he goes on with what he was saying.

Roxy starts going out with him on dates. And little by little he talks her into letting him go along on jobs with her. But Roxy's in business with her father and brother and they've got just the right amount of work. They don't need anybody else. Besides, who was this guy J.P.? J.P. what? Watch out, they warned her.

So she and J.P. saw some movies together. They went to a few dances. But mainly the courtship revolved around their cleaning chimneys together. Before you know it, J.P. says, they're talking about tying the knot. And after a while they do it, they get married. J.P.'s new father-in-law takes him in as a full partner. In a year or so, Roxy has a kid. She's quit being a chimney sweep. At any rate, she's quit doing the work. Pretty soon she has another kid. J.P.'s in his mid-twenties by now. He's buying a house. He says he was happy with his life. "I was happy with the way things were going," he says. "I had everything I wanted. I had a wife and kids I loved, and I was doing what I wanted to do with my life." But for some reason—who knows why we do what we do?—his drinking picks up. For a long time he drinks beer and beer only. Any kind of beer—it didn't matter. He says he could drink beer twenty-four hours a day. He'd drink beer at night while he watched TV. Sure, once in a while he drank hard stuff. But that was only if they went out on the town, which was not often, or else when they had company over. Then a time comes, he doesn't know why, when he makes the switch from beer to gin-and-tonic. And he'd have more gin-and-tonic after dinner, sitting in front of the TV. There was always a glass of gin-and-tonic in his hand. He says he actually liked the taste of it. He began stopping off after work for drinks before he went home to have more drinks. Then he began missing some dinners. He just wouldn't show up. Or else he'd show up, but he wouldn't want anything to eat. He'd filled up on snacks at the bar. Sometimes he'd walk in the door and for no good reason throw his lunch pail across the living room. When Roxy yelled at him, he'd turn around and go out again. He moved his drinking time up to early afternoon, while he was still supposed to be working. He tells me that he was starting off the morning with a couple of drinks. He'd have a belt of the stuff before he brushed his teeth. Then he'd have his coffee. He'd go to work with a thermos bottle of vodka in his lunch pail.

J.P. quits talking. He just clams up. What's going on? I'm listening. It's helping me relax, for one thing. It's taking me away from my own situation. After a minute, I say, "What the hell? Go on, J.P." He's pulling his chin. But pretty soon he starts talking again.

J.P. and Roxy are having some real fights now. I mean *fights*. J.P. says that one time she hit him in the face with her fist and broke his nose. "Look at this," he says. "Right here." He shows me a line across the bridge of his nose. "That's a broken nose." He returned the favor. He dislocated her shoulder for her. Another time he split her lip. they beat on each other in front of the kids. Things got out of hand. But he kept on drinking. He couldn't stop. And nothing could make him stop.

Not even with Roxy's dad and her brother threatening to beat the hell out of him. They told Roxy she should take the kids and clear out. But Roxy said it was her problem. She got herself into it, and she'd solve it.

Now J.P. gets real quiet again. He hunches his shoulders and pulls down in his chair. He watches a car driving down the road between this place and the hills.

I say, "I want to hear the rest of this, J.P. You better keep talking."

"I just don't know," he says. He shrugs.

"It's all right," I say. And I mean it's okay for him to tell it. "Go on, J.P."

One way she tried to fix things, J.P. says, was by finding a boyfriend. J.P. would like to know how she found the time with the house and kids.

I look at him and I'm surprised. He's a grown man. "If you want to do that," I say, "you find the time. You make the time."

J.P. shakes his head. "I guess so," he says.

Anyway, he found out about it—about Roxy's boyfriend—and he went wild. He manages to get Roxy's wedding ring off her finger. And when he does, she cuts it into several pieces with a pair of wire-cutters. Good, solid fun. They'd already gone a couple of rounds on this occasion. On his way to work the next morning, he gets arrested on a drunk charge. He loses his driver's license. He can't drive the truck to work anymore. Just as well, he says. He'd already fallen off a roof the week before and broken his thumb. It was just a matter of time until he broke his neck, he says.

He was here at Frank Martin's to dry out and to figure how to get his life back on track. But he wasn't here against his will, any more than I was. We weren't locked up. We could leave any time we wanted. But a minimum stay of a week was recommended, and two weeks or a month was, as they put it, "strongly advised."

As I said, this is my second time at Frank Martin's. When I was trying to sign a check to pay in advance for a week's stay, Frank Martin said, "The holidays are always bad. Maybe you should think of sticking around a little longer this time? Think in terms of a couple of weeks. Can you do a couple of weeks? Think about it, anyway. You don't have to decide anything right now," he said. He held his thumb on the check and I signed my name. Then I walked my girlfriend to the front door and said goodbye. "Goodbye," she said, and she lurched into the doorjamb and then onto the porch. It's late afternoon. It's raining. I go from the door to the window. I move the curtain and watch her drive away. She's in my car. She's drunk. But I'm drunk, too, and there's nothing I can do. I make it to a big chair that's close to the radiator, and I sit down. Some guys look up from their TV. Then they shift back to what they were watching. I just sit there. Now and then I look up at something that's happening on the screen.

Later that afternoon the front door banged open and J.P. was brought in between these two big guys—his father-in-law and brother-in-law, I find out afterward. They steered J.P. across the room. The old guy signed him in and gave Frank Martin a check. Then these two guys helped J.P. upstairs. I guess they put him to bed. Pretty soon the old guy and the other guy came downstairs and headed for the front door. They couldn't seem to get out of this place fast enough. It was like they couldn't wait to wash their hands of all this. I didn't blame them. Hell, no. I don't know how I'd act if I was in their shoes.

A day and a half later J.P. and I meet up on the front porch. We shake hands and comment on the weather. J.P. has a case of the shakes. We sit down and prop our feet up on the railing. We lean back in our chairs like we're just out there taking our ease, like we might be getting ready to talk about our bird dogs. That's when J.P. gets going with his story.

It's cold out, but not too cold. It's a little overcast. Frank Martin comes outside to finish his cigar. He has on a sweater buttoned all the way up. Frank Martin is short and heavy-set. He has curly gray hair and a small head. His head is too small for the rest of his body. Frank Martin puts the cigar in his mouth and stands with his arms crossed over his chest. He works that cigar in his mouth and looks across the valley. He stands there like a prizefighter, like somebody who knows the score.

J.P. gets quiet again. I mean, he's hardly breathing. I toss my cigarette into the coal bucket and look hard at J.P., who scoots farther down in his chair. J.P. pulls up his collar. What the hell's going on? I wonder. Frank Martin uncrosses his arms and takes a puff on the cigar. He lets the smoke carry out of his mouth. Then he raises his chin toward the hills and says, "Jack London used to have a big place on the other side of this valley. Right over there behind that green hill you're looking at. But alcohol killed him. Let that be a lesson to you. He was a better man than any of us. But he couldn't handle the stuff, either." Frank Martin looks at what's left of his cigar. It's gone out. He tosses it into the bucket. "You guys want to read something while you're here, read that book of his, *The Call of the Wild*. You know the one I'm talking about? We have it inside if you want to read something. It's about this animal that's half dog and half wolf. End of sermon," he says, and then hitches his pants up and tugs his sweater down. "I'm going inside," he says. "See you at lunch."

"I feel like a bug when he's around," J.P. says. "He makes me feel like a bug." J.P. shakes his head. Then he says, "Jack London. What a name! I wish I had me a name like that. Instead of the name I got."

My wife brought me up here the first time. That's when we were still together, trying to make things work out. She brought me here and she stayed around for an hour or two, talking to Frank Martin in private. Then she left. The next morning Frank Martin got me aside and said, "We can help you. If you want help and want to listen to what we say." But I didn't know if they could help me or not. Part of me wanted help. But there was another part.

This time around, it was my girlfriend who drove me here. She was driving my car. She drove us through a rainstorm. We drank champagne all the way. We were both drunk when she pulled up in the drive. She intended to drop me off, turn around, and drive home again. She had things to do. One thing she had to do was to go to work the next day. She was a secretary. She had an okay job with this electronic-parts firm. She also had this mouthy teenaged son. I wanted her to get a room in town, spend the night, and then drive home. I don't know if she got the room or not. I haven't heard from her since she led me up the front steps the other day and walked me into Frank Martin's office and said, "Guess who's here."

But I wasn't mad at her. In the first place, she didn't have any idea what she was letting herself in for when she said I could stay with her after my wife asked me to leave. I felt sorry for her. The reason I felt sorry for her was that on the day before Christmas her Pap smear came back, and the news was not cheery. She'd have to go back to the doctor, and real soon. That kind of news was reason enough for both of us to start drinking. So what we did was get ourselves good and drunk. And on Christmas Day we were still drunk. We had go to out to a restaurant to eat, because she didn't feel like cooking. The two of us and her mouthy teenaged son opened some presents, and then we went to this steakhouse near her apartment. I wasn't hungry. I had some soup and a hot roll. I drank a bottle of wine with the soup. She drank some wine, too. Then we started in on Bloody Marys. For the next couple of days, I didn't eat anything except salted nuts. But I drank a lot of bourbon. Then I said to her, "Sugar, I think I'd better pack up. I better go back to Frank Martin's."

She tried to explain to her son that she was going to be gone for a while and he'd have to get his own food. But right as we were going out the door, this mouthy kid screamed at us. He screamed, "The hell with you! I hope you never come back. I hope you kill yourselves!" Imagine this kid!

Before we left town, I had her stop at the package store, where I bought us the champagne. We stopped someplace else for plastic glasses. Then we picked up a bucket of fried chicken. We set out for Frank Martin's in this rainstorm, drinking and listening to music. She drove. I looked after the radio and poured. We tried to make a little party of it. But we were sad, too. There was that fried chicken, but we didn't eat any.

I guess she got home okay. I think I would have heard something if she didn't. But she hasn't called me, and I haven't called her. Maybe she's had some news about herself by now. Then again, maybe she

hasn't heard anything. Maybe it was all a mistake. Maybe it was somebody else's smear. But she has my car, and I have things at her house. I
know we'll be seeing each other again.

They clang an old farm bell here to call you for mealtime. J.P. and I
get out of our chairs and we go inside. It's starting to get too cold on the
porch, anyway. We can see our breath drifting out from us as we talk.

New Year's Eve morning I try to call my wife. There's no answer. It's
okay. But even if it wasn't okay, what am I supposed to do? The last time
we talked on the phone, a couple of weeks ago, we screamed at each
other. I hung a few names on her. "Wet brain!" she said, and put the
phone back where it belonged.

But I wanted to talk to her now. Something had to be done about my
stuff. I still had things at her house, too.

One of the guys here is a guy who travels. He goes to Europe and
places. That's what he says, anyway. Business, he says. He also says he
has his drinking under control and he doesn't have any idea why he's
here at Frank Martin's. But he doesn't remember getting here. He
laughs about it, about his not remembering. "Anyone can have a blackout," he says. "That doesn't prove a thing." He's not a drunk—he tells
us this and we listen. "That's a serious charge to make," he says. "That
kind of talk can ruin a good man's prospects." He says that if he'd only
stick to whiskey and water, no ice, he'd never have these blackouts. It's
the ice they put into your drink that does it. "Who do you know in
Egypt?" he asks me. "I can use a few names over there."

For New Year's Eve dinner Frank Martin serves steak and baked
potato. My appetite's coming back. I clean up everything on my plate
and I could eat more. I look over at Tiny's plate. Hell, he's hardly
touched a thing. His steak is just sitting there. Tiny is not the same old
Tiny. The poor bastard had planned to be at home tonight. He'd
planned to be in his robe and slippers in front of the TV, holding hands
with his wife. Now he's afraid to leave. I can understand. One seizure
means you're ready for another. Tiny hasn't told any more nutty stories
on himself since it happened. He's stayed quiet and kept to himself. I

ask him if I can have his steak, and he pushes his plate over to me.

Some of us are still up, sitting around the TV, watching Times square, when Frank Martin comes in to show us his cake. He brings it around and shows it to each of us. I know he didn't make it. It's just a bakery cake. But it's still a cake. It's a big white cake. Across the top there's writing in pink letters. The writing says, HAPPY NEW YEAR— ONE DAY AT A TIME.

"I don't want any stupid cake," says the guy who goes to Europe and places. "Where's the champagne?" he says, and laughs.

We all go into the dining room. Frank Martin cuts the cake. I sit next to J.P. J.P. eats two pieces and drinks a Coke. I eat a piece and wrap another piece in a napkin, thinking of later.

J.P. lights a cigarette—his hands are steady now—and he tells me his wife is coming in the morning, the first day of the new year.

"That's great," I say. I nod. I lick the frosting off my finger. "That's good news, J.P."

"I'll introduce you," he says.

"I look forward to it," I say.

We say goodnight. We say Happy New Year. I use a napkin on my fingers. We shake hands.

I go to a phone, put in a dime, and call my wife collect. But nobody answers this time, either. I think about calling my girlfriend, and I'm dialing her number when I realize I really don't want to talk to her. She's probably at home watching the same thing on TV that I've been watching. Anyway, I don't want to talk to her. I hope she's okay. But if she has something wrong with her, I don't want to know about it.

After breakfast, J.P. and I take coffee out to the porch. The sky is clear, but it's cold enough for sweaters and jackets.

"She asked me if she should bring the kids," J.P. says. "I told her she should keep the kids at home. Can you imagine? My God, I don't want my kids up here."

We use the coal bucket for an ashtray. We look across the valley to where Jack London used to live. We're drinking more coffee when this car turns off the road and comes down the drive.

"That's her!" J.P. says. He puts his cup next to his chair. He gets up and goes down the steps.

I see this woman stop the car and set the brake. I see J.P. open the door. I watch her get out, and I see them hug each other. I look away. Then I look back, J.P. takes her by the arm and they come up the stairs. This woman broke a man's nose once. She has had two kids, and much trouble, but she loves this man who has her by the arm. I get up from the chair.

"This is my friend," J.P. says to his wife. "Hey, this is Roxy."

Roxy takes my hand. She's a tall, good-looking woman in a knit cap. She has on a coat, a heavy sweater, and slacks. I recall what J.P. told me about the boyfriend and the wirecutters. I don't see any wedding ring. That's in pieces somewhere, I guess. Her hands are broad and the fingers have these big knuckles. This is a woman who can make fists if she has to.

"I've heard about you," I say. "J.P. told me how you got acquainted. Something about a chimney, J.P. said."

"Yes, a chimney," she says. "There's probably a lot else he didn't tell you," she says. "I bet he didn't tell you everything," she says, and laughs. Then—she can't wait any longer—she slips her arm around J.P. and kisses him on the cheek. They start to move to the door. "Nice meeting you," she says. "Hey, did he tell you he's the best sweep in the business?"

"Come on now, Roxy," J.P. says. He has his hand on the doorknob.

"He told me he learned everything he knew from you," I say.

"Well, that much is sure true," she says. She laughs again. But it's like she's thinking about something else. J.P. turns the doorknob. Roxy lays her hand over his. "Joe, can't we go into town for lunch? Can't I take you someplace?"

J.P. clears his throat. He says, "It hasn't been a week yet." He takes his hand off the doorknob and brings his fingers to his chin. "I think they'd like it if I didn't leave the place for a little while yet. We can have some coffee here," he says.

"That's fine," she says. Her eyes work over to me again. "I'm glad Joe's made a friend. Nice to meet you," she says.

They start to go inside. I know it's a dumb thing to do, but I do it any-way. "Roxy," I say. And they stop in the doorway and look at me. "I need some luck," I say. "No kidding. I could do with a kiss myself."

J.P. looks down. He's still holding the knob, even though the door is open. He turns the knob back and forth. But I keep looking at her. Roxy grins. "I'm not a sweep anymore," she says. "Not for years. Didn't Joe tell you that? But, sure, I'll kiss you, sure."

She moves over. She takes me by the shoulders—I'm a big man—and she plants this kiss on my lips. "How's that?" she says.

"That's fine," I say.

"Nothing to it," she says. She's still holding me by the shoulders. She's looking me right in the eyes. "Good luck," she says, and then she lets go of me.

"See you later, pal," J.P. says. He opens the door all the way, and they go in.

I sit down on the front steps and light a cigarette. I watch what my hand does, then I blow out the match. I've got the shakes. I started out with them this morning. This morning I wanted something to drink. It's depressing, but I didn't say anything about it to J.P. I try to put my mind on something else.

I'm thinking about chimney sweeps—all that stuff I heard from J.P.—when for some reason I start to think about a house my wife and I once lived in. That house didn't have a chimney, so I don't know what makes me remember it now. But I remember the house and how we'd only been in there a few weeks when I heard a noise outside one morn-ing. It was Sunday morning; and it was still dark in the bedroom. But there was this pale light coming in from the bedroom window. I listened. I could hear something scrape against the side of the house. I jumped out of bed and went to look.

"My God!" my wife says, sitting up in bed and shaking the hair away from her face. Then she starts to laugh. "It's Mr. Venturini," she says. "I forgot to tell you. He said he was coming to paint the house today. Early. Before it gets too hot. I forgot all about it," she says, and laughs. "Come on back to bed, honey. It's just him."

"In a minute," I say.

I push the curtain away from the window. Outside, this old guy in white coveralls is standing next to his ladder. The sun is just starting to break above the mountains. The old guy and I look each other over. It's the landlord, all right—this old guy in coveralls. But his coveralls are too big for him. He needs a shave, too. And he's wearing this baseball cap to cover his bald head. Goddamn it, I think, if he isn't a weird old fellow. And a wave of happiness comes over me that I'm not him—that I'm me and that I'm inside this bedroom with my wife.

He jerks his thumb toward the sun. He pretends to wipe his forehead. He's letting me know he doesn't have all that much time. The old fart breaks into a grin. It's then I realize I'm naked. I look down at myself. I look at him again and shrug. What did he expect?

My wife laughs. "Come *on*," she says. "Get back in this bed. Right now. This minute. Come on back to bed."

I let go of the curtain. But I keep standing there at the window. I can see the old fellow nod to himself like he's saying, "Go on, sonny, go back to bed. I understand." He tugs on the bill of his cap. Then he sets about his business. He picks up his bucket. He starts climbing the ladder.

I lean back into the step behind me now and cross one leg over the other. Maybe later this afternoon I'll try calling my wife again. And then I'll call to see what's happening with my girlfriend. But I don't want to get her mouthy kid on the line. If I do call, I hope he'll be out somewhere doing whatever he does when he's not around the house. I try to remember if I ever read any Jack London books. I can't remember. But there was a story of his I read in high school. "To Build a Fire," it was called. This guy in the Yukon is freezing. Imagine it—he's actually going to freeze to death if he can't get a fire going. With a fire, he can dry his socks and things and warm himself.

He gets his fire going, but then something happens to it. A branchful of snow drops on it. It goes out. Meanwhile, it's getting colder. Night is coming on.

I bring some change out of my pocket. I'll try my wife first. If she answers, I'll wish her a Happy New Year. But that's it. I won't bring up business. I won't raise my voice. Not even if she starts something. She'll ask me where I'm calling from, and I'll have to tell her. I won't say anything about New Year's resolutions. There's no way to make a joke out of this. After I talk to her, I'll call my girlfriend. Maybe I'll call her first. I'll just have to hope I don't get her kid on the line. "Hello, sugar," I'll say when she answers. "It's me."

R O B E R T   S T O N E

· · · · · · ·

Helping

O ne gray November day, Elliot went to Boston for the afternoon.
The wet streets seemed cold and lonely. He sensed a broken promise in the city's elegance and verve. Old hopes tormented him like
phantom limbs, but he did not drink. He had joined Alcoholics
Anonymous fifteen months before.

Christmas came, childless, a festival of regret. His wife went to Mass
and cooked a turkey. Sober, Elliot walked in the woods.

In January, blizzards swept down from the Arctic until the weather
became too cold for snow. The Shawmut Valley grew quiet and crystal-
line. In the white silences, Elliot could hear the boards of his house
contract and feel a shrinking in his bones. Each dusk, starving deer
came out of the wooded swamp behind the house to graze his orchard for
whatever raccoons had uncovered and left behind. At night he lay beside his sleeping wife listening to the baying of dog packs running them
down in the deep moon-shadowed snow.

Day in, day out, he was sober. At times it was almost stimulating.
But he could not shake off the sensations he had felt in Boston. In his
mind's eye he could see dead leaves rattling along brick gutters and
savor that day's desperation. The brief outing had undermined him.

Sober, however, he remained, until the day a man named
Blankenship came into the office at the state hospital for counselling.

Blankenship had red hair, a brutal face, and a sneaking manner. He was a sponger and petty thief whom Elliot had seen a number of times before.

"I been having this dream," Blankenship announced loudly. His voice was not pleasant. His skin was unwholesome. Every time he got arrested the court sent him to the psychiatrists and the psychiatrists, who spoke little English, sent him to Elliot.

Blankenship had joined the Army after his first burglary but had never served east of the Rhine. After a few months in Wiesbaden, he had been discharged for reasons of unsuitability, but he told everyone he was a veteran of the Vietnam War. He went about in a tiger suit. Elliot had had enough of him.

"Dreams are boring," Elliot told him.

Blankenship was outraged. "Whaddaya mean?" he demanded.

During counselling sessions Elliot usually moved his chair into the middle of the room in order to seem accessible to his clients. Now he stayed securely behind his desk. He did not care to seem accessible to Blankenship. "What I said, Mr. Blankenship. Other people's dreams are boring. Didn't you ever hear that?"

"Boring?" Blankenship frowned. He seemed unable to imagine a meaning for the word.

Elliot picked up a pencil and set its point quivering on his desk-top blotter. He gazed into his client's slack-jawed face. The Blankenship family made their way through life as strolling litigants, and young Blankenship's specialty was slipping on ice cubes. Hauled off the pavement, he would hassle the doctors in Emergency for pain pills and hurry to a law clinic. The Blankenships had threatened suit against half the property owners in the southern part of the state. What they could not extort at law they stole. But even the Blankenship family had abandoned Blankenship. His last visit to the hospital had been subsequent to an arrest for lifting a case of hot-dog rolls from Woolworth's. He lived in a Goodwill depository bin in Syndham.

"Now I suppose you want to tell me your dream? Is that right, Mr. Blankenship?"

Blankenship looked left and right like a dog surrendering eye contact. "Don't you want to hear it?" he asked humbly.

Elliot was unmoved. "Tell me something, Blankenship. Was your dream about Vietnam?"

At the mention of the word "Vietnam," Blankenship customarily broke into a broad smile. Now he looked guilty and guarded. He shrugged. "Ya."

"How come you have dreams about that place, Blankenship? You were never there."

"Whaddaya mean?" Blankenship began to say, but Elliot cut him off.

"You were never there, my man. You never saw the goddam place. You have no business dreaming about it! You better cut it out!"

He had raised his voice to the extent that the secretary outside his open door paused at her word processor.

"Lemme alone," Blankenship said fearfuly. "Some doctor you are."

"It's all right," Elliot assured him. "I'm not a doctor."

"Everybody's on my case," Blankenship said. His moods were volatile. He began to weep.

Elliot watched the tears roll down Elliot's chapped, pitted cheeks. He cleared his throat. "Look fella... " he began. He felt at a loss. He felt like telling Blankenship that things were tough all over.

Blankenship sniffed and telescoped his neck and after a moment looked at Elliot. His look was disconcertingly trustful; he was used to being counselled.

"Really, you know, it's ridiculous for you to tell me your problems have to do with Nam. You were never over there. It was me over there, Blankenship. Not you."

Blankenship leaned forward and put his forehead on the knees.

"Your troubles have to do with here and now," Elliot told his client. "Fantasies aren't helpful."

His voice sounded overripe and hypocritical in his own ears. What a dreadful business, he thought. What an awful job this is. Anger was driving him crazy.

Blankenship straightened up and spoke through his tears. "This dream. . . " he said. "I'm scared."

Elliot felt ready to endure a great deal in order not to hear Blankenship's dream.

"I'm not the one you see about that," he said. In the end he knew his duty. He sighed. "O.K. All right. Tell me about it."

"Yeah?" Blankenship asked with leaden sarcasm. "Yeah? You think dreams are friggin' boring?"

"No, no," Elliot said. He offered Blankenship a tissue and Blankenship took one. "That was sort of off the top of my head. I didn't really mean it."

Blankenship fixed his eyes on dreaming distance. "There's a feeling that goes with it. With the dream." Then he shook his head in revulsion and looked at Elliot as though he had only just awakened. "So what do you think? You think it's boring?"

"Of course not," Elliot said. "A physical feeling?"

"Ya. It's like I'm floating in rubber."

He watched Elliot stealthily, aware of quickened attention. Elliot had caught dengue in Vietnam and during his weeks of delirium had felt vaguely as though he were floating in rubber.

"What are you seeing in this dream?"

Blankenship only shook his head. Elliot suffered a brief but intense attack of rage.

"Hey, Blankenship," he said equably, "here I am, man. You can see I'm listening."

"What I saw was black," Blankenship said. He spoke in an odd tremolo. His behavior was quite different from anything Elliot had come to expect from him.

"Black? What was it?"

"Smoke. The sky maybe."

"The sky?" Elliot asked.

"It was all black. I was scared."

In a waking dream of his own, Elliot felt the muscles on his neck distend. He was looking up at a sky that was black, filled with smoke-swollen clouds, lit with fires, damped with blood and rain.

"What were you scared of?" he asked Blankenship.

"I don't know," Blankenship said.

Elliot could not drive the black sky from his inward eye. It was as though Blankenship's dream had infected his own mind.

"You don't know? You don't know what you were scared of?"

Blankenship's posture was rigid. Elliot, who knew the aspect of true fear, recognized it there in front of him.

"The Nam," Blankenship said.

"You're not even old enough," Elliot told him.

Blankenship sat trembling with joined palms between his thighs. His face was flushed and not in the least ennobled by pain. He had trouble with alcohol and drugs. He had trouble with everything.

"So wherever your black sky is, it isn't Vietnam."

Things were so unfair, Elliot thought. It was unafir of Blankenship to appropriate the condition of a Vietnam veteran. The trauma inducing his post-traumatic stress had been nothing more serious than his own birth, a routine procedure. Now, in addition to the poverty, anxiety, and confusion that would always be his life's lot, he had been visited with irony. It was all arbitrary and some people simply got elected. Everyone knew that who had been where Blankenship had not.

"Because, I assure you, Mr. Blankenship, you were never there."

"Whaddaya mean?" Blankenship asked.

When Blankenship was gone, Elliot leafed through his file and saw that the psychiatrists had passed him upstairs without recording a diagnosis. Disproportionately angry, he went out to the secretary's desk.

"Nobody wrote up that last patient," he said. "I'm not supposed to see people without a diagnosis. The shrinks are just passing the buck."

The secretary was a tall, solemn redhead with prominent front teeth and a slight speech disorder. "Dr. Sayyid will have kittens if he hears you call him a shrink, Chas. He's already complained. He hates being called a shrink."

"Then he came to the wrong country," Elliot said. "He can go back to his own."

The woman giggled. "He *is* the doctor, Chas."

"Hates being called a shrink?" He threw the file on the secretary's table and stormed back toward his office. "That fucking little zip couldn't give you a decent haircut. He's a prescription clerk."

The secretary looked about her guiltily and shook her head. She was used to him.

Elliot succeeded in calming himself down after a while, but the image of black sky remained with him. At first he thought he would be able to simply shrug the whole thing off. After a few minutes, he picked up his phone and dialled Blankenship's probation officer.

"The Vietnam thing is all he has," the probation officer explained. "I guess he picked it up around."

"His descriptions are vivid," Elliot said.

"You mean they sound authentic?"

"I mean he had me going today. He was ringing my bells."

"Good for Blanky. Think he believes it himself?"

"Yes," Elliot said. "He believes it himself now."

Elliot told the probation officer about Blankenship's current arrest, which was for showering illegally at midnight in the Wyndham Regional High School. He asked what Probation knew about Blankenship's present relationship with his family.

"You kiddin'?" the P.O. asked. "They're all locked down. The whole family's inside. The old man's in Bridgewater. Little Donny's in San Quentin or somewhere. Their dog's in the pound."

Elliot had lunch alone in the hospital staff cafeteria. On the far side of the double-glazed windows, the day was darkening as an expected snowstorm gathered. Along Route 7, ancient elms stood frozen against the gray sky. When he had finished his sandwich and coffee, he sat staring out at the winter afternoon. His anger had given way to an insistent anxiety.

On the way back to his office, he stopped at the hospital gift shop for a copy of *Sports Illustrated* and a candy bar. When he was inside again, he closed the door and put his feet up. It was Friday and he had no appointments for the remainder of the day, nothing to do but write a few letters and read the office mail.

Elliot's cubicle in the social-services department was windowless and lined with bookshelves. When he found himself unable to concentrate on the magazine and without any heart for his paperwork, he ran his eye over the row of books beside his chair. There were volumes by Heinrich Muller and Carlos Casteneda, Jones' life of Freud, and *The Golden Bough*. The books aroused a revulsion in Elliot. Their present uselessness repelled him.

Over and over again, detail by detail, he tried to recall his conversation with Blankenship.

"You were never there," he heard himself explaining. He was trying to get the whole incident straightened out after the fact. Something was wrong. Dread crept over him like a paralysis. He ate his candy bar without tasting it. He knew that the craving for sweets was itself a bad sign.

Blankenship had misappropriated someone else's dream and made it his own. It made no difference whether you had been there, after all. The dreams had crossed the ocean. They were in the air.

He took his glasses off and put them on his desk and sat with his arms folded, looking into the well of light from his desk lamp. There seemed to be nothing but whirl inside him. Unwelcome things came and went in his mind's eye. His heart beat faster. He could not control the headlong promiscuity of his thoughts.

It was possible to imagine larval dreams travelling in suspended animation undetectable in a host brain. They could be divided and regenerate like flatworms, hide in seams and bedding, in war stories, laughter, snapshots. They could rot your socks and turn your memory into a black-and-green blister. Green for the hills, black for the sky above. At daybreak they hung themselves up in rows like bats. At dusk they went out to look for dreamers.

Elliot put his jacket on and went into the outer office, where the secretary sat frowning into the measured sound and light of her machine. She must enjoy its sleekness and order, he thought. She was divorced. Four redheaded kids between ten and seventeen lived with her in an unpainted house across from Stop & Shop. Elliot liked her and had come to find her attractive. He managed a smile for her.

"Ethel, I think I'm going to pack it in," he declared. It seemed awkward to be leaving early without a reason.

"Jack wants to talk to you before you go, Chas."

Elliot looked at her blankly.

Then his colleague, Jack Sprague, having heard his voice, called from the adjoining cubicle. "Chas, what about Sunday's games? Shall I call you with the spread?"

"I don't know," Elliot said. "I'll phone you tomorrow."

"This is a big decision for him," Jack Sprague told the secretary. "He might lose twenty-five bucks."

At present, Elliot drew a slightly higher salary than Jack Sprague, although Jack had a Ph.D. and Elliot was simply an M.S.W. Different branches of the state government employed them.

"Twenty-five bucks," said the woman. "If you guys have no better use for twenty-five bucks, give it to me."

"Where are you off to, by the way?" Sprague asked.

Elliot began to answer, but for a moment no reply occurred to him. He shrugged. "I have to get back," he finally stammered. "I promised Grace."

"Was that Blankenship I saw leaving?"

Elliot nodded.

"It's February," Jack said. "How come he's not in Florida?"

"I don't know," Elliot said. He put on his coat and walked to the door. "I'll see you."

"Have a nice weekend," the secretary said. She and Sprague looked after him indulgently as he walked toward the main corridor.

"Are Chas and Grace going out on the town?" she said to Sprague. "What do you think?"

"That would be the day," Sprague said. "Tomorrow he'll come back over here and read all day. He spends every weekend holed up in this goddam office while she does something or other at the church." He shook his head. "Every night he's at A.A. and she's home alone."

Ethel savored her overbite. "Jack," she said teasingly, "are you thinking what I think you're thinking? Shame on you."

"I'm thinking I'm glad I'm not him, that's what I'm thinking. That's as much as I'll say."

"Yeah, well, I don't care," Ethel said. "Two salaries and no kids, that's the way to go, boy."

Elliot went out through the automatic doors of the emergency bay and the cold closed over him. He walked across the hospital parking lot with his eyes on the pavement, his hands thrust deep in his overcoat pockets, skirting patches of shattered ice. There was no wind, but the motionless air stung; the metal frames of his glasses burned his skin. Curlicues of mud-brown ice coated the soiled snowbanks along the street. Although it was still afternoon, the street lights had come on.

The lock on his car door had frozen and he had to breathe on the keyhole to fit the key. When the engine turned over, Jussi Björling's recording of the Handel Largo filled the car interior. He snapped it off at once.

Halted at the first stoplight, he began to feel the want of a destination. The fear and impulse to flight that had got him out of the office faded, and he had no desire to go home. He was troubled by a peculiar impatience that might have been with time itself. It was as though he were waiting for something. The sensation made him feel anxious; it was unfamiliar but not altogether unpleasant. When the light changed he drove on, past the Gulf station and the firehouse and between the greens of Ilford Common. At the far end of the common he swung into the parking lot of the Packard Conway Library and stopped with the engine running. What he was experiencing, he thought, was the principle of possibility.

He turned off the engine and went out again into the cold. Behind the leaded library windows he could see the librarian pouring coffee in her tiny private office. The librarian was a Quaker of socialist principles named Candace Music, who was Elliot's cousin.

The Conway Library was all dark wood and etched mirrors, a Gothic saloon. Years before, out of work and booze-whipped, Elliot had gone to hide there. Because Candace was a classicist's widow and knew some

Greek, she was one of the few people in the valley with whom Elliot had cared to speak in those days. Eventually, it had seemed to him that all their conversations tended toward Vietnam, so he had gone less and less often. Elliot was the only Vietnam veteran Candace knew well enough to chat with, and he had come to suspect that he was being probed for the edification of the East Ilford Friends Meeting. At that time he had still pretended to talk easily about his war and had prepared little discourses and picaresque anecdotes to recite on demand. Earnest seekers like Candace had caused him great secret distress.

Candace came out of her office to find him at the checkout desk. He watched her brow furrow with concern as she composed a smile. "Chas, what a surprise. You haven't been in for an age."

"Sure I have, Candace. I went to all the Wednesday films last fall. I work just across the road."

"I know, dear," Candace said. "I always seem to miss you."

A cozy fire burned in the hearth, an antique brass clock ticked along on the marble mantel above it. On a couch near the fireplace an old man sat upright, his mouth open, asleep among half a dozen soiled plastic bags. Two teen-age girls whispered over their homework at a table under the largest window.

"Now that I'm here," he said, laughing, "I can't remember what I came to get."

"Stay and get warm," Candace told him. "Got a minute? Have a cup of coffee."

Elliot had nothing but time, but he quickly realized that he did not want to stay and pass it with Candace. He had no clear idea of why he had come to the library. Standing at the checkout desk, he accepted coffee. She attended him with an air of benign supervision, as though he were a Chinese peasant and she a medical missionary, like her father. Candace was tall and plain, more handsome in her middle sixties than she had ever been.

"Why don't we sit down?"

He allowed her to gentle him into a chair by the fire. They made a threesome with the sleeping old man.

"Have you given up translating, Chas? I hope not."

"Not at all," he said. Together they had once rendered a few fragments of Sophocles into verse. She was good at clever rhymes.

"You come in so rarely, Chas. Ted's books go to waste."

After her husband's death, Candace had donated his books to the Conway, where they reposed in a reading room inscribed to his memory, untouched among foreign-language volumes, local genealogies, and books in large type for the elderly.

"I have a study in the barn," he told Candace. "I work there. When I have time." The lie was absurd, but he felt the need of it.

"And you're working with Vietnam veterans," Candace declared.

"Supposedly," Elliot said. He was growing impatient with her nodding solicitude.

"Actually," he said, "I came in for the new Oxford 'Classical World.' I thought you'd get it for the library and I could have a look before I spent my hard-earned cash."

Candace beamed. "You've come to the right place, Chas, I'm happy to say." He thought she looked disproportionately happy. "I have it."

"Good," Elliot said, standing. "I'll just take it, then. I can't really stay."

Candace took his cup and saucer and stood as he did. When the library telephone rang, she ignored it, reluctant to let him go. "How's Grace?" she asked.

"Fine," Elliot said. "Grace is well."

At the third ring she went to the desk. When her back was turned, he hesitated for a moment and then went outside.

The gray afternoon had softened into night, and it was snowing. The falling snow whirled like a furious mist in the headlight beams on Route 7 and settled implacably on Elliot's cheeks and eyelids. His heart, for no good reason, leaped up in childlike expectation. He had run away from a dream and encountered possibility. He felt in possession of a promise. He began to walk toward the roadside lights.

Only gradually did he begin to understand what had brought him there and what the happy anticipation was that fluttered in his breast.

Drinking, he had started his evenings from the Conway Library. He would arrive hung over in the early afternoon to browse and read. When the old pain rolled in with dusk, he would walk down to the Midway Tavern for a remedy. Standing in the snow outside the library, he realized that he had contrived to promise himself a drink.

Ahead, through the storm, he could see the beer signs in the Midway's window warm and welcoming. Snowflakes spun around his head like an excitement.

Outside the Midway's package store, he paused with his hand on the doorknob. There was an old man behind the counter whom Elliot remembered from his drinking days. When he was inside, he realized that the old man neither knew nor cared who he was. The package store was thick with dust; it was on the counter, the shelves, the bottles themselves. The old counterman looked dusty. Elliot bought a bottle of King William Scotch and put it in the inside pocket of his overcoat.

Passing the windows of the Midway Tavern, Elliot could see the ranks of bottles aglow behind the bar. The place was crowded with men leaving the afternoon shifts at the shoe and felt factories. No one turned to note him when he passed inside. There was a single stool vacant at the bar and he took it. His heart beat faster. Bruce Springsteen was on the jukebox.

The bartender was a club fighter from Pittsfield called Jackie G., with whom Elliot had often gossiped. Jackie G. greeted him as though he had been in the previous evening. "Say, babe?"

"How do," Elliot said.

A couple of the men at the bar eyed his shirt and tie. Confronted with the bartender, he felt impelled to explain his presence. "Just thought I'd stop by," he told Jackie G. "Just thought I'd have one. Saw the light. The snow . . . " He chuckled expansively.

"Good move," the bartender said. "Scotch?"

"Double," Elliot said.

When he shoved two dollars forward along the bar, Jackie G. pushed one of the bills back to him. "Happy hour, babe."

"Ah," Elliot said. He watched Jackie pour the double. "Not a moment too soon."

For five minutes or so, Elliot sat in his car in the barn with the engine running and his Handel tape on full volume. He had driven over from East Ilford in a Baroque ecstasy, swinging and swaying and singing along. When the tape ended, he turned off the engine and poured some Scotch into an apple-juice container to store providentially beneath the car seat. Then he took the tape and the Scotch into the house with him. He was lying on the sofa in the dark living room, listening to the Largo, when he heard his wife's car in the driveway. By the time Grace had made her way up the icy back-porch steps, he was able to hide the Scotch and rinse his glass clean in the kitchen sink. The drinking life, he thought, was lived moment by moment.

Soon she was in the tiny cloakroom struggling off with her overcoat. In the process she knocked over a cross-country ski, which stood propped against the cloakroom wall. It had been more than a year since Elliot had used the skis.

She came into the kitchen and sat down at the table to take off her boots. Her lean, freckled face was flushed with the cold, but her eyes looked weary. "I wish you'd put those skis down in the barn," she told him. "You never use them."

"I always like to think," Elliot said, "that I'll start the morning off skiing."

"Well, you never do," she said. "How long have you been home?"

"Practically just walked in," he said. Her pointing out that he no longer skied in the morning enraged him. "I stopped at the Conway Library to get the new Oxford 'Classical World.' Candace ordered it."

Her look grew troubled. She had caught something in his voice. With dread and bitter satisfaction, Elliot watched his wife detect the smell of whiskey.

"O God," she said. "I don't believe it."

Let's get it over with, he thought. Let's have the song and dance.

She sat up straight in her chair and looked at him in fear.

"Oh, Chas," she said, "how could you?"

For a moment he was tempted to try to explain it all.

"The fact is," Elliot told his wife, "I hate people who start the day cross-country skiing."

She shook her head in denial and leaned her forehead on her palm and cried.

He looked into the kitchen window and saw his own distorted image. "The fact is I think I'll start tomorrow morning by stringing head-high razor wire across Anderson's trail."

The Andersons were the Elliots' nearest neighbors. Loyall Anderson was a full professor of government at the state university, thirty miles away. Anderson and his wife were blond and both of them were over six feet tall. they had two blond children, who qualified for the gifted class in the local school but attended regular classes in token of the Andersons' opposition to elitism.

"Sure," Elliot said. "Stringing wire's good exercise. It's life-affirming in its own way."

The Andersons started each and every day with a brisk morning glide along a trail that they partly maintained. They skied well and presented a pleasing, wholesome sight. If, in the course of their adventure, they encountered a snowmobile, Darlene Anderson would affect to choke and cough, indicating her displeasure. If the snowmobile approached them from behind and the trail was narrow, the Andersons would decline to let it pass, asserting their statutory right-of-way.

"I don't want to hear your violent fantasies," Grace said.

Elliot was picturing razor wire, the Army kind. He was picturing the decapitated Andersons, their blood and jaunty ski caps bright on the white trail. He was picturing their severed heads, their earnest blue eyes and large white teeth reflecting the virginal morning snow. Although Elliot hated snowmobiles, he hated the Andersons far more.

He looked at his wife and saw that she had stopped crying. Her long, elegant face was rigid and lipless.

"Know what I mean? One string at Mommy and Daddy level for Loyall and Darlene. And a bitty wee string at kiddie level for Skippy and Samantha, those cunning little whizzes."

"Stop it," she said to him.

"Sorry," Elliot told her.

Stiff with shame, he went and took his bottle out of the cabinet into which he had thrust it and poured a drink. He was aware of her eyes on him. As he drank, a fragment from old Music's translation of "Medea" came into his mind. "Old friend, I have to weep. The gods and I went mad together and made things as they are." It was such a waste; eighteen months of struggle thrown away. But there was no way to get the stuff back in the bottle.

"I'm very sorry," he said. "You know I'm very sorry, don't you, Grace?"

The delectable Handel arias spun on in the next room.

"You must stop," she said. "You must make yourself stop before it takes over."

"It's out of my hands," Elliot said. He showed her his empty hands. "It's beyond me."

"You'll lose your job, Chas." She stood up at the table and leaned on it, staring wide-eyed at him. Drunk as he was, the panic in her voice frightened him. "You'll end up in jail again."

"One engages," Elliot said, "and then one sees."

"How can you have done it?" she demanded. "You promised me."

"First the promises," Elliot said, "and then the rest."

"Last time was supposed to be the last time," she said.

"Yes," he said, "I remember."

"I can't stand it," she said. "You reduce me to hysterics." She wrung her hands for him to see. "See? Here I am, I'm in hysterics."

"What can I say?" Elliot asked. He went to the bottle and refilled his glass. "Maybe you shouldn't watch."

"You want me to be forbearing, Chas? I'm not going to be."

"The last thing I want," Elliot said, "is an argument."

"I'll give you a fucking argument. You didn't have to drink. All you had to do was come home."

"That must have been the problem," he said.

Then he ducked, alert at the last possible second to the missile that came for him at hairline level. Covering up, he heard the shattering of glass, and a fine rain of crystals enveloped him. She had sailed the sugar bowl at him; it had smashed against the wall above his head and there was sugar and glass in his hair.

"You bastard!" she screamed. "You are undermining me!"

"You ought not to throw things at me," Elliot said. "I don't throw things at you."

He left her frozen into her follow-through and went into the living room to turn the music off. When he returned she was leaning back against the wall, rubbing her right elbow with her left hand. Her eyes were bright. She had picked up one of her boots from the middle of the kitchen floor and stood holding it.

"What the hell do you mean, that must have been the problem?"

He set his glass on the edge of the sink with an unsteady hand and turned to her. "What do I mean? I mean that most of the time I'm putting one foot in front of the other like a good soldier and I'm out of it from the neck up. But there are times when I don't think I will ever be dead enough—or dead long enough—to get the taste of this life off my teeth. That's what I mean!"

She looked at him dry-eyed. "Poor fella," she said.

"What you have to understand, Grace, is that this drink I'm having"—he raised the glass toward her in a gesture of salute—"is the only worthwhile thing I've done in the last year and a half. It's the only thing in my life that means jack shit, the closest thing to satisfaction I've had. Now how can you begrudge me that? It's the best I'm capable of."

"You'll go too far," she said to him. "You'll see."

"What's that, Grace? A threat to walk?" He was grinding his teeth. "Don't make me laugh. You, walk? You, the friend of the unfortunate?"

"Don't you hit me," she said when she looked at his face. "Don't you dare."

"You, the Christian Queen of Calvary, walk? Why, I don't believe that for a minute."

She ran a hand through her hair and bit her lip. "No, we stay," she said. Anger and distraction made her look young. Her cheeks blazed rosy against the general pallor of her skin. "In my family we stay until the fella dies. That's the tradition. We stay and pour it for them and they die."

He put his drink down and shook his head.

"I thought we'd come through," Grace said. "I was sure."

"No," Elliot said. "Not altogether."

They stood in silence for a minute. Elliot sat down at the oilcloth-covered table. Grace walked around it and poured herself a whiskey.

"You are undermining me, Chas. You are making things impossible for me and I just don't know." She drank and winced. "I'm not going to stay through another drunk. I'm telling you right now. I haven't got it in me. I'll die."

He did not want to look at her. He watched the flakes settle against the glass of the kitchen door. "Do what you feel the need of," he said.

"I just can't take it," she said. Her voice was not scolding but measured and reasonable. "It's February. And I went to court this morning and lost Vopotik."

Once again, he thought, my troubles are going to be obviated by those of the deserving poor. He said, "Which one was that?"

"Don't you remember them? The three-year-old with the broken fingers?"

He shrugged. Grace sipped her whiskey.

"I told you. I said I had a three-year-old with broken fingers, and you said, 'Maybe he owed somebody money.'"

"Yes," he said, "I remember now."

"You ought to see the Vopotiks, Chas. The woman is young and obese. She's so young that for a while I thought I could get to her as a juvenile. The guy is a biker. They believe the kid came from another planet to control their lives. They believe this literally, both of them."

"You shouldn't get involved that way," Elliot said. "You should leave it to the caseworkers."

"They scared their first caseworker all the way to California. They were following me to work."

"You didn't tell me."

"Are you kidding?" she asked. "Of course I didn't." To Elliot's surprise, his wife poured herself a second whiskey. "You know how they address the child? As 'dude.' She says to it, 'Hey, dude.'" Grace shuddered with loathing. "You can't imagine! The woman munching Twinkies. The kid smelling of shit. They're high morning, noon, and night, but you can't get anybody for that these days."

"People must really hate it," Elliot said, "when somebody tells them they're not treating their kids right."

"They definitely don't want to hear it," Grace said. "You're right." She sat stirring her drink, frowning into the glass. "The Vopotik child will die, I think."

"Surely not," Elliot said.

"This one I think will die," Grace said. She took a deep breath and puffed out her cheeks and looked at him forlornly. "The situation's extreme. Of course, sometimes you wonder whether it makes any difference. That's the big question, isn't it?"

"I would think," Elliot said, "that would be the one question you didn't ask."

"But you do," she said. "You wonder: Ought they to live at all? To continue the cycle?" She put a hand to her hair and shook her head as if in confusion. "Some of these folks, my God, the poor things cannot put Wednesday on top of Tuesday to save their lives."

"It's a trick," Elliot agreed, "a lot of them can't manage."

"And kids are small, they're handy and underfoot. They make noise. They can't hurt you back."

"I suppose child abuse is something people can do together," Elliot said.

"Some kids are obnoxious. No question about it."

"I wouldn't know," Elliot said.

"Maybe you should stop complaining. Maybe you're better off. Maybe your kids are better off unborn."

"Better off or not," Elliot said, "it looks like they'll stay that way."

"I mean our kids, of course," Grace said. "I'm not blaming you, understand? It's just that here we are with you drunk again and me losing Vopotik, so I thought why not get into the big unaskable questions." She got up and folded her arms and began to pace up and down the kitchen. "Oh," she said when her eye fell upon the bottle, "that's good stuff, Chas. You won't mind if I have another? I'll leave you enough to get loaded on."

Elliot watched her pour. So much pain, he thought; such anger and confusion. He was tired of pain, anger, and confusion; they were what had got him in trouble that very morning.

The liquor seemed to be giving him a perverse lucidity when all he now required was oblivion. His rage, especially, was intact in its salting of alcohol. Its contours were palpable and bleeding at the borders. Booze was good for rage. Booze could keep it burning through the darkest night.

"What happened in court?" he asked his wife.

She was leaning on one arm against the wall, her long, strong body flexed at the hip. Holding her glass, she stared angrily toward the invisible fields outside. "I lost the child," she said.

Elliot thought that a peculiar way of putting it. He said nothing.

"The court convened in an atmosphere of high hilarity. It may be Hate Month around here but it was buddy-buddy over at Ilford Courthouse. The room was full of bikers and bikers' lawyers. A colorful crowd. There was a lot of bonding." She drank and shivered. "They didn't think too well of me. They don't think too well of broads as lawyers. Neither does the judge. The judge has the common touch. He's one of the boys."

"Which judge?" Elliot asked.

"Buckley. A man of about sixty. Know him? Lots of veins on his nose?"

Elliot shrugged.

"I thought I had done my homework," Grace told him. "But suddenly I had nothing but paper. No witnesses. It was Margolis at Valley Hospital who spotted the radiator burns. He called us in the first place. Suddenly he's got to keep his reservation for a campsite in St. John. So Buckley threw his deposition out." She began to chew on a fingernail. "The caseworkers have vanished—one's in L.A., the other's in Nepal. I went in there and got run over. I lost the child."

"It happens all the time," Elliot said. "Doesn't it?"

"This one shouldn't have been lost, Chas. These people aren't simply confused. They're weird. They stink."

"You go messing into anybody's life," Elliot said, "that's what you'll find."

"If the child stays in that house," she said, "he's going to die."

"You did your best," he told his wife. "Forget it."

She pushed the bottle away. She was holding a water glass that was almost a third full of whiskey.

"That's what the commissioner said."

Elliot was thinking of how she must have looked in court to the cherry-faced judge and the bikers and their lawyers. Like the schoolteachers who had tormented their childhoods, earnest and tight-assed, humorless and self-righteous. It was not surprising that things had gone against her.

He walked over to the window and faced his reflection again. "Your optimism always surprises me."

"My optimism? Where I grew up our principal cultural expression was the funeral. Whatever keeps me going, it isn't optimism."

"No?" he asked. "What is it?"

"I forget," she said.

"Maybe it's your religious perspective. Your sense of the divine plan."

She sighed in exasperation. "Look, I don't think I want to fight anymore. I'm sorry I threw the sugar at you. I'm not your keeper. Pick on someone your own size."

"Sometimes," Elliot said, "I try to imagine what it's like to believe that the sky is full of care and concern."

"You want to take everything from me, do you?" She stood leaning against the back of her chair. "That you can't take. It's the only part of my life you can't mess up."

He was thinking that if it had not been for her he might not have survived. There could be no forgiveness for that. "Your life? You've got all this piety strung out between Monadnock and Central America. And look at yourself. Look at your life."

"Yes," she said, "look at it."

"You should have been a nun. You don't know how to live."

"I know that," she said. "That's why I stopped doing counselling. Because I'd rather talk the law than life." She turned to him. "You got everything I had, Chas. What's left I absolutely require."

"I swear I would rather be a drunk," Elliot said, 'than force myself to believe such trivial horseshit."

"Well, you're going to have to do it without a straight man," she said, "because this time I'm not going to be here for you. Believe it or not."

"I don't believe it," Elliot said. "Not my Grace."

"You're really good at this," she told him. "You make me feel ashamed of my own name."

"I love your name," he said.

The telephone rang. They let it ring three times, and then Elliot went over and answered it.

"Hey, who's that?" a good-humored voice on the phone demanded.

Elliot recited their phone number.

"Hey, I want to talk to your woman, man. Put her on."

"I'll give her a message," Elliot said.

"You put your woman on, man. Run and get her."

Elliot looked at the receiver. He shook his head. "Mr. Vopotik?"

"Never you fuckin' mind, man. I don't want to talk to you. I want to talk to the skinny bitch."

Elliot hung up.

"Is it him?" she asked.

"I guess so."

They waited for the phone to ring again and it shortly did.

"I'll talk to him," Grace said. But Elliot already had the phone.

"Who are you, asshole?" the voice inquired. "What's your fuckin' name, man?"

"Elliot," Elliot said.

"Hey, don't hang up on me, Elliot. I won't put up with that. I told you go get that skinny bitch, man. You go do it."

There were sounds of festivity in the background on the other end of the line—a stereo and drunken voices.

"Hey," the voice declared. "Hey, don't keep me waiting, man."

"What do you want to say to her?" Elliot asked.

"That's none of your fucking business, fool. Do what I told you."

"My wife is resting," Elliot said. "I'm taking her calls."

He was answered by a shout of rage. He put the phone aside for a moment and finished his glass of whiskey. When he picked it up again the man on the line was screaming at him. "That bitch tried to break up my family, man! She almost got away with it. You know what kind of pain my wife went through?"

"What kind?" Elliot asked.

For a few seconds he heard only the noise of the party. "Hey, you're not drunk, are you, fella?"

"Certainly not," Elliot insisted.

"You tell that skinny bitch she's gonna pay for what she did to my family, man. You tell her she can run but she can't hide. I don't care where you go—California, anywhere—I'll get to you."

"Now that I have you on the phone," Elliot said, "I'd like to ask you a couple of questions. Promise you won't get mad?"

"Stop it!" Grace said to him. She tried to wrench the phone from his grasp, but he clutched it to his chest.

"Do you keep a journal?" Elliot asked the man on the phone. "What's your hat size?"

"Maybe you think I can't get to you," the man said. "But I can get to you, man. I don't care who you are, I'll get to you. The brothers will get to you."

"Well, there's no need to go to California. You know where we live."

"For God's sake," Grace said.

"Fuckin' right," the man on the telephone said. "Fuckin' right I know."

"Come on over," Elliot said.

"How's that?" the man on the phone asked.

"I said come on over. We'll talk about space travel. Comets and stuff. We'll talk astral projection. The moons of Jupiter."

"You're making a mistake, fucker."

"Come on over," Elliot insisted. "Bring your fat wife and your beat-up kid. Don't be embarrassed if your head's a little small."

The telephone was full of music and shouting. Elliot held it away from his ear.

"Good work," Grace said to him when he had replaced the receiver.

"I hope he comes," Elliot said. "I'll pop him."

He went carefully down the cellar stairs, switched on the overhead light, and began searching among the spiderwebbed shadows and fouled fishing line for his shotgun. It took him fifteen minutes to find it and his cleaning case. While he was still downstairs, he heard the telephone ring again and his wife answer it. He came upstairs and spread his shooting gear across the kitchen table. "Was that him?"

She nodded wearily. "He called back to play us the chain saw."

"I've heard that melody before," Elliot said.

He assembled his cleaning rod and swabbed out the shotgun barrel. Grace watched him, a hand to her forehead. "God," she said. "What have I done? I'm so drunk."

"Most of the time," Elliot said, sighting down the barrel, "I'm helpless in the face of human misery. Tonight I'm ready to reach out."

"I'm finished," Grace said. "I'm through, Chas. I mean it."

Elliot rammed three red shells into the shotgun and pumped one forward into the breech with a satisfying report. "Me, I'm ready for some radical problem-solving. I'm going to spray that no-neck Slovak all over the year."

"He isn't a Slovak," Grace said. She stood in the middle of the kitchen with her eyes closed. Her face was chalk white.

"What do you mean?" Elliot demanded. "Certainly he's a Slovak."

"No he's not," Grace said.

"Fuck him anyway. I don't care what he is. I'll grease his ass."

He took a handful of deer shells from the box and stuffed them in his jacket pockets.

"I'm not going to stay with you, Chas. Do you understand me?"

Elliot walked to the window and peered out at his driveway. "He won't be alone. They travel in packs."

"For God's sake!" Grace cried, and in the next instant bolted for the downstairs bathroom. Elliot went out, turned off the porch light and switched on a spotlight over the barn door. Back inside, he could hear Grace in the toilet being sick. He turned off the light in the kitchen.

He was still standing by the window when she came up behind him. It seemed strange and fateful to be standing in the dark near her, holding the shotgun. He felt ready for anything.

"I can't leave you alone down here drunk with a loaded shotgun," she said. "How can I?"

"Go upstairs," he said.

"If I went upstairs it would mean I didn't care what happened. Do you understand? If I go it means I don't care anymore. Understand?"

"Stop asking me if I understand," Elliot said. "I understand fine."

"I can't think," she said in a sick voice. "Maybe I don't care. I don't know. I'm going upstairs."

"Good," Elliot said.

When she was upstairs, Elliot took his shotgun and the whiskey into the dark living room and sat down in an armchair beside one of the lace-curtained windows. The powerful barn light illuminated the length of his driveway and the whole of the back yard. From the window at which he sat, he commanded a view of several miles in the direction of East Il-ford. The two-lane blacktop road that ran there was the only one along which an enemy could pass.

He drank and watched the snow, toying with the safety of his 12-gauge Remington. He felt neither anxious nor angry now but only impatient to be done with whatever the night would bring. Drunkenness and the silent rhythm of the falling snow combined to make him feel outside of time and syntax.

Sitting in the dark room, he found himself confronting Blankenship's dream. He saw the bunkers and wire of some long-lost perimeter. The rank smell of night came back to him, the dread evening and quick dusk, the mysteries of outer darkness: fear, combat, and death. Enervated by liquor, he began to cry. Elliot was sympathetic with other people's tears but ashamed of his own. He thought of his own tears as childish and excremental. He stifled whatever it was that had started them.

Now his whiskey tasted thin as water. Beyond the lightly frosted glass, illuminated snowflakes spun and settled sleepily on weighted pine boughs. He had found a life beyond the war after all, but in it he was still sitting in darkness, armed, enraged, waiting.

His eyes grew heavy as the snow came down. He felt as though he could be drawn up into the storm and he began to imagine that. He imagined his life with all its artifacts and appetites easing up the spout into white oblivion, everything obviated and foreclosed. He thought maybe he could go for that.

When he awakened, his left hand had gone numb against the trigger guard of his shotgun. The living room was full of pale, delicate light. He looked outside and saw that the storm was done with and the sky radiant and cloudless. The sun was still below the horizon.

Slowly Elliot got to his feet. The throbbing poison in his limbs served to remind him of the state of things. He finished the glass of whiskey on the windowsill beside his easy chair. Then he went to the hall closet to get a ski jacket, shouldered his shotgun, and went outside.

There were two cleared acres behind his house; beyond them a trail descended into a hollow of pine forest and frozen swamp. Across the hollow, white pastures stretched to the ridgeline, lambent under the lightening sky. A line of skeletal elms weighted with snow marked the course of frozen Shawmut Brook.

He found a pair of ski goggles in a jacket pocket and put them on and set out toward the tree line, gripping the shotgun, step by careful step in the knee-deep snow. Two raucous crows wheeled high overhead, their cries exploding the morning's silence. When the sun came over the ridge, he stood where he was and took in a deep breath. The risen sun warmed his face and he closed his eyes. It was windless and very cold.

Only after he had stood there for a while did he realize how tired he had become. The weight of the gun taxed him. It seemed infinitely wearying to contemplate another single step in the snow. He opened his eyes and closed them again. With sunup the world had gone blazing blue and white, and even with his tinted goggles its whiteness dazzled him and made his head ache. Behind his eyes, the hypnagogic patterns formed a monsoon-heavy tropical sky. He yawned. More than anything, he wanted to lie down in the soft, pure snow. If he could do that, he was certain he could go to sleep at once.

He stood in the middle of the field and listened to the crows. Fear, anger, and sleep were the three primary conditions of life. He had learned that over there. Once he had thought fear the worst, but he had learned that the worst was anger. Nothing could fix it; neither alcohol nor medicine. It was a worm. It left him no peace. Sleep was the best.

He opened his eyes and pushed on until he came to the brow that overlooked the swamp. Just below, gliding along among the frozen cattails and bare scrub maple, was a man on skis. Elliot stopped to watch the man approach.

The skier's face was concealed by a red-and-blue ski mask. He wore snow goggles, a blue jumpsuit, and a red woolen Norwegian hat. As he came, he leaned into the turns of the trail, moving silently and gracefully along. At the foot of the slope on which Elliot stood, the man looked up, saw him, and slid to a halt. The man stood staring at him for a moment and then began to herringbone up the slope. In no time at all the skier stood no more than ten feet away, removing his goggles, and inside the woolen mask Elliot recognized the clear blue eyes of his neighbor, Professor Loyall Anderson. The shotgun Elliot was carrying seemed to grow heavier. He yawned and shook his head, trying unsuccessfully to clear it. The sight of Anderson's eyes gave him a little thrill of revulsion.

"What are you after?" the young professor asked him, nodding toward the shotgun Elliot was cradling.

"Whatever there is," Elliot said.

Anderson took a quick look at the distant pasture behind him and then turned back to Elliot. The mouth hole of the Professor's mask filled with teeth. Elliot thought that Anderson's teeth were quite as he had imagined them earlier. "Well, Polonski's cows are locked up," the professor said. "So they at least are safe."

Elliot realized that the professor had made a joke and was smiling. "Yes," he agreed.

Professor Anderson and his wife had been the moving force behind an initiative to outlaw the discharge of firearms within the boundaries of East Ilford Township. The initiative had been defeated, because East Ilford was not that kind of town.

"I think I'll go over by the river," Elliot said. He said it only to have something to say, to fill the silence before Anderson spoke again. He was afraid of what Anderson might say to him and of what might happen.

"You know," Anderson said, "that's all bird sanctuary over there now."

"Sure," Elliot agreed.

Outfitted as he was, the professor attracted Elliot's anger in an elemental manner. The mask made him appear a kind of doll, a china figure or a marionette. His eyes and mouth, all on their own, were disagreeable.

Elliot began to wonder if Anderson could smell the whiskey on his breath. He pushed the little red bull's-eye safety button on his gun to Off.

"Seriously," Anderson said, "I'm always having to run hunters out of there. Some people don't understand the word 'posted.'"

"I would never do that," Elliot said. "I would be afraid."

Anderson nodded his head. He seemed to be laughing. "Would you?" he asked Elliot merrily.

In imagination, Elliot rested the tip of his shotgun barrel against Anderson's smiling teeth. If he fired a load of deer shot into them, he thought, they might make a noise like broken china. "Yes," Elliot said. "I wouldn't know who they were or where they'd been. They might resent my being alive. Telling them where they could shoot and where not."

Anderson's teeth remained in place. "That's pretty strange," he said. "I mean, to talk about resenting someone for being alive."

"It's all relative," Elliot said. "They might think, 'Why should he be alive when some brother of mine isn't?' Or they might think, 'Why should he be alive when I'm not?'"

"Oh," Anderson said.

"You see?" Elliot said. Facing Anderson, he took a long step backward. "All relative."

"Yes," Anderson said.

"That's so often true, isn't it?" Elliot asked. "Values are often relative."

"Yes," Anderson said. Elliot was relieved to see that he had stopped smiling.

"I've hardly slept, you know," Elliot told Professor Anderson.

"Hardly at all. All night. I've been drinking."

"Oh," Anderson said. He licked his lips in the mouth of the mask. "You should get some rest."

"You're right," Anderson said.

"Well," Anderson said, "got to go now."

Elliot thought he sounded a little thick in the tongue. A little slow in the jaw.

"It's a nice day," Elliot said, wanting now to be agreeable.

"It's great," Anderson said, shuffling on his skis.

"Have a nice day," Elliot said.

"Yes," Anderson said, and pushed off.

Elliot rested the shotgun across his shoulders and watched Anderson withdraw through the frozen swamp. It was in fact a nice day, but Elliot took no comfort in the weather. He missed night and the falling snow.

As he walked back toward his house, he realized that now there would be whole days to get through, running before the antic energy of whiskey. The whiskey would drive him until he dropped. He shook his head in regret. "It's a revolution," he said aloud. He imagined himself talking to his wife.

Getting drunk was an insurrection, a revolution—a bad one. There would be outsize bogus emotions. There would be petty moral blackmail and cheap remorse. He had said dreadful things to his wife. He had bullied Anderson with his violence and unhappiness, and Anderson would not forgive him. There would be damn little justice and no mercy.

Nearly to the house, he was startled by the desperate feathered drumming of a pheasant's rush. He froze, and out of instinct brought the gun up in the direction of the sound. When he saw the bird break from its cover and take wing, he tracked it, took a breath, and fired once. The bird was a little flash of opulent color against the bright-blue sky. Elliot felt himself flying for a moment. The shot missed.

Lowering the gun, he remembered the deer shells he had loaded. A hit with the concentrated shot would have pulverized the bird, and he was glad he had missed. He wished no harm to any creature. Then he thought of himself wishing no harm to any creature and began to feel fond and sorry for himself. As soon as he grew aware of the emotion he was indulging, he suppressed it. Pissing and moaning, mourning and weeping, that was the nature of the drug.

The shot echoed from the distant hills. Smoke hung in the air. He turned and looked behind him and saw, far away across the pasture, the tiny blue-and-red figure of Professor Anderson motionless against the snow. Then Elliot turned again toward his house and took a few labored steps and looked up to see his wife at the bedroom window. She stood perfectly still, and the morning sun lit her nakedness. He stopped where he was. She had heard the shot and run to the window. What had she thought to see? Burnt rags and blood on the snow. How relieved was she now? How disappointed?

Elliot thought he could feel his wife trembling at the window. She was hugging herself. Her hands clasped her shoulders. Elliot took his snow goggles off and shaded his eyes with his hand. He stood in the field staring.

The length of the gun was between them, he thought. Somehow she had got out in front of it, to the wrong side of the wire. If he looked long enough he would find everything out there. He would find himself down the sight.

How beautiful she is, he thought. The effect was striking. The window was so clear because he had washed it himself, with vinegar. At the best of times he was a difficult, fussy man.

Elliot began to hope for forgiveness. He leaned the shotgun on his forearm and raised his left hand and waved to her. Show a hand, he thought. Please just show a hand.

He was cold, but it had got light. He wanted no more than the gesture. It seemed to him that he could build another day on it. Another day was all you needed. He raised his hand higher and waited.

In Greenwich There Are Many Gravelled Walks

On an afternoon in early August, Peter Birge, just returned from driving his mother to the Greenwich sanitarium she had to frequent at intervals, sat down heavily on a furbelowed sofa in the small apartment he and she had shared ever since his return from the Army a year ago. He was thinking that his usually competent solitude had become more than he could bear. He was a tall, well-built young man of about twenty-three, with a pleasant face whose even, standardized look was the effect of proper food, a good dentist, the best schools, and a brush haircut. The heat, which bored steadily into the room through a Venetian blind lowered over a half-open window, made his white T shirt cling to his chest and arms, which were still brown from a week's sailing in July at a cousin's place on the Sound. The family of cousins, one cut according to the pattern of a two-car-and-country-club suburbia, had always looked with distaste on his precocious childhood with his mother in the Village and, the few times he had been farmed out to them during those early years, had received his healthy normality with ill-concealed surprise, as if they had clearly expected to have to fatten up what they undoubtedly referred to in private as "poor Anne's boy." He had only gone there at all, this time, when it became certain that the money saved up for a summer abroad, where his Army stint had not sent him, would have to be spent on one of his mother's trips to Greenwich, leaving barely enough, as it was, for his next, and final, year at the School of Journalism. Half out of disheartenment over his collapsed summer, half to provide himself with a credible "out" for the too jovially pressing cousins at Rye, he had registered for some courses at the Columbia summer session. Now these were almost over, too, leaving a gap before the fall semester began. He had cut this morning's classes in order to drive his mother up to the place in Connecticut.

He stepped to the window and looked through the blind at the convertible parked below, on West Tenth Street. He ought to call the garage for the pickup man, or else, until he thought of someplace to go, he ought to hop down and put up the top. Otherwise, baking there in the hot sun, the car would be like a griddle when he went to use it, and the leather seats were cracking badly anyway.

It had been cool when he and his mother started, just after dawn that morning, and the air of the well-ordered countryside had had that almost speaking freshness of early day. With her head bound in a silk scarf and her chubby little chin tucked into the cardigan which he had buttoned on her without forcing her arms into the sleeves, his mother, peering up at him with the near-gaiety born of relief, had had the exhausted charm of a child who has just been promised the thing for which it has nagged. Anyone looking at the shingled hair, the feet in small brogues—anyone not close enough to see how drawn and beakish her nose looked in the middle of her little, round face, which never reddened much with drink but at the worst times took on a sagging, quilted whiteness—might have thought the two of them were a couple, any couple, just off for a day in the country. No one would have thought only a few hours before, some time after two, he had been awakened, pounded straight up on his feet, by the sharp familiar cry and then the agonized susurrus of prattling that went on and on and on, that was different from her everyday, artless confidential prattle only in that now she could not stop, she could not stop, *she could not stop,* and above the small, working mouth with its eliding, spinning voice, the glazed button eyes opened wider and wider, as if she were trying to breathe through them. Later, after the triple bromide, the warm bath, and the crooning, practiced soothing he administered so well, she had hiccuped into crying, then into stillness at last, and had fallen asleep on his breast. Later still, she had awakened him, for he must have fallen asleep there in the big chair with her, and with the weak, humiliated goodness which always followed these times she had even tried to help him with the preparations for the journey—preparations which, without a word between them, they had set about at once. There'd been no doubt, of course, that she would have to go. There never was.

He left the window and sat down again in the big chair, and smoked one cigarette after another. Actually, for a drunkard—or an alcoholic, as people preferred to say these days—his mother was the least troublesome of any. He had thought of it while he packed the pairs of daintily kept shoes, the sweet-smelling blouses and froufrou underwear, the tiny, perfect dresses—of what a comfort it was that she had never grown raddled or blowzy. Years ago, she had perfected the routine within which she could feel safe for months at a time. It had gone on for longer than he could remember: from before the death of his father, a Swedish engineer, on the income of whose patents they had always been able to live fairly comfortably; probably even during her life with that other long-dead man, the painter whose model and mistress she had been in the years before she married his father. There would be the long, drugged sleep of the morning, then the unsteady hours when she manicured herself back into cleanliness and reality. Then, at about four or five in the afternoon, she and the dog (for there was always a dog) would make their short pilgrimage to the clubby, cozy little hangout where she would be a fixture until far into the morning, where she had been a fixture for the last twenty years.

Once, while he was at boarding school, she had made a supreme effort to get herself out of the routine—for his sake, no doubt—and he had returned at Easter to a new apartment, uptown, on Central Park West. All that this had resulted in was inordinate taxi fares and the repetitious nightmare evenings when she had gotten lost and he had found her, a small, untidy heap, in front of their old place. After a few months, they had moved back to the Village, to those few important blocks where she felt safe and known and loved. For they all knew her there, or got to know her—the aging painters, the new-comer poets, the omniscient news hacks, the military spinsters who bred dogs, the anomalous, sandalled young men. And they accepted her, this dainty hanger-on who neither painted nor wrote but hung their paintings on her walls, faithfully read their parti-colored magazines, and knew them all—their shibboleths, their feuds, the whole vocabulary of their disintegration, and, in a mild, occasional manner, their beds.

Even this, he could not remember not knowing. At ten, he had been an expert compounder of remedies for hangover, and of an evening, standing sleepily in his pajamas to be admired by the friends his mother sometimes brought home, he could have predicted accurately whether the party would end in a brawl or in a murmurous coupling in the dark.

It was curious, he supposed now, stubbing out a final cigarette, that he had never judged resentfully either his mother or her world. By the accepted standards, his mother had done her best; he had been well housed, well schooled, even better loved than some of the familied boys he had known. Wisely, too, she had kept out of his other life, so that he had never had to be embarrassed there except once, and this when he was grown, when she had visited his Army camp. Watching her at a post party for visitors, poised there, so chic, so distinctive, he had suddenly seen it begin: the fear, the scare, then the compulsive talking, which always started so innocently that only he would have noticed at first—that warm, excited buttery flow of harmless little lies and pretensions which gathered its dreadful speed and content and ended then, after he had whipped her away, just as it had ended this morning.

On the way up this morning, he had been too clever to subject her to a restaurant, but at a drive-in place he was able to get her to take some coffee. How grateful they had both been for the coffee, she looking up at him, tremulous, her lips pecking at the cup, he blessing the coffee as it went down her! And afterward, as they flew onward, he could feel her straining like a homing pigeon toward their destination, toward the place where she felt safest of all, where she would gladly have stayed forever if she had just had enough money for it, if they would only let her stay. For there the pretty little woman and her dog—a poodle, this time—would be received like the honored guest that she was, so trusted and docile a guest, who asked only to hide there during the season of her discomfort, who was surely the least troublesome of them all.

He had no complaints, then, he assured himself as he sat on the burning front seat of the convertible trying to think of somewhere to go. It was just that while others of his age still shared a communal wonder at what life might hold, he had long since been solitary in his knowledge of what life was.

Up in a sky as honestly blue as a flag, an airplane droned smartly toward Jersey. Out at Rye, the younger crowd at the club would be commandeering the hot blue day, the sand, and the water, as if they were all extensions of themselves. They would use the evening this way, too, disappearing from the veranda after a dance, exploring each other's rhythm-and-whiskey-whetted appetites in the backs of cars. They all thought themselves a pretty sophisticated bunch, the young men who had graduated not into a war but into its hung-over peace, the young girls attending junior colleges so modern that the deans had to spend all their time declaring that their girls were being trained for the family and the community. But when Peter looked close and saw how academic their sophistication was, how their undamaged eyes were still starry with expectancy, their lips still avidly open for what life would surely bring, then he became envious and awkward with them, like a guest at a party to whose members he carried bad news he had no right to know, no right to tell.

He turned on the ignition and let the humming motor prod him into a decision. He would drop in at Robert Veilum's, where he had dropped in quite often until recently, for the same reason that others stopped by at Vielum's—because there was always likely to be somebody there. The door of Robert's old-fashioned apartment, on Clarmont Avenue, almost always opened on a heartening jangle of conversation and music, which meant that others had gathered there, too, to help themselves over the pauses so endemic to university life—the life of the mind—and there were usually several members of Robert's large acquaintance among the sub-literary, quasi-artistic, who had strayed in, ostensibly en route somewhere, and who lingered on hopefully on the chance that in each other's company they might find out what that somewhere was.

Robert was a perennial taker of courses—one of those nonmatriculated students of indefinable age and income, some of whom pursued, with monkish zeal and no apparent regard for time, this or that freakishly peripheral research project of their own conception, and others of whom, like Robert, seemed to derive a Ponce de Leon sustenance from the young. Robert himself, a large man of between forty and fifty, whose small features were somewhat cramped together in a wide face, never seemed bothered by his own lack of direction, implying rather that this was really the catholic approach of the "whole man," alongside of which the serious pursuit of a degree was somehow foolish, possibly vulgar. Rumor connected him with a rich Boston family that had remittanced him at least as far as New York, but he never spoke about himself, although he was extraordinarily alert to gossip. Whatever income he had he supplemented by renting his extra room to a series of young men students. The one opulence among his dun-colored, perhaps consciously Spartan effects was a really fine record-player, which he kept going at all hours with selections from his massive collection. Occasionally he annotated the music, or the advance copy novel that lay on his table, with foreign-language tags drawn from the wide, if obscure, latitudes of his travels, and it was his magic talent for assuming that his young friends, too, had known, had experienced, that, more than anything, kept them enthralled.

"*Fabelhaft!* Isn't it?" he would say of the Mozart. "Remember how they did it that last time at Salzburg!" and they would all sit there, included, belonging, headily remembering the Salzburg to which they had never been. Or he would pick up the novel and lay it down again. "La plume de mon oncle, I'm afraid. *La plume de mon oncle Gide. Eheu,* poor Gide!"—and they would each make note of the fact that one need not read that particular book, that even, possibly, it was no longer necessary to read Gide.

Peter parked the car and walked into the entrance of Robert's apartment house, smiling to himself, lightened by the prospect of company. After all, he had been weaned on the salon talk of such circles; these self-fancying little bohemias at least made him feel at home. And Robert was cleverer than most—it was amusing to watch him. For just as soon as his satellites thought themselves secure on the promontory of some "trend" he had pointed out to them, they would find that he had deserted them, had gone to another trend, another eminence, from which he beckoned, cocksure and just faintly malicious. He harmed no one permanently. And if he concealed some skeleton of a weakness, some closeted Difference with the Authorities, he kept it decently interred.

As Peter stood in the dark, soiled hallway and rang the bell of Robert's apartment, he found himself as suddenly depressed again, unaccountably reminded of his mother. There were so many of them, and they affected you so, these charmers who, if they could not offer you the large strength, could still atone for the lack with so many small decencies. It was admirable, surely, the way they managed this. And surely, after all, they harmed no one.

Robert opened the door. "Why, hello—Why, hello, Peter!" He seemed surprised, almost relieved. "Greetings!" he added, in a voice whose boom was more in the manner than the substance. "Come in, Pietro, come in!" He wore white linen shorts, a zebra-striped beach shirt, and huaraches, in which he moved easilyy, leading the way down the dark hall of the apartment, past the two bedrooms, into the living room. All of the apartment was on a court, but on the top floor, so it received a medium, dingy light from above. The living room, long and pleasant, with an old white mantel, a gas log, and many books, always came as a surprise after the rest of the place, and at any time of day Robert kept a few lamps lit, which rouged the room with an evening excitement.

As they entered, Robert reached over in passing and turned on the record-player. Music filled the room, muted but insistent, as if he wanted it to patch up some lull he had left behind. Two young men sat in front of the dead gas log. Between them was a table littered with maps,

an open atlas, travel folders, glass beer steins. Vince, the current
roomer, had his head on his clenched fists. The other man, a stranger,
indolently raised a dark, handsome head as they entered.

"Vince!" Robert spoke sharply. "You know Peter Birge. And this is
Mario Osti. Peter Birge."

The dark young man nodded and smiled, lounging in his chair.
Vince nodded. His red-rimmed eyes looked beyond Peter into some
distance he seemed to prefer.

"God, isn't it but hot!" Robert said. "I'll get you a beer." He bent
over Mario with an inquiring look, a caressing hand on the empty glass
in front of him.

Mario stretched back on the chair, smiled upward at Robert, and
shook his head sleepily. "Only makes me hotter." He yawned, spread
his arms langourously, and let them fall. He had the animal self-
possession of the very handsome; it was almost a shock to hear him
speak.

Robert bustled off to the kitchen.

"Robert!" Vince called, in his light, pouting voice. "Get me a drink.
Not a beer. A drink." He scratched at the blond stubble on his cheek
with a nervous, pointed nail. On his round head and retroussé face, the
stubble produced the illusion of a desiccated baby, until, looking
closer, one imagined that he might never have been one, but might have
been spawned at the age he was, to mummify perhaps but not to grow.
He wore white shorts exactly like Robert's, and his blue-and-white
striped shirt was a smaller version of Robert's brown-and-white, so that
the two of them made an ensemble, like the twin outfits the children
wore on the beach at Rye.

"You know I don't keep whiskey here." Robert held three steins
deftly balanced, his heavy hips neatly avoiding the small tables which
scattered the room. "You've had enough, wherever you got it." It was
true, Peter remembered, that Robert was fonder of drinks with a flutter
of ceremony about them—*café brûlé* perhaps, or, in the spring, a
Maibowle, over which he could chant the triumphant details of his pursuit of the necessary woodruff. But actually one tippled here on the ex-

hilarating effect of wearing one's newest facade, in the fit company of others similarly attired.

Peter picked up his stein. "You and Vince all set for Morocco, I gather."

"Morocco?" Robert took a long pull at his beer. "No. No, that's been changed. I forgot you hadn't been around. Mario's been brushing up my Italian. He and I are off for Rome the day after tomorrow."

The last record on the changer ended in an archaic battery of horns. In the silence while Robert slid on a new batch of records, Peter heard Vince's nail scrape, scrape along his cheek. Still leaning back, Mario shaped smoke with his lips. Large and facilely drawn, they looked, more than anything, accessible—to a stream of smoke, of food, to another mouth, to any plum that might drop.

"You going to study over there?" Peter said to him.

"Paint." Mario shaped and let drift another corolla of smoke.

"No," Robert said, clicking on the record arm. "I'm afraid Africa's démodé." A harpsichord began to play, its dwarf notes hollow and perfect. Robert raised his voice a shade above the music. "Full of fashion photographers. And little come-lately writers." He sucked in his cheeks and made a face. "Trying out their passions under the beeg, bad sun."

"*Eheu*, poor Africa?" said Peter.

Robert laughed. Vince stared at him out of wizened eyes. Not drink, so much, after all, Peter decided, looking professionally at the mottled cherub face before he realized that he was comparing it with another face, but lately left. He looked away.

"Weren't you going over, Peter?" Robert leaned against the machine.

"Not this year." Carefully Peter kept out of his voice the knell the words made in his mind. In Greenwich, there were many gravelled walks, unshrubbed except for the nurses who dotted them, silent and attitudinized as trees. "Isn't that Landowska playing?"

"Hmm. Nice and cooling on a hot day. Or a fevered brow." Robert fiddled with the volume control. The music became louder, then lowered. "Vince wrote a poem about that once. About the Mozart, really, wasn't it, Vince? 'A lovely clock between ourselves and time.' " He enunciated daintily, pushing the words away from him with his tongue.

"Turn it off!" Vince stood up, his small fists clenched, hanging at his sides.

"No, let her finish." Robert turned deliberately and closed the lid of the machine, so that the faint hiss of the needle vanished from the frail, metronomic notes. He smiled. "What a time-obsessed crowd writers are. Now Mario doesn't have to bother with that dimension."

"Not unless I paint portraits," Mario said. His parted lips exposed his teeth, like some white, unexpected flint of intelligence.

"*Dolce far niente*," Robert said softly. He repeated the phrase dreamily, so that half-known Italian words—"*loggia*," the "Ponte Vecchio," the "Lungarno"—imprinted themselves one by one on Peter's mind, and he saw the two of them, Mario and Robert now, already in the frayed-gold light of Florence, in the umber dusk of half-imagined towns.

A word, muffled, came out of Vince's throat. He lunged for the record-player. Robert seized his wrist and held it down on the lid. They were locked that way, staring at each other, when the doorbell rang.

"That must be Susan," Robert said. He released Vince and looked down, watching the blood return to his fingers, flexing his palm.

With a second choked sound, Vince flung out his fist in an awkward attempt at a punch. It grazed Robert's cheek, clawing downward. A thin line of red appeared on Robert's cheek. Fist to mouth, Vince stood a moment; then he rushed from the room. They heard the nearer bedroom door slam and the lock click. The bell rang again, a short, hesitant burr.

Robert clapped his hand to his cheek, shrugged, and left the room.

Mario got up out of his chair for the first time. "Aren't you going to ask who Susan is?"

"Should I?" Peter leaned away from the face bent confidentially near, curly with glee.

"His daughter," Mario whispered. "He said he was expecting his *daughter*. Can you imagine? *Robert!*"

Peter moved farther away from the mobile, pressing face and, standing at the window, studied the gritty details of the courtyard. A vertical line of lighted windows, each with a glimpse of stair, marked the hallways on each of the five floors. Most of the other windows were dim and closed, or opened just a few inches above their white ledges, and the yard was quiet. People would be away or out in the sun, or in their brighter front rooms dressing for dinner, all of them avoiding this dark shaft that connected the backs of their lives. Or, here and there, was there someone sitting in the facing light, someone lying on a bed with his face pressed to a pillow? The window a few feet to the right, around the corner of the court, must be the window of the room into which Vince had gone. There was no light in it.

Robert returned, a Kleenex held against his cheek. With him was a pretty, ruffle-headed girl in a navy-blue dress with a red arrow at each shoulder. He switched on another lamp. For the next arrival, Peter thought, surely he will tug back a velvet curtain or break out with a heraldic flourish of drums, recorded by Red Seal. Or perhaps the musty wardrobe was opening at last and was this the skeleton—this girl who had just shaken hands with Mario, and now extended her hand toward Peter, tentatively, timidly, as if she did not habitually shake hands but today would observe every custom she could.

"How do you do?"

"How do you do?" Peter said. The hand he held for a moment was small and childish, the nails unpainted, but the rest of her was very correct for the eye of the beholder, like the young models one sees in magazines, sitting or standing against a column, always in three-quarter view, so that the picture, the ensemble, will not be marred by the human glance. Mario took from her a red dressing case that she held in her free hand, bent to pick up a pair of white gloves that she had dropped, and returned them with an avid interest which overbalanced, like a waiter's gallantry. She sat down, brushing at the gloves.

"The train was awfully dusty—and crowded." She smiled tightly at Robert, looked hastily and obliquely at each of the other two, and bent over the gloves brushing earnestly, stopping as if someone had said something, and, when no one did, brushing again.

"Well, well, well," Robert said. His manners, always good, were never so to the point of cliches, which would be for him what nervous *gaffes* were for other people. He coughed, rubbed his cheek with the back of his hand, looked at the hand, and stuffed the Kleenex into the pocket of his shorts. "How was camp?"

Mario's eyebrows went up. The girl was twenty, surely, Peter thought.

"All right," she said. She gave Robert the stiff smile again and looked down into her lap. "I like helping children. They can use it." Her hands folded on top of the gloves, then inched under and hid beneath them.

"Susan's been counselling at a camp which broke up early because of a polio scare," Robert said as he sat down. "She's going to use Vince's room while I'm away, until college opens."

"Oh—" She looked up at Peter. "Then you aren't Vince?"

"No. I just dropped in. I'm Peter Birge."

She gave him a neat nod of acknowledgment. "I'm glad, because I certainly wouldn't want to inconvenience—"

"Did you get hold of your mother in Reno?" Robert asked quickly.

"Not yet. But she couldn't break up her residence term anyway. And Arthur must have closed up the house here. The phone was disconnected."

"Arthur's Susan's stepfather," Robert explained with a little laugh. "Number three, I think. Or is it *four*, Sue?"

Without moving, she seemed to retreat, so that again there was nothing left for the observer except the girl against the column, any one of a dozen with the short, anonymous nose, the capped hair, the foot arched in the trim shoe, and half an iris glossed with an expertly aimed photoflood. "Three," she said. Then one of the hidden hands stole out from under the gloves, and she began to munch evenly on a fingernail.

"Heavens, you haven't still got that *habit!*" Robert said.

"What a heavy papa you make, Robert," Mario said.

She flushed, and put the hand back in her lap, tucking the fingers under. She looked from Peter to Mario and back again. "Then you're not Vince," she said. "I didn't think you were."

The darkness increased around the lamps. Behind Peter, the court had become brisk with lights, windows sliding up, and the sound of taps running.

"Guess Vince fell asleep. I'd better get him up and send him on his way." Robert shrugged, and rose.

"Oh, don't! I wouldn't want to be an inconvenience," the girl said, with a polite terror which suggested she might often have been one.

"On the contrary." Robert spread his palms, with a smile, and walked down the hall. They heard him knocking on a door, then his indistinct voice.

In the triangular silence, Mario stepped past Peter and slid the window up softly. He leaned out to listen, peering sidewise at the window to the right. As he was pulling himself back in, he looked down. His hands stiffened on the ledge. Very slowly he pulled himself all the way in and stood up. Behind him a tin ventilator clattered inward and fell to the floor. In the shadowy lamplight his too classic face was like marble which moved numbly. He swayed a little, as if with vertigo.

"I'd better get out of here!"

They heard his heavy breath as he dashed from the room. The slam of the outer door blended with Robert's battering, louder now, on the door down the hall.

"What's down there?" She was beside Peter, otherwise he could not have heard her. They took hands, like strangers met on a narrow footbridge or on one of those steep places where people cling together more for anchorage against their own impulse than for balance. Carefully they leaned out over the sill. Yes—it was down there, the shirt, zebra-striped, just decipherable on the merged shadow of the courtyard below.

Carefully, as if they were made of eggshell, as if by some guarded movement they could still rescue themselves from disaster, they drew back and straightened up. Robert, his face askew with the impossible question, was behind them.

After this, there was the hubbub—the ambulance from St. Luke's, the prowl car, the two detectives from the precinct station house, and finally the "super," a vague man with the grub pallor and shamble of those who live in basements. He pawed over the keys on the thong around his wrist and, after several tries, opened the bedroom door. It was a quiet, unviolent room with a tossed bed and an open window, with a stagy significance acquired only momentarily in the minds of those who gathered in a group at its door.

Much later, after midnight, Peter and Susan sat in the bald glare of an all-night restaurant. With hysterical eagerness, Robert had gone on to the station house with the two detectives to register the salient facts, to help ferret out the relatives in Ohio, to arrange, in fact, anything that might still be arrangeable about Vince. Almost without noticing, he had acquiesced in Peter's proposal to look after Susan. Susan herself, after silently watching the gratuitous burbling of her father, as if it were a phenomenon she could neither believe nor leave, had followed Peter without comment. At his suggestion, they had stopped off at the restaurant on their way to her step-father's house, for which she had a key.

"Thanks. I was starved." She leaned back and pushed at the short bang of hair on her forehead.

"Hadn't you eaten at all?"

"Just those pasty sandwiches they sell on the train. There wasn't any dinner."

"Smoke?"

"I do, but I'm just too tired. I can get into a hotel all right, don't you think? If I can't get in at Arthur's?"

"I know the manager of a small one near us," Peter said. "But if you don't mind coming to my place, you can use my mother's room for tonight. Or for as long as you need, probably."

"What about your mother?"

"She's away. She'll be away for quite a while."

"Not in Reno, by any chance?" There was a roughness, almost a coarseness, in her tone, like that in the overdone camaraderie of the shy.

"No. My father died when I was eight. Why?"

"Oh, something in the way you spoke. And then you're so competent. Does she work?"

"No. My father left something. Does yours?"

She stood up and picked up her bedraggled gloves. "No," she said, and her voice was suddenly distant and delicate again. "She married." She turned and walked out ahead of him.

He paid, rushed out of the restaurant, and caught up with her.

"Thought maybe you'd run out on me," he said.

She got in the car without answering.

They drove through the Park, toward the address in the East Seventies that she had given him. A weak smell of grass underlay the gas-blended air, but the Park seemed limp and worn, as if the strain of the day's effluvia had been too much for it. At the Seventy-second Street stop signal, the blank light of a street lamp invaded the car.

"Thought you might be feeling Mrs. Grundyish at my suggesting the apartment," Peter said.

"Mrs. Grundy wasn't around much when I grew up." The signal changed and they moved ahead.

They stopped in a street which had almost no lights along its smartly converted house fronts. This was one of the streets, still sequestered by money, whose houses came alive only under the accelerated, febrile glitter of winter and would dream through the gross summer days, their interiors deadened with muslin or stirred faintly with the subterranean clinkings of caretakers. No. 4 was dark.

"I would rather stay over at your place, if I have to," the girl said. Her voice was offhand and prim. "I hate hotels. We always stopped at them in between."

"Let's get out and see."

They stepped down into the areaway in front of the entrance, the car door banging hollowly behind them. She fumbled in her purse and took out a key, although it was already obvious that it would not be usable. In his childhood, he had often hung around in the areaways of old brownstones such as this had been. In the corners there had always been a soft, decaying smell, and the ironwork, bent and smeared, always hung loose and broken-toothed. The areaway of this house had been repaved with slippery flag; even in the humid night there was no smell. Black-tongued grillwork, with an oily shine and padlocked, secured the windows and the smooth door. Fastened on the grillwork in front of the door was the neat, square proclamation of a protection agency.

"You don't have a key for the padlocks, do you?"

"No." She stood on the curb, looking up at the house. "It was a nice room I had there. Nicest one I ever did have, really." She crossed to the car and got in.

He followed her over to the car and got in beside her. She had her head in her hands.

"Don't worry. We'll get in touch with somebody in the morning."

"I don't. I don't care about any of it, really." She sat up, her face averted. "My parents, or any of the people they tangle with." She wound the lever on the door slowly, then reversed it. "Robert, or my mother, or Arthur," she said, "although he was always pleasant enough. Even Vince—even if I'd known him."

"He was just a screwed-up kid. It could have been anybody's window."

"No." Suddenly she turned and faced him. "I should think it would be the best privilege there is, though. To care, I mean."

When he did not immediately reply, she gave him a little pat on the arm and sat back. "Excuse it, please. I guess I'm groggy." She turned around and put her head on the crook of her arm. Her words came faintly through it. "Wake me when we get there."

She was asleep by the time they reached his street. He parked the car as quietly as possible beneath his own windows. He himself had never felt more awake in his life. He could have sat there until morning with her sleep-secured beside him. He sat thinking of how different it would be at Rye, or anywhere, with her along, with someone along who was the same age. For they were the same age, whatever that was, whatever the age was of people like them. There was nothing he would be unable to tell her.

To the north, above the rooftops, the electric mauve of midtown blanked out any auguries in the sky, but he wasn't looking for anything like that. Tomorrow he would take her for a drive—whatever the weather. There were a lot of good roads around Greenwich.

The Editors

M I R I A M D O W is a high school English teacher at the Nichols School in Buffalo, New York, where she is a member of her school's faculty group for drug abuse. She grew up in Boston, graduated from Radcliffe, and has a master of arts degree from the Harvard Graduate School of Education. She and her husband are members of Al-Anon and have four grown children.

J E N N I F E R R E G A N, a writer from Katonah, New York, grew up in Buffalo. She graduated from Smith College and received a master of arts degree from the State University of New York in Buffalo. She is a poet and short-story writer and also reviews books for the *Buffalo News*. Regan is currently working on a book about quilts. She is a recovering alcoholic and the mother of three grown children.

The Authors

A L I C E A D A M S' six novels include *Listening to Billy* and *Second Chances*. Her three story collections are *Beautiful Girl*, *To See You Again* and *Return Trips*.

A R N A B O N T E M P S (d. 1973) had a varied and active literary career as a poet, novelist, and short-story writer. He is perhaps best known for his anthologies, such as *Golden Slippers*, a collection of Negro poetry for children, and *The Poetry of the Negro: 1746–1949*, which he co-edited with Langston Hughes.

H O R T E N S E C A L I S H E R is the author of 11 novels and six short-story collections, including *Mysteries of Motion* and *Saratoga Hot*. *The Collected Stories of Hortense Calisher* and the novel *False Entry* were nominated for the National Book Award. Calisher has won four O. Henry Awards.

R A Y M O N D C A R V E R (d. 1988) wrote four volumes of short stories, including *What We Talk About When We Talk About Love*, *Would You Please Be Quiet Please* and *Cathedral*, as well as four volumes of poetry. *Where I'm Calling From: New and Collected Stories* was published in 1988. In 1983 Carver was the co-winner of the first Mildred and Harold Strauss Living Award and in 1985 he won the Levinson Prize from *Poetry* magazine.

JOHN CHEEVER (d. 1982) was the author of five novels. His first novel, *The Wapshot Chronicle,* won the 1958 National Book Award. His other novels include *Bullet Park* and *Falconer*. He wrote over 100 short stories and won the Pulitzer Prize in 1979 following the publication of his *Collected Stories*.

LOUISE ERDRICH's first novel, *Love Medicine* won the 1984 National Book Critics Circle Award. She has published two other novels, *Beet Queen* and *Tracks,* as well as a volume of poetry called *Jacklight* and several short stories.

WILLIAM GOYEN (d. 1983) published several novels, including *House of Breath* and *Arcadio*. His *Collected Stories* was nominated in 1975 for the Pulitzer Prize. Goyen wrote plays and story collections, the last of which, *Had I A Hundred Mouths,* was published posthumously.

JULIE HAYDEN (d. 1981) published a collection of short stories called *The Lists of the Past*.

LANGSTON HUGHES (d. 1967) wrote non-fiction, fiction, poetry and plays. One of his most famous fictional characters was Jesse B. Simple who was featured in *Simple Speaks His Mind*. Hughes considered himself mainly a poet. Among his volumes of poetry are *The Dream Keeper, Shakespeare in Harlem* and *Fields of Wonder*.

SUSAN MINOT's first novel *Monkeys* received the French Prix Femina Etranger award for 1987.

JOYCE CAROL OATES's 18th novel is *You Must Remember This* and the 19th, *American Appetities*. Her other works include *Them,* which won the National Book Award in 1970, *Bellefleur* and *Wonderland*. Her short-story collections include *Marriage and Other Infidelities* and *Where Are You Going, Where Have You Been?* Oates has also written an essay, "On Boxing." And, under the pen name of Rosamund Smith, Oates wrote *Lives of the Twins*.

FRANK O'CONNOR (d. 1966) wrote one-act plays, poetry, history, literary criticism and novels, one of which was *Dutch Interiors*. O'Connor's many volumes of short stories include *Guests of the Nation, The Stories of Frank O'Connor* and *More Stories by Frank O'Connor*.

TILLIE OLSEN's collection of short stories is called *Tell Me A Riddle*. The title story won the O. Henry Award for Best Short Story in 1961. Olsen wrote the novel *Yonnondio: From the Thirties* and a book of non-fiction called *Silences*.

ROBERT STONE's novel *A Hall of Mirrors* won the Faulkner Award for first novel in 1967. His book *Dog Soldiers* received the National Book Award in 1975. His other novels include *A Flag for Sunrise* and *Children of Light*.

PETER TAYLOR won the Ritz-Hemingway Award and the Pulitzer Prize for fiction for *A Summons to Memphis*. He has published seven collections of short stories, including *The Collected Stories of Peter Taylor*, and *The Old Forest and Other Stories*, which won the PEN Award for the best work of fiction in 1985.

The cover image, "Poema de Omar," is by Oscar Rodriguez,

from the collection of Tess Gallagher.

Book design is by Tree Swenson.

The Bodoni type was set by The Typeworks.

Book manufactured by Edwards Brothers.